Along the Border Lies

Along the Border Lies

PAUL S. FLORES

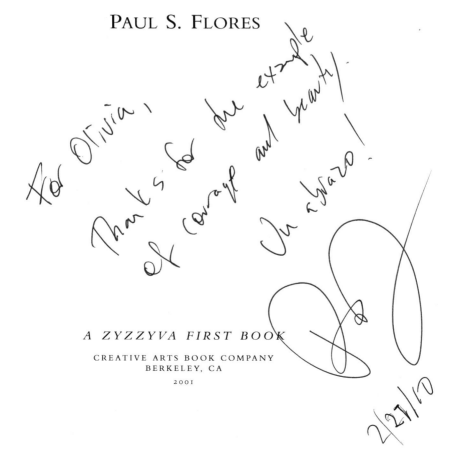

A ZYZZYVA FIRST BOOK

CREATIVE ARTS BOOK COMPANY
BERKELEY, CA
2001

Publication of this book was made possible by a grant
from the Creative Work Fund.

Cover design: Ingalls + Associates, San Francisco

Cover photograph: U.S. Geological Survey

Author photograph: Patricia Flores

Printed: Publishers Press, Salt Lake City

For information contact:
Creative Arts Book Company
833 Bancroft Way
Berkeley, CA 94710

ISBN 978-0-88739-478-2
Library of Congress Catalog Number 2001095295

Printed in the United States of America

The characters in this book are fictional. If there is any resemblance to the lives of real people, it was meant for the purpose of metaphoric dialogue. The Mexican border is a real space, with real people who share many common experiences and legends. Any fabulous information held within these pages is meant to be shared with the public in order to further discussion about the real issues that border residents face.

Acknowledgments

There are many people without whose inspiration and support I could not have written this book. I wish first and foremost to thank my mother, Patricia Flores; the Flores family, who inspire so much pride and laughter; my father, George Stoya, and the Stojsavljevic family.

Thanks to the writing instructors who encouraged and believed in me: Melvyn Freilicher, Quincy Troupe, Victor Hernández Cruz, Maxine Chernoff, and Jewel Gomez.

Thanks to my editor, Howard Junker, and publisher, Don Ellis, of Creative Arts Book Company; I sincerely appreciate your faith and patience.

Thanks to the Creative Work Fund for a grant to *ZYZZYVA* that made publication of this book possible.

Thanks also to my colleagues Ethriam Brammer, Brandon Downing, Darren J. de León, Norman Antonio Zelaya.

Finally, my thanks and love to Karina Hodoyán, without whom all of this would still be just an idea.

For Karina

I. Silhouettes in the Flag

"A Mexicano, a Salvadoreño, and a Nicaraguense are all riding together in a car heading south on the 5. Who do you think is driving?"

"I give up. Who's driving?"

"The migra. Who else?"

*A*lfredo hiked the sidewalk through seven suburban blocks of new one-story tract homes, marching in his red beret and green camouflage fatigues with ROTC stamped boldly on them. The Remington was slung on his shoulder, naked across his back, and his green canteen flapped on his hip. Inside his backpack he carried a thin wool blanket, mini first-aid kit, duct tape, beef jerky, notebook, pens, blackface paint, iridescent oil sticks, flashlight, night-vision scope, extra ammo, a dozen M-80 "explosives," and a Bic lighter. He refused to hurry. Instead, he kept an erect and determined stride, thinking somebody might admire the open display of his gun—and be persuaded to join him.

But nobody in this new community three miles from the Tijuana border paid any attention to what went on outside their windows. If illegal immigrants could emerge from the San Ysidro Canyon and stroll through the neighborhood without fear of capture, who would notice 19-year-old Alfredo in full commando gear out to catch them? Even if they had, who would have been able to guess his mission?

Alfredo hated Tijuana: its dank smell of sewer and waste, its scattered poverty, chaos, and virtual namelessness. He hated the Mexicans who waited by the fence for night to fall so they could cross into the canyon illegally. This endless, lawless game drove him insane.

And he hated his own Mexican inheritance, the genetic nightmare he now suffered, epilepsy, passed down from the same ambiguous bloodlines that had also poisoned his grandfather with foaming fits of rage and uncontrollable seizures. He lived in constant fear of these attacks. He knew that his grandfather,

Alfredo Guadalupe, had carved his way from Michoacán to el norte with a mahogany-handled machete; he now kept this ridiculously folkloric weapon in his closet. He himself would use more powerful means to destroy all doubts about who he was and where he came from. Now Alfredo would blow the canyon wide open and leave no trace of his private frustration.

He code-named his mission Operation Black Flag. He had presented it to some of his most trusted friends among the Junior ROTC cadets. Black Flag would stamp out the cucarachas at the border and resurrect the spirit of Corporal Gerald Scott Peterson, a POW/MIA in Vietnam, Alfredo's biological father.

Last night, his Commandos—Jesse, Erica, Gil—had rehearsed the mission with Alfredo, tracking the route he had carved from the elementary school fence to the border fence, and home. Black Flag was set to begin on the eve of Memorial Day.

There was still the matter of correctly arming the Commandos. Every time they had been in the canyon with Alfredo, they could only manage to bring their paintball guns. They had tried to convince Alfredo to use paint, rather than live ammunition, as a suitably symbolic substitute, like the wooden guns they used at school for drill-team.

Fuck that! Alfredo had insisted. To show people you were serious, you had to use live rounds. Besides, how could you stop the pollos from crossing if you shot them with paint? They would only laugh it off. He wanted to teach the illegals that this was indeed a war. His father would have done no less; therefore, Alfredo could accept no less than blood for blood.

Everything had better be taken care of soon, he thought. Until the time was right, however, he would have to wait and watch. As he did now, from a ridge overlooking the Tijuana River reservoir, watching illegal immigrants climb out of a small dirt tunnel below the border fence. The particular spot Alfredo had staked out had been busy of late. Previously, he had kept a count of how many had passed through the tunnel in his notebook. When the number absurdly eclipsed a thousand in three weeks, he stopped keeping track.

He lay on his belly and peered through the nightscope on the rifle he had again snuck out of his stepfather's closet. Alfredo adjusted the scope to bring the bodies into focus: one, two, three, four, five gray silhouettes scurrying out from beneath the ten-foot, rusted, flimsy excuse for a wall separating Tijuana and San Diego.

He unlocked the safety and stroked the trigger. He felt his whole body condense and rediscover itself. He wished he himself could be shot like a rocket through the rifle—to explode into the group of illegals gathering at the wall.

"Fucking wetbacks."

He lowered the gun and looked again into the canyon around him, into the glowing horizon of the eastern hills. The floodlights of the borderline seemed to vibrate with intense illumination. The night was clear and moonless. At the center of the horizon was the swarming mist of car smog beneath the booming stadium lights, where cars wheezed in line to cross into San Diego. Busy Saturday night or not, there was always that miserable wheezing coming from the traffic of the border. Alfredo looked for dust clouds between the bald peaks of the hills and listened for any rumbling motors or helicopter blades. He knew the Border Patrol lurked somewhere at the edge of the lights with the coyotes and hijackers, drug smugglers, and vigilantes like himself. Alfredo feared la migra and dreaded their potential intrusion on his mission.

A dry desert gust brought the hot smell of piss and sewage from the mud-patched remains of the Tijuana River; the rainy season had ended three months ago. Alfredo watched another group of shadows scramble up the reservoir embankments. A hundred yards away, a dozen more silhouettes rustled in and out of the bushes and shadows, having successfully crossed. They gathered near the fence, helping each other from the hole. Alfredo could make out that a few wore cowboy hats.

"Dumb-ass mojados. Those shitty hats are a dead giveaway."

Mojado was his mother's word. It wasn't a bad one for her, or her family. We all crossed the river, she would say, high or dry. Y por ser mexicano en los estados unidos, sigues mojado, pues.

¡Sigues mojado! Alfredo wanted to yell at them. You'll always be wetbacks! His elbow gave out; he lost their location. He lowered the rifle and scanned below, squinting into the gray and black shadows. When he placed his eye to the scope again, he rediscovered the figures dipping and darting in and out of sight like a family of cockroaches running for cover.

Alfredo knew that path was bumpy and loopy. Many times he had fallen, running it himself. The sand was thick and soft near the wall. You had to step lightly or your feet would churn in the thick sand and you would get nowhere fast.

They would be impossible to hit once they got into that sand, into the brush, into the hedge. That's why we've got to get them right when they pop out of the burrow. Right when they hit American soil.

POP

POP

POP

Just like brown bubbles.

ALFREDO WOKE AND STARED ABOVE HIS BED INTO the silhouette of his father's face outlined in white against the black POW/MIA flag fastened to his ceiling. Surrounding the flag were several maps of Vietnam, whose important borders, rivers, and battlesites Alfredo had highlighted with a glow-in-the-dark pen so that he could study them at night, like constellations, wondering where his father might be held. Hanoi. Da Nang. Ho Chi Minh City. Khe Sanh. The Gulf of Tonkin. Each place was a prison in which his father was held against his will.

He tried to sit up, but felt something pinch his waist. He pulled a hardbound book from under his blankets and realized he had fallen asleep reading _Heart of Darkness_. It had been a difficult task to read last night. He must have read each page a dozen times before being able to concentrate over his stepfather's loud "It's not the feel of a gun that kills, it's the caliber. But it really depends on the make of the .45." In any case, he thought, _Apocalypse Now_ was better. He was supposed to write an essay comparing the two; he had a hard time getting over the fact that there was no mention of the Viet Cong, gooks, or Communists in the book. He didn't really know who Conrad thought the enemy was supposed to be. Nonetheless, Alfredo had begun to imagine himself as Marlow in search of Kurtz, the father figure. He had been dreaming of going up river…until a wailing mariachi had jolted him out of sleep. He told himself he needed to begin going to bed with earplugs.

The music came from the living room stereo blasting one of his mother's favorite rancheras. Alfredo could recognize Dora's flat voice singing over the mariachi's baritone, "Ando borracho. Ando tomando. Porque el destino cambió mi suerte." Dora and her husband, Shawn, had been on a binge since Thursday. First there were his friends from work, then his gun club, and now his family down for Memorial Day. Alfredo wasn't getting enough sleep. He had hoped to be out of the house for his daily jog before the sun broke. But when the long-suffering gritos ended his dreams, he began the day in aggravation, consumed with self-pity, while ridiculous Spanish lyrics assaulted him. "Si has pensado dejar mi cariño, recuerda el camino donde te encontré."

Once downstairs, Alfredo found his mother in the kitchen pouring vodka into a red mixture. His tongue quickly became thick and dry. The image of running water became vodka rushing into the blender—the tap would smell like rotten potatoes. Dora picked up a can of clams and began to open it with the manual opener. Alfredo wondered where the pancakes or bacon and eggs were. Was this breakfast? A little Vitamin C with Vitamin Alcohol? Dora wrenched the can opener around the sharp aluminum edge. She swayed with the mariachi and happily spun herself to the sink, draining the clam juice. When his stepfather came down, the music would change to Dwight Yoakam or Garth Brooks.

"Why do you put clams in a Bloody Mary?" Alfredo asked.

"Ay, mijo, you scared me." She hit the blender and yelled, "Do you want a Clamato?" Then she turned it off, and added pepper and Tabasco. "Perfect for breakfast. Lots of vitamins, hmm?"

Alfredo shook his head. He'd caught a whiff of clam musk and shuddered. He needed some coffee.

"Your father's family is coming over," Dora said above the blender as ice cracked and loudly zoomed. "All the way down from Santa Barbara. ¿Qué bueno, eh? I wish we lived in Santa Barbara."

"He's not my dad."

Maybe she remembered that today was Alfredo's birthday. Maybe she remembered that he was epileptic and that alcohol didn't mix well with the anticonvulsants that he was supposed to be taking. Maybe she remembered that his prescription had run out many months ago. Maybe not. Their relationship had changed since Dora had married Shawn. So had her ability to remember things.

"Why are you all made up this morning?" Alfredo asked her.

"What's that, querido?"

"Nothing. Is there any breakfast?"

"There's Clamato."

She lifted the lid off the blender, checked inside, and pressed the whirl button. Next month would be his last, Alfredo thought. School's out, I'm gone—with or without the Marines.

As Alfredo walked past his mother toward the coffee pot, he could smell her perfume. She smelled good. He could tell she had gotten some sleep. With her gold hoop earrings and bangle bracelets shining and clinking, she looked bright and pretty this morning. She had combed out her shoulder-length, copper-streaked brown hair, and pinned it back with a black plastic clasp. Her Coca-Cola-colored eyes weren't darkly circled and red this morning, but cleanly painted with light brown eye shadow and black eyeliner. You couldn't tell she had been up until three, fixing Jack Daniel's and Cokes for Shawn and his Gun Collectors Association.

Alfredo caught himself in a daze. The mariachi screamed at him, "Y te voy a enseñar a querrer. Porque tu no has querido."

Alfredo found the coffee was already turned off. He would have to make a cup of instant.

"Enough caffeine to wake up and have a drink, right, Mom?"

She was singing along with the mariachi as she added the clams. Alfredo cringed.

"What'd you say, mi amor?"

Dora turned around and stood smiling at him with an empty glass in her one hand, the full blender-pitcher in the other. She gestured them both at him and then poured more of the lumpy red liquid into the glass.

"Umm," she said. "Now for the best part."

Alfredo watched as the gray clams slid from the pitcher and plopped one by one into the full glass.

"Oh, Jesus."

Dora took a drink, smiled, and winked. "¡Ay! I forgot the ápio. And more tomatoes. Go to the store, please, mijo, and pick up some ripe tomatoes and some, some ápio—"

"Celery," Alfredo said into the floor.

"I know. Don't raise your voice at me."

"Sorry."

"O.K. Now I need you to pick up that and—and I need more tomatoes for the salsa. I used them all on the ceviche. Did you see it in the fridge? I make a hell of ceviche, if I may say so myself. We're going to have a real Mexican barbecue today, honey."

Alfredo watched the red digital numbers blink zeros and

pulled the instant coffee out of the microwave. Chunks of unmelted brown crystals floated to the top. Alfredo liked it boiling hot. If he didn't burn his tongue, he felt he might as well go back to bed.

"Brush your teeth and get money out of my purse," Dora commanded.

"I'm trying to have a cup of coffee."

"This has to be ready before Shawn gets out of the shower. If you go now, you might have time to beat him downstairs, eh?"

On weekends Alfredo's stepfather took long showers. And he took a small cooler into the bathroom in order to have cold beers to drink inside the hot shower. Shawn would cool his skin with a can of Coors after he shaved.

"My sisters will be arriving soon," Dora continued between sips at the Clamato. "That means you have to be back here to watch your cousins. So come on. Get going."

Dora bent over to kiss him goodbye, but Alfredo moved away. She glared at him. Alfredo gazed back at her, then at the green, red, and white writing on her black sweatshirt: When all is said and done, Mezcal's the one. Ensenada to San Diego, 1987. There was a picture of a green worm riding a ten-speed, one hand raised, gulping a bottle of mezcal. A long time ago, Shawn had sponsored bike races in Baja California. That was where he had met Dora Moreno. She had been one of the people catering the event, serving bottles of water and shots of mezcal to road-race enthusiasts. Alfredo seriously doubted they had met under such normal circumstances. He couldn't imagine his mother doing any catering for bike-race events. Dora had been a waitress most of her life, and she rarely went into Mexico anymore, except for holiday visits to Tijuana. Most of the family had moved to San Diego by now. Shawn still went to the rides there, though not to race; he told everyone marriage had taken his stamina. He went just to drink the free bottles of mezcal with his other ex-road-racer friends.

"Where's your purse?" Alfredo asked Dora.

"On the kitchen table, I think. Or the comedor."

"I don't know which is which," Alfredo said, confused by her irksome habit of mixing Spanish and English.

"You should know which is which. Don't pretend you don't understand Spanish."

"The dining room table or the kitchen table, Mother?"

"What's the matter with you? Did you wake up on the wrong side of the bed again this morning?"

Dora punched the blender again and ice cracked in the pitcher.

"Haven't had a good night's sleep in five years."

"I can't hear you. What'd you say?"

Five years since he'd become a Burns.

Alfredo found his mother's purse on the large faux oak dining table. He set his coffee cup down on a wool place mat and opened Dora's camel-colored leather wallet, thick with pictures of her infinite family to whom Alfredo was told he was related. The relatives from Mexico no longer came over to Alfredo's house. Shawn wouldn't allow Dora's family to stay overnight for fear they might decide to stay too long, refuse to leave. He told Dora he didn't want to be forced to call Immigration. Only the few who already lived in San Diego ever came for a couple hours on special occasions. Even this made Shawn nervous. He suspected Dora's brothers and sisters of pretending not to speak English in order to frustrate him and talk about him in a bad way. However, they simply refused to try to communicate with him. Coming from Tijuana, Shawn's rough gringo attitude was something they were all too familiar with. It was only the visitors from deep Mexico who were frightened by Shawn; they were the only ones unaccustomed to such paranoia.

Alfredo flipped through the pictures with names written in ink on the back, as if to remind his mother of who the people were: Tía Magdalena with her daughters, Milagro and Navidad; Tío Osvaldo from Veracruz with his sons, Chapulín (Alfredo didn't know his real name), Oscar, and Ramón, who had been the last two family members to stay with Alfredo before being deported back to Mexico. They had all come through his mother's apartment at one time or another. Some of the pictures were taken outside Coco's Diner, where Dora had worked before she married Shawn and where she had gotten her family jobs in the kitchen as cooks and dishwashers. They had all stayed with Alfredo and his mother, arriving with humble smiles, unannounced, like an army of ants to a picnic basket, only leaving when everything had been devoured—food, space, money—or when the exterminators showed up.

Hidden between his Aunt Norma and her son, Fat Fernando, Alfredo found the photo he really wanted to see. The rigid jaw stood out the most, shiny and clean, as if the man had swallowed an iron. Round cheekbones. Ice blue eyes, determined and solid. Blond hair severely cropped beneath a shiny dark blue bill pulled low over his square brow. Alfredo admired the multicolored, many-sized squares and badges over the heart of the blue coat. He wanted his uniform to look the same one day. A prideful chill consumed him when he located the Purple Heart among the collage of medals. He turned the photo over. The blue lines written on the back were muddy and fading:

> If you kiss this picture tonight and rub it
> over your belly, I'll be home soon enough
> to kiss you back and hold my son on his birthday.
> > Marine Corporal Gerald Scott Peterson,
> > your husband to be
> > November 1974

When Alfredo had learned from his mother that he was the son of a prisoner of war, he was not quite sure how to react, nor whether to accept if this was true or not. After his sixth-grade graduation ceremony, Dora had urged him into the boys' bathroom in order to confess something to him. She had stressed the word *confess* with rum-and-Coke sticking to her breath like a tight flannel sheet. She told Alfredo he was conceived at a Travelodge in Oceanside, not far from Camp Pendleton, hours before Corporal Peterson went back to Vietnam for a final tour—an evacuation mission. Peterson had never returned. His side of the family was handling all the POW/MIA paperwork. Corporal Peterson was from Nebraska, and the Peterson family acknowledged no responsibility for Alfredo—at least, that's how she understood it. Dora had written letters to Gerry's parents about Alfredo, but received a Xeroxed letter stating that the Peterson family had received four other letters similar to hers. If she'd be willing to come to Nebraska and have her son's blood tested, they'd be willing to consider adopting Alfredo. She handed Alfredo the photo of his father so he could see for himself, along with the typed letter, without a return address, signed by Gerald Peterson, Sr. More than overwhelmed by the story, Alfredo asked his mother to keep both for him.

"So, what would you say if I told you I'm going to marry Shawn?" Dora had asked.

Alfredo wanted to pee, but couldn't with his mother in the boys' bathroom. He was worried someone would come in and find them there.

"Why do you want to marry Shawn?"

"Because I need help."

"Help with what?"

"Help with you. Help with everything, mijo. I'm alone with you. I don't wanna be a waitress forever. Don't you want to live in a house? Don't you think you need a family?"

The word *family* echoed off the gray bathroom walls and stuck like a wet clump of toilet paper to the ceiling. He began to feel queasy. Alfredo wasn't sure what his mother meant. He'd only had Dora and her Spanish-speaking relatives—they sometimes treated Alfredo more like a visitor from another country than a family member.

"I don't want you to marry Shawn."

"You don't know what you're saying, Alfredo. I'll be able to give you what my parents could never give me."

"But I don't want anything else."

"That's because you don't know what to ask for. You're just a kid."

Alfredo knew he was a burden to his mother, and he'd often dreamed of a time when he could give her everything she needed. He often felt guilty when the Anglo and black children at school made fun of Dora's Spanish accent; when they said she was a Mexican prostitute who fucked white men for money and a green card; when they called Alfredo beaner, wetback, or spic. At recess, kids would shout "La migra!" at Alfredo to see if he would get scared and start to run. He fought with other kids all the time and spent many days in the principal's office, waiting for his mother to come from work to pick him up. While he waited, he blamed her for it all. Alfredo began to believe he was what everyone said about him.

Now he would be a burden to a stranger. Shawn would adopt him, his mother said. There would be nothing more to fear from anyone. No more forged birth certificates, no more false addresses. Alfredo Moreno would become Alfredo Burns. He would have all the opportunities to succeed that an American citizen deserved.

Alfredo had wanted to cry in that bathroom after his mother had "confessed." He was confused, because he felt Dora was selling out to Shawn. Alfredo was more afraid than ever of what was to become of them in a strange man's house.

Alfredo felt he didn't look much like his father, at least not in that picture. Only his father's blue eyes were the same. Nonetheless, his name was Peterson. Not Burns, not Moreno, but Peterson. It was important that he claim that name. His biological father was not a beaner or wetback, and neither was Alfredo. The cold, fierce vision in his father's blue eyes convinced Alfredo that he had to rescue the memory of his father. Only then might he reclaim his own identity from the wetbacks and beaners who poisoned his self-respect.

With Operation Black Flag, his feelings of self-pity would finally become pride. The American tradition of courage, destiny, and power was his to take.

"Why aren't you dressed, Alfredo?"

He heard his stepfather behind him and put away the photo.

"You hear me, son? I said, why aren't you dressed yet?"

Shawn was wearing a Hawaiian shirt and blue jeans. His pink face was glazed red with a mixture of steam and drunken sweat. Shawn had not been in the military, but he knew how Alfredo admired the gung-ho, so he tried to imitate the style and speech as best he knew how.

"I woke up late," Alfredo said. "I was on my way up right now to get dressed."

Shawn stopped at the bottom of the stairs. He held one hand behind his back, in the other a can of Coors.

"Did you take my rifle out last night without permission?"

Alfredo didn't answer. He feared Shawn, who was over six feet tall, husky, and red-bearded with a baritone voice.

"Well, don't just stand there, son. Answer the question."

Dora came into the dining room.

"What is it?" she asked.

"It's a surprise," Shawn said. "Don't ruin it."

Alfredo never liked the way Shawn ordered his mother around, but he was too confused about what he should say about the gun to give it much attention. He didn't want to look at Shawn for fear of making him angry, so he kept his head down.

"I know you did, Alfredo. So just say yes, like a man."

"Did what?" Dora asked.

"Yes," Alfredo said.

"What are you talking about, Shawn?"

Alfredo waited to hear Shawn's heavy voice come down on

him for taking the rifle without permission. Alfredo had been caught several times before sneaking the rifle out. He was only supposed to touch the rifle if Shawn took him target shooting or hunting in the canyon. It was the only time they ever "bonded." Guns and sports were the only things Shawn could bond over. For everything else, there was beer and country music. Alfredo had cleaned the rifle last night, though he hadn't fired it. He had emptied the rounds and returned it to its case in the closet, exactly the way he had found it. Or so he thought.

Shawn suddenly pulled his hand from behind his back and whipped it in front of Alfredo, making him flinch.

"Gotcha!"

Shawn held out a small box wrapped in newspaper.

"I bet you thought we forgot your birthday, didn't you?" Shawn said with a mischievous smile. "Well, your mother may be losing a little bit of memory, but I'm still sharp as an elephant. Happy Birthday, Alfredo."

"You shouldn't say things like that, Shawn," Dora said.

"Say what?"

Dora frowned.

"You should have at least told me you bought him something. I could have wrapped it much better for you."

"Who cares?" Shawn said. He sipped from his beer.

Alfredo had been frightened, but Shawn's cruel sense of humor hadn't kept him from getting excited over receiving a gift. When Alfredo had torn away the paper, what remained was a cardboard box that Shawn usually filled with his old baseball cards. Alfredo frowned, figuring the contents to be something undesirable and boring as baseball cards. But when he opened the small package, he found a gleaming silver night-vision scope similar to the one Shawn had mounted on his hunting rifle. HAPPY 19, ALFREDO was engraved on the silver shell.

"Yes!" Alfredo shouted.

"Oh my God, Shawn," Dora gasped. "What is that?"

She reached for the small box, but Alfredo turned away.

"What does it fit?" Alfredo asked, holding the scope up to his eye, peering through the front window. He could see nothing through it. The living room was far too bright.

"Guess." said Shawn.

"The Remington?" Alfredo said.

"That's right, soldier. It's all yours."

"The rifle, too?" Alfredo asked, his face lighting up like a child on Santa Claus's lap.

"The whole kit and caboodle," Shawn said, grinning. "Just make sure you take good care of that weapon. It needs to be cleaned once a week. And you still have to ask me before you take it out, all right?"

"When can we go down to the Army/Navy exchange and get my gun license?"

"I'll put in the change of registration on Wednesday," Shawn said. "Then we'll make it legally yours."

"Wait a minute, por favór," Dora protested. She stood in front of her husband. "He's my son, Shawn, and I don't want him to have a gun. He doesn't need one."

"Why not? Alfredo shoots like a marksman, and he can hunt almost better than me."

Alfredo peered back through the scope again, pretending to ignore Dora and Shawn as they continued to argue. There was no stopping him now. Everything was falling into place, and he wanted to report the good news to Jesse and the others. Alfredo hoped their luck was as good as his, and the operation could now go forward.

ONCE HE HAD DRESSED, ALFREDO DROVE DORA'S Toyota Camry to the neighborhood supermarket. Instead of returning home with the celery and tomatoes his mother had sent him for, he then drove to Jesse's house. Jesse Treviño's house was big, quiet, and always full of food and video games. But the best thing was that his parents were never home. The Treviños owned a maquiladora in Tijuana and were working on buying another. They left early in the morning and came home late at night. Sometimes they wouldn't come home for days, and Jesse and his older brother, Tavo, would have the house all to themselves. They had a Mexican servant named Chela, who cooked and cleaned during the week, and sometimes stayed over on the weekends when she couldn't get a ride back to San Ysidro. When she asked Jesse to drop her at the trolley, he reminded her he still didn't have his driver's license, though he drove his mother's car whenever he felt like it. Jesse could order Chela to do just about whatever he wanted, despite the fact she had raised him from a baby, and was more a mother to him than his own. Nevertheless, Alfredo suspected Chela was an illegal, and he despised her.

"Aló, Alfredo. ¿Como estás?" Chela greeted him. She was heavy and wore a white shirt with dark blue polyester slacks. She seemed to always be at Jesse's house. Alfredo didn't know how she had time to raise her own children.

"Is Jesse home?"

"Sí. Está con los amigos. Pase."

If Chela understood him, why didn't she try to answer in English, Alfredo thought. He felt the same contempt for Chela that he did for cats, which Alfredo loved to torture.

"You need to quit acting like you own the place," Alfredo said with a completely straight face.

Chela frowned.

"¿Qué dijo?"

"Which room are the amigos in?"

"La oficina. Suba por arriba."

They were in the guest room, which was really Jesse's game and music room. He kept all his video games, books, and musical instruments there, along with an extra bed—Alfredo slept in Jesse's bunk bed when he spent the night. It used to be Mr. Treviño's office, but then Jesse's room became too crowded with gadgets, and he needed extra space to enjoy playing his guitar and his Playstation.

Alfredo had known Jesse Treviño since ninth grade; the two of them were given the nickname "Mexican Jumping Beans," after they had been trashed so many times by older jocks and bullies. "Trashing" was a traditional rite of passage for ninth graders at their high school. Alfredo and Jesse had each been thrown headfirst into a trashcan, while a senior had sat on top of the lid, holding it down. While Alfredo kicked and screamed, other seniors banged the can and sang the alma mater. The claustrophobia was excruciating. It conjured memories of Alfredo's first seizure.

Alfredo and Jesse had come to depend on each other for support and survival because it seemed everywhere they looked, people like them—short, dark-skinned Mexicans and Mexican Americans—were treated shamefully. The seniors one year even got away with trashing Dr. Muñoz, the Spanish teacher. Most students liked him because he didn't teach Spanish, but Spanglish;

his lessons were given mostly in English, spiced with Spanish words. But the Anglos hated him because he dressed like a cholo, a Mexican gangbanger, even though in class he was always going on about how he was a Chicano. As if that made any difference.

Alfredo found Gil and Erica playing Doom. The volume was way up, so Gil's shots sounded real, although the groans of his victims sounded like an audio sample. There were posters of Devo, Peter Murphy, and Blondie pinned on the walls; Jesse had inherited them from his older brother, Tavo, who had also given him a keyboard, a white trapset with cymbals, and an electric guitar. Though all four of them played in the school band, Jesse actually wrote his own songs and even played all the parts on his four-track recordings.

"Where's Jesse?" Alfredo asked.

"They're in the other room," Gil replied, "seeing if Tavo knows anyone who can get us some real weapons for tonight."

Alfredo shook his head. Tavo was a 26-year-old unemployed drug fiend, who was either always stoned or hanging out all night at the clubs on Revolution Avenue in Tijuana. Jesse thought Tavo was a homosexual, because he never brought any girlfriends over to the house.

"What if we get caught and Tavo rats on us?" Alfredo asked.

"Stop being so paranoid," Gil said. His eyes were glued to the TV as he maneuvered his 3-D character through underground mazes, while firing into his enemies. "Jesse's taking care of it."

"Jesse said Tavo knows people like that," Erica said. "Drug dealers and stuff, who have tons of guns. If we got the cash, we can get anything we want."

"You guys are pathetic," Alfredo said. "This is supposed to be a clean operation. And now we're buying guns from drug dealers? We had an agreement that no more people would—"

"Would you shut up? You're breaking my concentration."

"Ask me if I care."

"Do you have a serious problem?"

"You're a serious problem."

Gil dropped the joystick onto the carpet, turned around, and faced Alfredo.

"Why don't you do something about it?"

Gil was a lanky and lean Filipino. He had an authority complex. His father was a midrank naval officer who was often at sea. When he was home, he came down hard on Gil about not being good enough, not determined enough, not competitive enough, to be a Marine. He wanted Gil to go to the Naval Academy and learn to be an engineer. It drove him crazy that Alfredo, not Gil, had the highest marks in ROTC, the fastest time through the obstacle course, the best form when marching, all the correct rifle stations. And Gil passed on his father's resentment by trying to undermine Alfredo's leadership of the class. Gil always seemed to have something to prove, and he refused to be reviewed by Alfredo during exercises and drills.

"I found out that my grandfather has a double-barreled shotgun," Erica said, breaking the standoff. She was 16, with short blond hair, a bit on the chunky side. She played snare drum in the school marching band, beside Alfredo and Jesse. She was the newest member of the ROTC, having joined when she became infatuated with Jesse. Alfredo thought she fixed the balance of power in his favor, because Jesse was his best friend and he assumed that since Jesse would always side with him against Gil, Erica would, too.

"I don't think a shotgun will work for what we're going to do," Alfredo said. "But where is it?"

"In Arizona," Erica said, "at my grandfather's ranch. But I'm not going out there until Fourth of July."

"Why did you even bother to mention it, then?"

"You talk like you know it all, Alfredo, but where's your hardware?" Gil said.

"At home." Alfredo picked up Gil's discarded joystick. He sat down and began killing the armed men who peeked out around corners and from behind pillars. "My stepfather gave me his rifle for my birthday. You'll see. It's even got a nightscope with my name on it."

"You got a gun for your birthday?" Erica asked.

"Who got a gun for their birthday?" Jesse asked. He stood in the doorway, adjusting his glasses. He was dressed in T-shirt, fatigues, and army boots just like everyone else.

"Alfredo did," Erica said.

"Happy Birthday, Alfredo," Jesse said. "This is definitely going to be one to remember."

Erica went over to the keyboard and began pressing the keys without turning it on. Jesse watched her finger the chords. After recognizing what she was playing, he reached over and turned the keyboard on for her.

"I love Bach," Jesse said, smiling at Erica.

"Oh, please," Alfredo said. "You guys make me sick."

"What did Tavo say?" Gil asked.

"He's thinking about it," Jesse said. "But he also wants a finder's fee if we end up purchasing anything from his connections."

"A finder's fee? That's blackmail."

"Tavo calls it business," Jesse said. "That's his job."

"What did you expect?" Alfredo said. "He's unemployed."

"He's got an old friend he says can get a hold of almost anything. Even AK-47s with banana clips."

"No way," Alfredo said. "If we get caught with AKs, we'll be called Communists. Or worse, terrorists. That totally defeats the purpose of this mission. We have to calculate the cause and effect of every move we make."

"You're too paranoid, Alfredo," Gil said. "I say we postpone it until we get correctly armed. Whoever's in favor of postponing Operation Black Flag until we can get a real leader and real guns say 'aye.'"

"Whoever's in favor of kicking Gil Garcia out of this operation, effective immediately—"

"Hold on," Jesse said. "We can't go changing everything at the last minute. Let's just wait till my brother gets back to us. We'll go from there."

A heavy silence signaled that they would wait on Tavo's word. Though Alfredo had introduced Operation Black Flag to this group, he was bothered that there was ambiguity concerning who was actually leading the troops to battle. They had not yet come together as a team; they were still learning to trust one another.

THE MEMORIAL DAY PARTY WAS AS IF THERE HAD been two parties, with Alfredo and his mother perhaps having taken part in a third, more private, more awkward party between the segregated in-laws. The Morenos remained in the living room and kitchen where they could speak Spanish to each other, where they could yell at their children and complain about money without worrying about who was listening, who was ridiculing who. Shawn's family drank, ate, joked, and cursed on the back patio. The Morenos didn't drink. Many of Alfredo's uncles were recovering alcoholics, which prohibited their wives from drinking by macho default. The ambivalence toward alcohol had mostly to do with his uncles' inability to drive while intoxicated and, at the same time, avoid the police. After three DUIs, many of his uncles lost everything; having spent time in jail, they plunged deep in debt and could no longer even afford to drive. Sobriety was their cross to bear as born-again Christians.

Once the food had been devoured and the conversation wasted, all 26 aunts, uncles, and cousins hit the road. Nothing but dirty paper plates, half-full cans of Coca-Cola and Tupperware cups, hidden in all corners of the house, were left to be found. Alfredo cleaned up after his family, while his mother attended to Shawn's.

For most of the party, Alfredo had played babysitter over his younger cousins, watching them as they played little kid games, screaming and running around the house, upstairs, in and out of the bedrooms and bathrooms. He had little time for adult conversation. Tending his cousins was actually a relief compared to talking with his uncles or aunts, who kept trying to discourage him from joining the Marines. Wasn't he smarter than that? Did he commit a crime or something? Where was his novia, after all? What happened to the cute guerita girl he was dating last year? They had been mistaken, Alfredo told them. He'd never had a girlfriend. No one ever asked what he thought about his real father being a Vietnam vet missing in action. Neither did they ask Alfredo what he felt about Shawn. All he had to do was put his faith in Jesus and everything would work out right.

He was finally given a rest when Tía Marta brought out the chocolate cake she had made for Alfredo with two boxes of Betty Crocker cake mix. Alfredo sat at the head of the table with the rest of his mother's family while Tía Marta brought out the cake in a large tinfoil pan with "Happy 18th Birthday, Alfredo," written in pink on the chocolate frosting. Alfredo was positive he was the only one who even knew it was a mistake. He didn't even bother counting the candles. But before Alfredo blew them out, Tía Marta's six-year-old son, Beto, stabbed his five-year-old brother Miguel in the ear with a plastic fork as they both fought over who would get to help Alfredo blow out the candles. This happened to at least one pair of brothers in their family at every birthday party.

After the blood was cleaned up with wet paper towels, everyone was given a small piece of chocolate cake and a melted scoop of Neapolitan ice cream. ¡Buen Provecho! By the time it was all over, Alfredo was exhausted and glad to see them leave.

Wisps of charcoal smoke and lighter-fluid fumes shifted around Alfredo as he sat by himself near the black bulb of the covered barbecue in the back yard. Shawn's family circled around the redwood table on the patio, drinking Coors in cans. They were arguing, and, as usual, Shawn argued the loudest.

"Do you know what the cost of illegal immigration is to this country?" Shawn asked. "To feed them, educate them, care for them, birth their babies, clean up after them?"

"They don't pay taxes, either," one of his brothers added.

"Exactly."

"That's not true," Shawn's sister said. "They put most of their income back into the economy to buy food and pay rent. They only send a very small percentage home."

"Well, if they walk through people's back yards just like they were their own, it's no wonder people are shooting at them," Shawn said. "It's trespassing. It's a goddamn crime!"

There was a snicker of agreement. Shawn gulped at his Coors; Alfredo counted 15 seconds before the foam completely sank into the rusty wire of Shawn's thick red beard.

"You can't take the law into your own hands," Shawn's sister continued. "That is illegal."

"How can it be illegal if the law doesn't recognize that these people exist?"

"The law recognizes that they exist. It just doesn't afford them the same rights as naturalized citizens like you and me."

"What do you know? You live in Santa Barbara."

Alfredo remembered Shawn's sister was a professor at a community college. She had long red hair wrapped in a yellow bandanna. Shawn called her a hippie because she taught astronomy and had her own opinions. They argued all the time.

But once the conversation switched from illegal immigration to personal stories, Alfredo decided to return to his room to read *Heart of Darkness*. He had a hard time concentrating. The language was monotonous and archaic, almost as bad as Shakespeare. His paper was due in a few days, and he had yet to start on it. Alfredo found it difficult to read novels, or "literature," as his English teacher called it. Everything they read in class seemed to be written by one dead guy or another. Which made it hard for Alfredo to believe that it had any immediate value. What was the heart of darkness? Where? Whose? He kept scanning the page, looking for shorter paragraphs to grasp the meat of the plot. Was he the heart of darkness, or was the book? Nature or science? He finally put the book down and prepared to make his move to the canyon.

He painted his face with black and green paint, like the jungle soldiers in *Apocalypse Now*. His forehead and mouth were solid green with a thick black stripe across the bridge of his nose. He put on his red beret with his gold ROTC pin in front. He looked at himself in the bathroom mirror in full light, candlelight, and then with no light.

He sneaked into the master bedroom closet, cleared away Dora's many boxes of shoes, and, leaning on his stepfather's Hawaiian and polo shirts, eased the long black leather case from the top shelf, and put it on the bed. He pulled the heavy rifle out of the case. The smell of oil and polish gave him a rush. Shawn had already mounted the nightscope for him: the rifle was now his own. He strapped it on. He was ready.

No one saw him go down the stairs. He heard the low rumble of adult talk. No one heard him slip out the front door and into the street.

Alfredo set his internal snare, synchronizing the rimshot with the clip of his boots on the sidewalk. Thump-thump, thump-thump. Click. Thump-thump, thump-thump. Click. Thump-thump, thump-thump. Click. He always tried to march at a drummer's pace. It was part of his internal discipline.

A car passed, shining its headlights on Alfredo. It pulled into a driveway somewhere behind him. The newly paved sidewalks and bright stop signs ended at the chain-link limit of Loma Verde Elementary School and the edge of the canyon.

As Alfredo swung his leg over the top of the fence, straddling it, he paused with the rifle braced between his underarm and rib cage. Looking into the dotted horizon, he saw the lights of the Tijuana hills constelled in the distance. The indigo sky was pitted with charcoal-colored clouds that appeared to bounce, Alfredo realized, because he was panting. He took a deep breath and stayed on the fence a moment longer, above the steep bank of slick ice plant on the other side. The toes of his boots hooked into the chain links, and both hands gripped the cross-pole slick with dew.

The canyon stretched out before him, dark and murky. He heard crickets singing like an electric current. He took a deep breath and jumped from the fence. He fought to keep his feet as he slid down the slick bank, bending over and back, straining to keep his balance.

He was reminded of the jungle-gym slide at his elementary school, the one he had thrown sand on in order to go down it standing up, showing off for the others still too afraid to try it for themselves. Alfredo had shown remarkable daring on the playground slide, but, like the other fifth graders, he didn't have the courage to venture out beyond the sandbox and onto the grass field where the sixth graders ran around playing tackle football and grab-ass. He remembered being on top of the slide and seeing a few of the assgrabbers escaping the teacher on lunch duty by climbing over into the canyon. Each descended and disappeared into the trees to play the game the way they wanted, without adult supervision. Then, just as Alfredo was about to go speeding down the sandy slide standing up, he had seen a group of men climbing up out of the canyon where the assgrabbers had gone in. Short, dark men in dirty jeans and tattered shirts—they looked around, nervously. They walked toward the end of the playground, toward the gravel lot at the back of the school. While Alfredo watched them, the bullhorn began wailing, which usually meant five minutes to the end of recess. But lunch recess had just started.

The teacher shouted something at Alfredo, while he stood at the top of the slide. Probably telling him to get down. Everyone stared at Alfredo as if he had set off the bullhorn. Suddenly, Alfredo realized he indeed had. It was against the rules to go down the slide standing up, yet he felt responsible for another crime. When all the students who were gathered around the monkey bars noticed the teacher running down the asphalt ramp, waving the bullhorn, Alfredo heard someone say, "Look, Mrs. Donoghue is going after the wetbacks. Come on, Alfredo. Come down before Mrs. Donoghue gets you." But instead of going down standing up, Alfredo went down on his ass.

He could still hear the bullhorn wailing in his memory, as he clenched his jaw and carved down the ice plant, keeping himself stiff as a board. He was determined not to fall. Alfredo dug the rubber soles of his boots into the sharp, snapping fingers of the ice plant, and gained better control of his momentum by balancing his stepfather's rifle in front of him. He sped down the wet incline until he hit the sand at the edge of the canyon. He did not fall.

THE RENDEZVOUS POINT WAS BENEATH THE cover of a large juniper tree. There were several small, dusty boulders with flat tops arranged in a semicircle around a half-burnt tree trunk that served as a kind of forum. It was well hidden and marked the halfway point between the school and the top of the sandy ridge near the border fence. Alfredo sat in the dark against one of the rocks. He could smell the spicy juniper seeds and his own sweat-dampened fatigues. He pulled a flashlight from his backpack, opened his notebook, and marked the place, date, and time. It was 1:43 in the morning; his Commandos were over an hour late. You couldn't be late for something like this. Being on time was the first rule. Why weren't they better prepared? How could they have waited until the last moment to collect their weapons?

Alfredo was trying to bring the black flag to life. Otherwise, it was all just talk. Talk, talk, talk. Alfredo was prepared to act. His colleagues were obviously not. Maybe he was meant to go alone. After all, the assault was his idea. Maybe Gil had discouraged them from following through as a way to subvert Alfredo's leadership. If Gil was a traitor, Alfredo would have to eliminate him.

In case of a delay, Jesse had assured Alfredo they could get to the border on their own, once they had picked up the rifles from Tavo's connection. But maybe they had lost their way through the canyon. Alfredo knew the territory the best and had rehearsed the path to the rendezvous point with them several times before. But the sprawling locust and juniper trees looked the same all over the canyon. Alfredo had discovered many similar campsites in the canyon—inhabited by illegals. He had burst in on one group at dawn as they squatted around a smoldering fire. They spoke rapid Spanish, drank soda from cans, and laughed while searching for a good ember to light their cigarettes. It was as if they were in their own living room. Alfredo emerged, in camouflage and backpack, holding a long black flashlight, and threatened to light up their camp with a bomb. But they laughed at him and said, "Cálmate, guey. No hay problema. Ya nos vamos."

Alfredo was enraged by their nonchalance. He pulled out two

M-80s, lit one, and screamed "¡Fuego!" They scattered in a dust cloud of Spanish cuss words.

Alfredo extinguished their fire with sand and buried their sacks of trash along with the embers.

The Border Patrol searched the canyon for new migrant settlements all the time. Maybe Alfredo's partners had been apprehended. The police were always in the canyon looking for arsonists, drug dealers, rapists on the lam. Criminals of all types, from Mexico and the United States, had used the canyon for cover. It was becoming like the ninth level of hell. All the more reason to destroy it.

Alfredo did not want to miss his chance. He repacked his things and left the rendezvous camp. He passed swiftly through the canyon. He heard bats screech above him and spotted a coyote sprinting for cover. Once he reached the sandy clearing on the ridge above the border fence, he fell on his belly. The Tijuana reservoir below was empty. The surrounding hills had been shaved of their vegetation by the Border Patrol. If he stood up to take aim and shoot, he might be seen. He stretched out, gripping the glossy wood-and-steel muzzle of his rifle. He released the safety and squeezed the rifle tighter around the neck with his thumb. He hated all those who failed to deliver, who were or were not out in the void and distance. They were nothing more than a mute audience for his voice and vision. They were useless as death. Their role was passive. And his fellow vigilantes, he decided, were worse than useless, they were unreliable.

Alfredo could smell a vapor of sewage. He heard whispers like faraway footsteps scurrying across gravel, but saw no movement. He raised the scope and looked across the deep cement reservoir and saw nothing but slanting lines of telephone poles, gray treetops, and abandoned cars on a faraway empty street of Colonia Libertad. He could faintly hear cars speeding down I-5.

There was a thunk of metal on metal below that Alfredo felt shake the ground. He wiggled out farther on the ledge and squinted into grayness. He heard the thunk again. They were digging. He heard more whispers in greater volume. A panic came over him as he thought it might be the only group that came through tonight. The Border Patrol could pass by and find the large hole below the fence, stake the place out for who knew how long. Or worse, fill it with cement. Then Alfredo would have to spend time looking for a new spot. There was no time for that.

The clouds cleared as the wind picked up. Inside the gray tunnel of his night-vision scope, one silhouette peeked out from the base of the wall and then disappeared. Alfredo knew that when all had been pulled through, they would pair off in twos and threes, fearing capture by the Border Patrol.

At least a dozen bodies had already been pulled out from beneath the fence. They would break at any moment. He slapped his cheek against the neck of the rifle, and braced the butt tight against his shoulder. He squinted into the scope and shot.

CLACK

Chink-chink

CLACK

Chink-chink

CLACK CLACK CLACK

Chink-chink

Alfredo saw bodies scrambling, some falling and getting up. He had to have hit at least two of them. He knew they were bunched up, clinging to each other, frozen to the wall, shitting their pants. He fired again.

BOOM BOOM

BOOM BOOM BOOM

BOOM

BOOM BOOM BOOM BOOM

"Yooooh! Whoooo! Yeah!"

BOOM BOOM BOOM

BOOM BOOM BOOM BOOM

BOOM BOOM

"Did you hit anyone?"

"What? I can't hear."

"Did you get anyone?"

"I don't know. Everything's gray."

BOOM

"You fuck!" Alfredo screamed. He'd momentarily lost his hearing and wasn't sure how loud he had shouted. Gil was standing directly above him. His face was painted black, and his eyes glowed like Spanish olives in deviled eggs. Alfredo jumped up and shoved him in the chest with the flat side of his rifle.

"Back off, Alfredo," Gil said. He braced his own rifle at his shoulder and pointed it at Alfredo's nose. "Unless you wanna get it like one of them."

"Calm down," Jesse said. "Come on, Gil, put it down."

"This fucker attacked me!" Gil said.

"We can't have you guys fighting," Jesse said. "It's bad for morale."

"Yeah. And it's stupid, too," Erica added. "You guys need to get over it."

Gil relented and lowered his rifle across his chest.

"This isn't over," he told Alfredo.

"Everybody move back," Alfredo said. He scrambled back from the edge of the cliff and retrieved his backpack from the bushes. "You guys were too loud and too late. The Border Patrol will be looking for us."

"You think they care if a few pollos got wasted?" Jesse said, squatting near the tumbleweeds and mustard plants 15 yards from the edge of the cliff.

"I want to go down and see who we got," Gil said. "Soldiers always confirm their kills."

"We don't have time for that," Alfredo hissed. "Besides you guys were late. Where were you? We could have had them all."

"What do you mean?" Jesse said. "We must have each gotten off half a dozen rounds."

"What did you hit?"

"A woman, I think," Jesse said. "Somebody."

"You hit shit," Alfredo challenged. "That was totally unorganized."

"Look. My chamber's empty, and it held seven rounds."

"You probably just made holes in the fence. Where were you?"

"We got delayed," Erica said, giggling. "At Lolita's." The whites of her front teeth gleamed in her black face.

"What the hell?" Alfredo said in disbelief. "You were eating when you knew you were supposed to meet me at 12:30?"

"First, we had to meet Tavo and the guy he set us up with at midnight," Jesse explained. "To get the guns."

"Some gangster dude. He was as big as a blimp, I swear."

They were all speaking rapidly, the excitement electrifying their voices and shortening their breath.

"There was a miscommunication, and we had to wait for the hardware to arrive," Jesse continued. "But we came straight here as soon as we could. Gil led us to you."

"I don't know what you're arguing about," Gil said. "I watched my targets fall. I know what I hit."

"I don't think I hit anything," Erica said. "The first shot hurt too much. I need more practice." She took off her beret and shook out her short blond hair. "Alfredo's right, though. We were late."

"Let's go down. I'll show you exactly who I killed," Gil said. "He was wearing a baseball hat and a loose poncho. And there was a woman. It looked like she was carrying groceries. You should have seen how everything shot up in her arms when I hit her. It was like being at the carnival. We have to go down and see."

Alfredo remembered seeing the woman with a swaddle in her arms through his scope. He'd thought she was holding a baby and had chosen another target, a skinny man with a big pumpkin head. He'd aimed for the pumpkin head, but wasn't sure whether he'd hit it. He was sure he'd killed another man who had moved slow during the shooting, as well as the one in the baseball hat Gil claimed to have taken out. But it wasn't necessary to confirm the kills. It would take too much time, and they were already behind schedule.

Alfredo thought he heard large engines gassing and gears shifting. Alfredo looked up into the hills above the border and through the misty haze of lights. Dark clouds of dust seemed to be descending upon them.

"No, we have to get back to the school," Alfredo said. "The Border Patrol will be looking for us."

"You can all follow me," Gil commanded. "I know how to get down there."

Jesse was the first to break away with Gil. Then all were running behind Gil, down into another ravine thick with tumbleweeds and soft sand. They had left the ridge and were supposedly circling around toward the border fence. Alfredo doubted Gil knew where he was going, but reluctantly followed, distracted between the aftershock of the shooting, his rage at Gil, and the disappointment of their late arrival. He felt disoriented and betrayed by Jesse, his best friend. Alfredo wanted to yell for them to stop and let him lead before they got lost. But he was bringing up the rear and could not tell how far ahead Gil had run.

Alfredo's boots got heavier as soil clumped and clung with the dampness, spitting up sand onto his back. He was scratched on his face by uncleared branches and bushes. This wasn't the right path. It was difficult to run with his rifle catching on everything, but it helped him get up and out of the sand when his knees buckled or when he lost his footing. He realized he was tired; he tried to focus on measured breathing between the thumps of his steps.

The woman Gil claimed to have shot kept coming to his mind. What if she really was carrying a baby? What was the difference between an illegal infant and an adult?

What had made Alfredo decide, in that moment of recognition, that he couldn't shoot her? Why had Gil been able to? Alfredo needed to stay on task. But the operation was falling apart, and instead of leading, he was now following.

"Alfredo!" he heard ahead of him. "They're here!"

It was Jesse calling out his name—for anyone to hear. As Alfredo approached the bottom of the ravine, he heard more shouting.

"Get down! On your knees!"

"Espérate. Por favór. No nos disparen. Please...don't...shoot. No tenemos dinero ni nada. Lo llevaron todo. Por favór..."

"¡A las rodillas!" Jesse shouted. "¡Y cállense!"

Alfredo emerged from the brush and found Gil and Jesse standing over three Mexicans: two men and a woman on their knees, sobbing. Alfredo hadn't prepared to deal with survivors. This was a guerrilla operation—shoot and run. He had not expected to take any prisoners.

Erica had gone to cry—and vomit—in the bushes.

"Did you ever wonder why there was a girl in the group, Jesse?" Gil asked sardonically.

"She'll come around," Jesse said, defending his girlfriend. "You all right, Erica?"

Erica groaned and spit back at them.

"Alfredo, cover the old guy," Gil commanded. "I got this one right here." He aimed at a young man with a thick head of black hair, dressed in a sweatshirt and jeans, who had been shot in the stomach and was now visibly in severe pain. His voice was high, short of breath, and frightened as he rocked back and forth, speaking to the woman in the language none of them could understand. By the sound of their clip-clopping speech, Alfredo guessed they were Indians.

Alfredo did what he was told and pointed his gun at a man

with short gray hair and thick gray mustache, his shirt and jeans soaked in blood. He had been shot in the left shoulder and in the right thigh.

"I don't see any dead bodies anywhere," Alfredo said. "We've only got prisoners. Which is exactly what we didn't want. I say we get outta here now before—"

"Shut up," Gil said. "We're not going anywhere."

"Por favór. Mi esposa está grave. Mi hijo también. Mi hijo..."

"¡Callate lo hocico!" Jesse hissed at the young man clutching his stomach. He lifted his gun at the woman and pointed it at her head. "O la matamos."

The plump forearm of her baby peeked out of the colored bundle she cradled, and then the baby start to cry.

"It's alive," Alfredo said.

"For now," Gil responded. "Tell that baby to shut up."

Alfredo could hear rustling in the bushes behind him. Now that they did not have a dead baby on their hands, Erica's guilty conscience might be eased, and she could try to make her way back to the circle.

"¿Por qué?" the woman sobbed. "¿Por qué? Ay. Ay. Pero, por qué?"

"What is she saying?" Gil asked.

"She wants to know why," Jesse said.

"Why? Why what?"

The woman repeated herself several times in the language none of them could understand. Then the younger man spoke. He was having a hard time drawing breath, and Alfredo was certain he would die soon. He wanted to leave them. He did not want to watch them die. He wanted to break. But he couldn't.

"I think something's wrong with the baby," Jesse said. "I don't know. They're all freaked out."

"¿Por qué? ¿Por qué?" the woman cried.

"Tell her, they're all going to die," Gil commanded. "Tell her why. Tell her it was your idea to shoot them."

"You shot her," Alfredo answered. "You tell her why."

"I may have shot her. But you're going to take her out. This is all you, Alfredo. They're all going to die because of you. It was your idea to murder some wetbacks. Tell her why."

Alfredo tried to ignore Gil's taunts. He pushed the barrel of the Remington closer to the old man's face.

If he were alive and living with Alfredo, his father would probably be as old as this man, whose brown eyes awaited death. But this man knew nothing about Vietnam, much less about POW/MIAs. Alfredo's father had been taken prisoner by the Viet Cong, made to kneel before the enemy, and submit to torture. This man knew he was going to die, and yet he was fighting to keep his dignity. Had Corporal Peterson kept his dignity? Or had he begged for his life? Had the VC forced him to turn on his fellow soldiers, give away secret positions, commit treason?

What drove a man to lose his dignity, if not the threat of death? Alfredo refused to imagine his father as a rat. No matter how frightening it may have been, or how much infighting took place, Corporal Peterson would have been the last to turn on his own. He had been a hero, a man willing to die for his country and his beliefs. Just like Alfredo.

There was indeed a reason why. But Alfredo knew Gil didn't care. Gil's hatred was not the same as Alfredo's, but instead aimed at Alfredo. To Gil, Alfredo was one of the wetbacks. Alfredo was Mexican, so was Jesse. Gil was Filipino. Did he think himself better because he wasn't Mexican? Or because his father was a naval officer? He would have liked Alfredo to be kneeling, facing the barrel of his rifle, begging for his life. This was simply a chance for Gil to show that his cruelty was stronger. Gil wanted to kill them all and blame Alfredo for it. He had taken complete control of the operation. Alfredo would have to tell them why, if only to let Gil know that the shoe was on the other foot and that this was still Alfredo's vision.

"You're our prisoners," Alfredo began. "You have no rights, because you chose to enter our country illegally. You are fugitives, border-crossing criminals. We, as American citizens, have the right to detain you. You are invaders and don't belong here. You have no name, no one knows you, and you can't speak our language. You trespass on our land, our property, and our freedom. You contribute nothing to society, nor to the good of the whole. You don't pay taxes. You are completely anti-American, anti-family, and anti-flag. You bring poverty, corruption, and chaos with you from Mexico. You endanger the lives of law-abiding citizens. You are a public nuisance, a health hazard, and you contaminate our welfare system. You stress our local, state, and federal budgets by overburdening our hospitals and schools with your sick families and your illiterate children. You undermine the economy by working for less than minimum wage. You are the black market. You transport illegal substances and diseases. You are human contraband. Your lives are corrupt; your presence corrupts our lives."

As Alfredo stopped speaking, the hum of their prayers grew louder.

Alfredo fought to remain focused on his original plan, the one that Gil had wrested from his control. He tried to focus on the image of his father's face on the black POW/MIA flag. And louder now, to make sure the others heard him above the Nuestro Señors, Ave Marias, and prayers to Juan Soldado, Alfredo continued his executioner's song.

"You are weak, helpless, dirty. You wander through our neighborhoods like stray dogs looking for handouts. You give hard-working Mexican Americans a bad name. You overcrowd our homes and take our hospitality for granted. You get drunk and harass our mothers, sisters, and daughters. You leave trash in our streets and yards. You flush tons of dirty diapers down the toilet, clogging up the pipes. You break up families by taking jobs from the people who were born here. You bring gangs to our neighborhoods and schools. You put us all in danger of the police, the Border Patrol, and deportation—even we who are citizens. You set bad examples for Americans.

"As patriots, as vigilantes of the memory of all American POWs missing in action, as defenders and vanguards of the American way, we condemn you to suffer merciless humiliation at our hands."

"Bravo!" Jesse said.

BOOM

BOOM

BOOM

The young man fell over on his side with the force of the shots fired at close range from Gil's rifle. An echo rippled through the canyon. There was silence, except for the woman who held her baby and collapsed in tears.

Gil moved beside Jesse: "Take her out."

Jesse stalled and shook his head.

"I can't. I don't want to."

"Yes, you can," Gil said. "She's already dying."

But Jesse wouldn't do it, and Gil began to taunt him and call

42

names. Jesse began yelling back at Gil.

"You can't tell me what to do. This isn't ROTC class."

"Don't do it, Jesse," Erica said. She had watched from behind, and now she was ready to protest. "Let's just leave them how they are, and get out of here before it's too late."

"She's right," Alfredo said. "We're asking to be caught if we don't leave right now. Let's go."

"Who's gonna catch us?" Gil shouted. "The Border Patrol? The army? The police? They're on our side. Right, Alfredo? You said it all before. We're the good guys."

"You're a fool, Gil," Erica said. "You're the one who wanted to come down here to see what they looked like. Now you've seen. If we all get caught, it'll be your fault."

"No, it won't," Gil laughed. "This is all Alfredo's idea."

"But if we get caught, we're all going to jail for murder because of your stupidity."

A rumbling wind descended upon them. Dust and sand kicked up around the bushes. Alfredo lost a breath when he spotted a searchlight hitting a few hundred yards ahead. It was what he feared. They had made too much noise and wasted too much time. The Border Patrol had sent out a chopper and now they would all be caught.

Alfredo ran, even though he knew they would not escape. As he ran, the spotlight kept getting closer, waving to the right. Now it circled to the left, and then out of sight behind him, where he felt the heat of its beam on his back. The chopper was riding them tightly, its thunder blades rumbling and rolling up on him like a roaring jaguar climbing his back. He was doomed. He kept his eyes on the bleach-burned horizon without needing to look at the ground. He repeated the letters of the alphabet backward: Zorro— gay blade; Yucca (ughhcc!); Ximena—his mother's middle name; Wool—warts (the way his aunts said it, supposedly imitating his grandmother); Verguenza—not mine!

At least he had chosen for himself. Alfredo felt he could still salvage a moral victory. Perhaps word would get out about his father, and something would be done to reunite them. Even if it was confirmation of his death, it was something he could hope for despite all that had gone wrong.

The foot of the ice plant hill was in sight. Alfredo stopped running. There were two helicopters now, two beaming rays striking the ice plant. He turned around to look for the others. Gil had been right behind him, had almost tripped over Alfredo. They gripped each other by the arms to keep from falling.

"Are they coming?" Alfredo asked, turning himself out of Gil's hands.

"Think so. What are you waiting for? Go!" Gil pushed Alfredo ahead. Alfredo stumbled and and then steadied himself. He turned around quickly, his finger searching for the safety on his rifle. Gil passed by him and began to climb the ice plant. Alfredo lifted his rifle and aimed for his back as Jesse and Erica finally reached him. They stopped behind him and waited silently for Alfredo to shoot.

"DON'T MOVE!"

The voice boomed through a bullhorn. Light streamed down the ice plant.

"¡NO SE MUEVAN!" another shouted.

The lights crisscrossed until two fell on Alfredo. He ducked back down, raising up his arm and the rifle to shield himself from the light. He saw the headlights of two white Ford Broncos parked at the edge of the fence.

"THIS IS THE U.S. BORDER PATROL! DISCARD ALL WEAPONS NOW, OR YOU WILL BE SHOT! REPEAT! DITCH THE GUNS OR YOU'LL BE SHOT RIGHT WHERE YOU STAND! WE ARE AGENTS OF UNITED STATES BORDER PATROL!"

"¡TIREN LAS ARMAS!" the Spanish voiced raked, thick with norteño accent. "¡SOMOS DE INMIGRACIÓN ESTADOUNIDENSE! DEJEN LAS ARMAS Y ARRIBA LAS MANOS O—"

"We speak English!" Gil shouted. "American citizens! We're throwing away our guns!"

"DROP THEM WHERE YOU STAND. GET ON YOUR KNEES!"

Alfredo watched Shawn's rifle fall with a thud onto the ice plant that covered the hill like a net of sharp, glistening emerald fingers. He dropped his hands at his sides and kneeled.

II. BLOOD ON THE RAZORWIRE

Everyone has two dreams: one of home, and one of leaving.
Salman Rushdie

"*911.* What's your emergency?"

"I want to report un asesinato."

"Excuse me?

"I want to report a murder."

"Would you like to report a homicide?"

"A homicide? Yes. Three homicidios."

"Can you give me your name, please?"

"Can't I be anonymous?"

"You don't want to tell me your name?"

"No. I want to talk to the police. It's very important. Someone will want to hear about this. Can you put me through to somebody quickly? This is a life-or-death situation."

"I understand. Can you tell me what happened?"

"I told you. I want to report a murder. And two others."

"Are they inside the premises?"

"Inside? Where? Here?"

"Yes. Should I send an ambulance?"

"No. No. They're not here. I'm not at home."

"Where exactly are you, ma'am?"

"I'm at my boyfriend's studio in Chula Vista."

"O.K. What's the address?"

"The address? Don't you have that on your computer?"

"No."

"13…what's the number here, Edgar? No. La direción. 322 D Street."

"All right. And how long ago did this happen?"

"This morning. About 9:30."

"9:30 this morning. On 3rd and D in Chula Vista?"

"No. In Tijuana."

"I'm sorry, ma'am. Do you mean Tijuana, Mexico?"

"Yes. Tijuana, México. But I am a resident here in the U.S. How long before you can put me through to someone?"

"I don't think we're authorized to handle international crimes. Can you hold on while I check with my supervisor?"

"No. No. You don't understand. SOMEONE FROM LOS REYES DRUG CARTEL IS GOING TO KILL ME IF I DON'T TALK TO THE POLICE RIGHT NOW! Can you just please give me somebody?"

"Hold, please."

THE COCAINE HAD BEEN PACKED AWAY IN A compartment inside the roof of the 4Runner, where Tavo kept his CDs and tapes, but which were now spread beneath the seats and on the floorboards in back. Miranda had suggested Edgar walk it across the border and wait on the other side of the fence in San Ysidro for Tavo to pick him up. The customs agents working the x-ray machines and metal detectors inside the U.S. customs complex were trained to identify and detain suspiciously short, shabbily dressed, dark-skinned Mexicans trying to illegally enter the United States. Edgar was over six feet, an olive color, dressed in hip clothes, with a cleanly shaven head. Other than being Chicano, Edgar did not fit the description. He could have easily stated his U.S. citizenship and walked right through without a second glance from the red-eyed agent on graveyard duty. But the cocaine could not be secured on his body. It was too bulky a package for Edgar to swallow in a balloon or simply put down his pants. It was too big for him to walk it across in a shopping bag. It had barely fit inside the roof compartment of the 4Runner.

They were at a complete stop near the yellow painted line that "officially" separated Mexico and the United States. It was after three a.m. and the line at the Tijuana border was extra messy with high school and college students jumping in and out of each other's cars like drunken turkeys, shouting, stumbling, and vomiting. A few blond surfer boys had to be pulled back into their cars, while others were left behind to sleep it off next to the curb, lying in their own piss. The pickups returning to San Diego from Tijuana, Rosarito, Ensenada, and Tecate were loaded up with moto-cross bikes and quadrunners, yellowish Baja mud, and sand caked over the paint disguising their California license plates. Gusts of sulfuric exhaust blew from their tailpipes. Edgar looked ahead at the customs agent in his starched blue-and-white uniform; he was yanking on the leash of a German shepherd as it barked and lunged from one car to another. Edgar counted the cars ahead: a dozen more and the dog would be on them. It stopped at a purple VW Bug and began barking, whining, and impatiently clawing at the passenger door. The agent poked his head into the window and asked the passenger to get out.

"Miranda would love for me to get strip-searched," Edgar told Tavo. "That's why she asked me to cross this shit. She wants to torture me."

"You're talking paranoid," Tavo said. He bounced his hand off the steering wheel. "You know how easy it is to pass through. We look just as clean as the next guy."

"Or dirty. Or ugly. Or suspicious. Or—"

"Whatever. Miranda's not even with us."

"The coke's taken her place."

"Don't act like you didn't know she was hooked up with Los Reyes," Tavo said. "You should have expected she would ask something from you. Why do you think she always has it? Her cousin Julián is like their number-one guy."

"That's why he's dead now."

"Disappeared."

Edgar wanted to do one more key shot before the dog arrived. One more for confidence. But there was no time to risk it. Tavo turned down his stereo and slumped over the wheel. He was listening for something wrong with the engine. His nostrils quivered like he was trying to smell something. The cab of the 4Runner filled with the scattered buzz of Mexican electro-pop and norteño bass, as sharp bites of Metallica and House of Pain crackled through the flies and dust swarming around the cars in line. It was too hot to roll up the window.

"Saraaapes, elooooote, empanaaaaadas. ¿Cuál le gusta, señor?"

"No. No quiero, gracias," Tavo said, lifting his head up from the dash. He tossed his cigarette out the window in front of a man wearing ten straw sombreros and carrying a dozen multicolored blankets on his shoulders.

Edgar heard the dog bark again.

"How do those dogs smell drugs through all this shit?" he asked.

"Call it the inhumane treatment of animals," Tavo said. "Like monkeys sent into space."

"What do you know?" Edgar said coldly. "You don't have dog sense."

"You're right," Tavo said. "I guess you'd have to be a dog or a real Mexican to know."

"Or a fucking Hoover, like you," Edgar snapped.

"If that's not calling the kettle black."

Tavo stuck his hand out the window, gesturing forward with his many silver and turquoise rings at the rows upon rows of chrome, metal, and steel jammed together in front of him. There looked to be at least 500 cars waiting to pass through six customs booths that flashed a green light above, signaling that they were open for inspection.

"Pinche gringos," Tavo said. "I swear, one thing about gringos is they love to make a line. Fucking wait in line for anything."

"Good things come to those who wait," Edgar said. "Didn't they teach you that in Tijuana?"

"Yeah, right. The Mexicans are the ones trying to sneak in, jamming up the whole thing."

They had only moved a hundred yards in 45 minutes since Tavo had kamikazied into the middle of a line, skidding to a stop in front of an Astrovan loaded with fraternity boys from Oregon.

Tavo wrenched the wheel between his hands and grimaced at the drunken faces in front of him. "Tu puta madre," he said under his breath.

"Shouldn't you turn the heat on?" Edgar asked. "So you won't overheat?"

"As if hell wasn't already fucking hot enough. But maybe just for a minute." Tavo reached beneath the dashboard and flipped on the heater.

"Would they search an overheated car we both pushed to the front?" Edgar asked, watching as three more customs agents appeared from behind the front of a Winnebago in the next lane. They followed their dog as it bobbed its black-and-tan head under fenders and mufflers.

"Give them any reason," Tavo said, shaking his head. "Give them any reason to search your ass, Edgar, and they'll be feeding you laxatives and dissecting your shit before you have the chance to say rapidillo."

"¿Rapidillo?"

"Diarrhea."

"Oh."

Cocaine brought out the deviant, perverted, and redundant in you, Edgar thought. Not that Tavo was ever a completely sober and conscientious individual. Yet being drug smugglers put them both in the same boat as the Customs and Immigration shit-collectors. They played their game. Everyone did. As far as Edgar knew, everyone in line was a criminal, a liar, and a smuggler. And there could be no redemption except safe passage into San Diego.

If they caught him, Edgar could say the coke belonged to Los Reyes, the powerful Baja California drug cartel Miranda was involved with—or trying to escape. Which was it? Her cousin, Julián, was also linked to Los Reyes. He had disappeared, and she needed help getting their remaining stash across the border so Los Reyes couldn't catch her with it. Maybe Edgar could trade information for immunity. He could say Los Reyes forced him into it, even if really Edgar was trying to help Miranda. Being the ingenious friend he was, Tavo offered to share the responsibility with Edgar and drive the coke into San Diego in exchange for enough drugs to remain insomniac for two weeks. They had helped themselves to heavy portions before deciding to go through customs. Now they were stuck in line on one of the busiest Saturday nights of the year.

A little boy appeared at Edgar's window. His head was just taller than the door. One tiny hand gripped the black interior where the window was rolled down, while the other pressed a box of multicolored Chiclets inside. He stuck a finger in his ear and waited beside Edgar with the box of gum suspended into the car.

"Tell him, Edgar, que no, you don't want any."

Edgar remained silent, entranced by the boy's disassociated gaze.

"Don't stare, Edgar. They think you want to buy."

Edgar watched the boy's tiny fingers curve over the truck's windowsill like dark, wrinkled wings, each fingernail thickly striped with dirt. Edgar felt his own body moving in slow motion as he touched the boy's hand. The boy looked bored, but he hung onto the window, staring through the truck cab and into more cars.

"Chicle," the boy said.

"Where's your mamá?" Edgar asked.

"Allá," the boy said, shaking his head toward the back of the line.

Tavo reached into his pocket for a few pesos. A car beeped, reminding him to move up.

"Oh, que la chingada. Here. Toma, niño." Tavo reached across Edgar and handed the boy some coins. "Para que comas, O.K.? Only for food."

The boy tossed some gum inside the cab and moved on.

Tavo twisted the wheel between his hands and inched forward. Edgar began to fiddle with the radio.

A Mexican judicial on a moto-cross bike chased a group of tiny indígena children and their mother in and out of traffic. The children ran from this Mexican policeman, whose job it was to stop any unlicensed vending, but who could not cross the yellow line into the United States; the kids leaped back and forth across the line, laughing at him.

Beneath the full moon, shadows crept over the wheat-colored hills on the U.S. side of the canyon. The government had burned the brush and trees to make it easier to spot illegals trying to cross. Edgar could see bulky white Ford Broncos parked at odd angles, observing the busy border. Suddenly, all the noise around them was drowned by a helicopter buzzing the hills, its Night Sun spotlight looking to squeeze undocumented immigrants out from the cracks of the earth.

Such bright light at three in the morning struck Edgar like a waking nightmare, where everyone was exposed and vulnerable, as if the border was a world where the worst things could happen at any time.

Tavo found a space to cut in and jerked the 4Runner in front of a Nissan Sentra full of teenage girls fighting over what looked like a magazine. Farther up the new lane, Edgar watched more German shepherds sniff everything rapidly, hunting for something worse than addiction.

"I wonder if the NEA will ask for the money back after they find out I got arrested for smuggling drugs," Edgar said.

"Tell them you were doing research," Tavo said. "Tell them your girlfriend's a dealer and you did it for love. They can't take that away from you."

"What kind of joke is that?"

"A bad one," Tavo said. "But funny."

Tavo was very adept at the philosophy of laughing now and crying later. He could equate complete tragedy with complete relajo, a ridiculously sad joke. A particularly Mexican quality. Miranda had the same talent. With the $25,000 grant Edgar had won—to produce paintings for the annual Sites on the Border show—he had given Tavo a job as a research assistant. Perhaps that was the real joke.

"What were you thinking hooking me up with a dealer, Tavo? I could have found one in Chula Vista."

"Come on." Tavo hunched his shoulders and turned his palms up in his best Robert De Niro. "I didn't say you had to fall in love with her. I thought you wanted to party and meet some new people. You wanted to learn about Tijuana. That's why you hired me, right? I mean, I couldn't tell Vincent van Gogh from Dick Van Dyke."

"I hope, when the migra has their finger up your ass, Tavo, I hope you can still laugh."

"All you have to do is relax, breathe deep, and think of your favorite song," Tavo whispered. "And it'll all be over in no time."

"Fuck you. You're a real motherfucker. I cannot believe you're my best friend."

"I'm your only friend."

Edgar gripped the door handle and wedged his sweaty forearms against the interior, wanting to burst out of the truck and head for San Ysidro. The trolley would start running at 5 a.m. He could ride it back to Chula Vista. And then what? It made Edgar sick to think of facing Miranda again. Until tonight, trust hadn't been a serious issue between Edgar and Miranda. Nothing had been taken very seriously between them. There hadn't been much interest in trust.

Even if Miranda came from a well-known family in Tijuana, she was just a hustler. She had a daughter and was trying to earn money from cocaine. It was not unheard of. She had never made any type of emotional confession to Edgar. And he had kept quiet about his past. Their relationship had been purely physical. But now Edgar burned for her. He could feel her venom seize hold of his veins. He remembered love was physical. As physical as pain.

"Now you see how we live here," Tavo said, smiling. "The

thing is to feel paranoia, but not to become paranoid."

"Laugh so as not to cry, right? Ha, ha. Very funny, motherfucker."

"For me to laugh about how gringo laws rape Mexicans is not such a bad way of dealing with it," Tavo said. "It's a defense mechanism, hmm?"

"Jail is not funny."

"Come on. What happened to all that San Diego optimism?"

"Optimism? What are you talking about?"

Tavo waved his hand in front of him and smirked at the truckload of college boys jumping around, playing like apes and throwing empty beer cans and Chiclets at one another.

"You think those guys are afraid of customs?" Tavo said. "Those fuckers will be sleeping tight in their beds tonight, and so will you. So quit being a pussy."

"What are you talking about?"

"I'm talking about all this border-hype shit," Tavo said, lighting another cigarette. "Gringos don't have to live with the humiliation of la fucking migra up their ass, waiting in line all day. They treat Tijuana like a dump and then act like it's our fault it stinks."

"Do you really want to argue about this right now? Now is not the time for identity crisis."

"Who's arguing? It's the truth. You have nothing to fear, Edgar. You're a gringo first, a Mexican second. Accept it. Let it be, and we'll get through, no problem."

But weren't they all part of the same experience? That's what Edgar had wanted to believe. Smuggling the cocaine simply reinforced that philosophy.

Which reminded Edgar of his sister, Cristina, who had her own theories about the border: Power always searches for a way to exploit ambiguity, she'd said. If you can't decide to be on one side or the other, they'll pick it for you. According to Cristina and Tavo, Edgar couldn't escape being a gringo, even if he was Mexican. Chicanos were at least U.S. citizens. On the U.S. side, perhaps even rich Mexicans were seen as a class below Chicanos.

Edgar was as nameless—though no less an integral part of the whole picture—as everyone else in line tonight, gringo and Mexican. They were all being taken advantage of by the power players, one of whom, Edgar realized, was Miranda Cascabel.

Edgar had challenged Miranda and Tavo to hold nothing back when introducing him to "their" Tijuana. He wanted material for his new show. Tavo had been born in Tijuana, but now lived in Chula Vista. He had known Edgar since high school, and was determined to lead the crash course and take full advantage of his new self-proclaimed title as "research assistant." Edgar actually paid him to help him gather anthropological material, which now included cocaine. Tavo had brought Miranda around to the studio as a potential art collector and border liaison. She delivered cocaine to Tavo at Edgar's studio during her shopping trips to San Diego. Tavo insisted she was someone who had the right connections. Being from one of Tijuana's best-known families, she was connected to some powerful people, the majority of them drug dealers.

Edgar was now linked to something beyond art. Tavo and Miranda often took the opportunity to criticize him, as if he were the sole gringo to blame for the hyperfanaticism and heavy militarization. His experience of Tijuana had made it hard for him to tell where the border stopped and his personal relationships with Miranda, Tavo, Humberto, San Diego, and the rest of his own family began. Edgar's last few months of kaleidoscopic clubbing, cocaine, and concerts in the surreal company of painters, performers, pickpockets, and repo-men posing as middle-aged collectors for the Mexican Mafia—all of whom had either worked with, studied, used, bought, sold, or smuggled some form of contraband (the most common being narcotics) between San Diego and Tijuana—had been a perfect example of someone being utterly —and willingly—devoured by his surroundings.

Edgar knew now that Tijuana could not be understood except in direct relationship to San Diego, and vice versa. They were not separate. Beneath all the laws and beefed-up security tactics, it was really the war on drugs that allowed the U.S. government to push its racist agenda throughout Latin America. And the ultimate victims of the huge drug market the United States had created were the lower-class blacks and browns of the border towns of Tijuana and San Diego, Nogales, El Paso, and Juarez.

At any moment now, a German shepherd would determine Edgar's life. In his current state of identity crisis, the question WHICH SIDE ARE YOU ON??? became magnified, running across

55

the digital marquee above the customs portal, preparing him to declare any and all things Mexican.

"¡Siguen, pendejos!" Tavo yelled. "¡Vamonos!"

The college boys in the truck in front of them were throwing chewed gum at each other, with some landing and sticking on Tavo's hood like chunks of confetti. The driver kept stopping and getting out of his car to throw more gum into the crowded bed of the truck.

Edgar was sweating. He felt flies landing on his face. The dogs were out of sight at the moment. He watched Mexican children pick up the discarded shirts and baseball caps the rowdy college boys had tossed from the truck.

"My grandmother told me that before all these cars, helicopters, and soldiers," Tavo began, "there was just a kind of desert post, an office for the border patrol on the other side of the river. My grandmother would just walk across, no problem, in front of the migra without showing any ID or anything. Tijuana was small then, and the migra knew almost everybody that crossed by first and last name."

Edgar felt the sucking sensation on his memory affect his ability to comprehend. It was his own defense mechanism against trauma.

"Are you listening to me, Edgar?"

"I'm listening."

Tavo hesitated.

"What happened?" Edgar asked, impatient with the noise around him creeping in again, the dog barking up ahead, the buzzing lights, the cars, the smell of piss. Unwanted memories. The line always wanted to suck the private out of you, Edgar thought, spit you out and make you part of the noise.

"When my grandmother was walking back from one of her shopping trips, one of the Border Patrol agents had waited for her and a girlfriend walking along the river. There wasn't much built around the border then, in the twenties. There was the casino in Tijuana, but you had to go all the way to National City just to cash an American check. It was all just canyon, river, and sand."

Tavo chewed on the gum he'd bought from the boy, then spit it out before popping another piece in his mouth.

"The migra agent followed my grandmother and raped her, while another migra raped her friend. Both of them in the middle of the day, by the river. Probably not far from where we're sitting right now. That was the whole reason they joined the Border Patrol back then—to rape Mexican women. Can you imagine some migra raping your grandmother? Nobody was there to help them. Nobody saw anything. The worst was afterward—the migra even tried to help my grandmother put her groceries back into the bags she had spilled to fight him off of her." Tavo shook his head and spit out his gum. Edgar wondered why he was being told this now.

"Did she ever see that guy again?"

"Almost every time she crossed the border. But she tried to forget about it."

"I'm sure."

"What do you mean?"

"I'm just saying that's something to forget. Not forgive. Forget."

"That's easier for some people than it is for others," Tavo responded. "If you don't remember the bad things that happen to you, then who will?"

The line began moving rapidly all of a sudden. Tavo shifted into gear and jerked the 4Runner past the customs agent with the dog. Edgar looked the customs agent in the eye as he passed. Tavo kept looking in the rearview mirror. They were only four cars from the portal. But the migra and the dog had not moved.

"He's looking at us," Tavo said. "The dog's up somebody's else's ass, but the migra's looking at us."

The 4Runner moved up again and Edgar could see Interstate 5. Soon Edgar would have to proclaim his allegiance to the flag with the simple answer of "U.S.," while hoping the statement was enough to pardon the premature crime he and Tavo were about to commit. If Edgar could not convince the agent with a simple and confident answer, if the agent went as far as asking Edgar for his identification, then chances were that today would be the first day of the rest of their lives as certified felons. Tavo would, of course, have to show his green card, which meant he was only a resident. After all, what grandmother would encourage her family to become citizens of the state that raped her? On the other hand, here they were, virtually asking to be punished.

Only the agent at the portal was left to deal with now. He circled Tavo's 4Runner, jotting things down on his clipboard.

"Is this your automobile?" the agent asked Tavo, taking his

green card from him, examining the picture and dates on it.

"Yes. This is my car."

The agent was short, with a full head of dark brown hair cropped on the sides. He looked to be in his late thirties with crow's feet stretching around his brown eyes. He pushed inside Tavo's window, close enough for Edgar to see the agent's black-and-gold name plaque that read Martinez. He looked into the back seat with all the CDs and tapes spread over the floor and then backed his head out of the window and looked at Edgar.

"Citizenship?"

"U.S."

"What are you bringing back from Mexico this morning?"

"Nothing," Edgar said.

"Nothing," Tavo said.

"All right. Go ahead."

The agent waved them on. Just before Tavo pulled out of the portal, Edgar thought he heard what sounded like rapid pops of firecrackers somewhere off to the right and behind him in the line. He turned back half expecting to see colorful fireworks.

But perhaps their safe passage was not really something to celebrate. Maybe Edgar had really wanted to be caught and only imagined the fireworks in his mind. Tavo didn't bother to look back, appearing not to have heard anything. He eased the 4Runner toward the white median dividers arranged in zigzag angles to keep cars from speeding onto the freeway.

Four camouflaged soldiers who guarded the customs office watched the 4Runner pass. They did not move from their positions.

MY FAMILY COMES FROM EL CENTRO DE TIJUANA. Downtown Revalooshun Avenoo, where thousands of teenaged white girls and gringo sailors go to get drunk and have a good time. We live next to the old Tilley's Bar. You know the one always advertised on the radio by some guy in a monster-truck voice: The hottest club in downtown TJ! Two-for-one drink specials, ladies free before 9 p.m., wet T-shirt contests and tons of door prizes. And then a repeat of the whole thing in Spanish. That's us. That's Tijuana. That's Revolution: one big disco full of little girls, cops, drugs, and gringo tourists up the ass, man. It's overcrowded with homeless immigrants and indigenous refugees from Guatemala and El Salvador begging on the street. They send their kids out to sell Chiclets so they can pay the coyotes to get them across the border. Sometimes there isn't enough feria to bring the niños across. So they get left behind, and that's why Tijuana is famous for its orphanages, también. For tons of ceramic Virgen de Guadalupes. For the infamous "Donkey Show." If you're looking for the perfect Mexican stereotype, you can be sure to find it in Tijuana. It's like they say: Mexicanos son los más jodidos, por estar tan lejos de Diós y tan cerca de los Estados Unidos. Which basically means Mexicans will do anything for a dollar.

It wasn't always that way. Back when my grandfather Cascabel started his produce business, which became the famous CascaMax supermarket chain, La Revu was pura tienditas y gente cachanilla. Family businesses owned by people from Tijuana. We were upper-class by Tijuana standards, even though we lived downtown, and not on a ranch. My grandfather had actually sold the little ranch he owned in Tecate in order to build the first modern supermarket in Tijuana in the late fifties. My grandfather was a generous, loving, sober, and honest man, whose hard work and good luck paid off. Our family became one of the most well known in Tijuana because of him. All my uncles worked for the family. My aunts had big homes in Tijuana, with plenty of maids and private tutors to teach us all how to speak English. The Cascabel name was clean and respectable, then. It could get you a long line of credit, excellent business connections, a good marriage, the best table at any downtown restaurant. Then my grandfather died, and things weren't so good anymore. I guess we had counted on him too much. No one could really pick up the pieces after he left us.

I remember there was talk of naming a park for him after he died, but for some reason no one had the strength to follow through with the paperwork. Which is for the better. Because he'd probably have another stroke after seeing what we've done to his good name.

My grandfather died in 1987, around the time when things were really bad in Mexico. I remember during the early eighties there were crises everywhere. Economic crashes in Mexico City. Civil wars in Centro America. Scared refugees immigrating north. The border was flooded with refugees, and, like any sudden change, it was violent for a while. A lot of rich Tijuaneros were taking their money out of Mexico and beginning to buy property in safer, more exclusive areas in San Diego, Los Angeles, and Arizona. Everyone was afraid of being robbed or kidnapped. Or of losing their cash to the government, which had already frozen and seized many of our bank accounts. Mexico City has always taken advantage of Tijuana like that, mistreating us like a red-headed stepchild. Which is why we all hate Chilangos. Ellos son los mas culeros.

I would like to blame corruption. But everyone's corrupt. I want to say it's the pinche gringo tourism that forces Tijuana to cater to their wants and dollars. And that would probably be a good enough reason for most politically correct people—but Mexicans are not politically correct. It's no secret that there are more Yankee dollars in Tijuana than pesos. Just look at all the billboards in English, the Blockbuster Videos, the Carl's Jrs. in every shopping center. Tijuaneros are business people. We were able to avoid the crashes and devaluations that the rest of Mexico suffered because we have a tourist economy. The only recessions we experience come when too many Mexicans pull their dollars out of our national banks at the same time. For a couple of weeks nobody in Tijuana has any dollars—at least, those without U.S. bank accounts—and all of a sudden we have to use pesos. I think the government believes that forcing us to use pesos will actually cause us to be more Mexican. But it's all a conspiracy, because then some narco deposits millions of dollars into the state cash reserve and everybody's happy again. There's nothing like a fresh stack of Alexander Hamiltons to promote Mexican patriotism.

The truth is, a Mexican can't get any more sold out than being born and raised in Tijuana. The nationalist fever, famous in the rest of Mexico, doesn't make it to la frontera del norte. We're more like the Mexican part of San Diego. Everybody else already thinks we're gringos. Even the gringos think we're gringos. They don't even bother to learn Spanish, because Tijuaneros speak English, buy everything in gringo malls, eat too many Big Macs, and watch "Jeopardy." Half of my family and friends don't even speak Spanish at home. But, as you'll see, my friends and family are a little different.

You could call them yummies. Young urban Mexicans raised with money. Sons and daughters of mayors, politicos, and rich businessmen, who drive fancy cars and wear nice clothes, who go to the exclusive clubs and expensive restaurants, who drink French champagne and scotch, who travel to Europe once a year to shop. Most of my cousins and friends from Tijuana grew up to become fresas and juniors. The kind who think they're Mexican royalty, but are really just one or two generations removed from the working class—getting drunk all the time, wrecking automobile after automobile, paying off one cop or another, hanging out with drug dealers and narcos. Like the only way they can enjoy themselves is by destroying everything their parents worked for, everything that gives them privilege. They're the best gamblers and the worst losers.

Anything dangerous excites them. Cocaine and bullfighting, especially. On the other hand, some juniors resent their parents for actually having worked for something. They're jealous, even. Because, believe it or not, estos chiquiados also want something to believe in, something to struggle for. We don't like being part of a double standard we can't get out of. The one that tells us to be Mexican, look European, but whenever necessary, sing "The Star-Spangled Banner" and kiss Uncle Sam's hairy ass. Some run away and become like wounded artists. You know, musicians and painters who are always suffering the unexplainable loss of something—usually it's their inheritance. Some became weirdos and freaks, drug addicts with psychological disorders. Some died painful, ugly deaths.

I guess being young, bored, and rich made us easy targets for infiltration, and the narcos saw that. Or maybe we were just too afraid to say no. Either way, they knew how to prey on our weaknesses. They were ready to take all we had—as easy as we were ready to give it. Our money, our connections, our privileges, our identities, our lives.

I almost married one. I got pregnant and had a daughter with one. And then, like that, I became one. It was like *Invasion of the Body Snatchers*. It was just like that in Tijuana. Now the whole world is under attack. But the thing to remember is that narcos aren't Martians. They don't have any extraterrestrial mind-powers. Ni siquiera son genios. They aren't gods. They're regular people capable of wearing many masks and good at telling you what you want to hear. Sound familiar? It should, because many are middle class from traditional families in suburban parts of the country with a lot of ambition and no patience. Which shows what narcos have in common with juniors. Rebellion and immaturity. Fear of real responsibility. They can't hack a regular job. They're scared of a predictable life. Their main concern is covering their own ass—and getting paid.

Is it any different in the U.S.? At least in gringolandia, you have the law, the courts, the Constitution, and a witness protection program. People respect that. People in Mexico, and everywhere else in the world, respect American liberty and American law. We have no choice in the matter. But I don't want to argue about politics. I want to tell you what happened to me and my family. I want to tell you so maybe you won't be afraid to do something. God knows, no one is doing anything about it in Mexico. The so-called officials are too afraid to rock the boat, too deeply involved with the narcos. Gringos may think the war on drugs is a moral war. That drugs are bad, and peace is good. But whoever made any money in times of peace? Maybe you can take my story and let everyone know what's really going on. Gringos have to stop pretending we don't share a border. I mean, your children are our grandchildren. Maybe you can do something about the killing, the madness, la impunidad in Mexico, before it's too late, before it gets any worse for everyone. Your family, too. Maybe.

I SHOULD START BY GOING BACK FIVE YEARS TO when I met Platón. My cousin, Julián, and his new wife, Eva, had invited us over for a dinner party at the house Julián's father had given him in the Coronado Cays in San Diego. Julián was 29 at the time. As vice president of two stores in Tijuana, he didn't do much besides collect whatever salary his father decided to pay him. In fact, the house wasn't really Julián's. It wasn't even in his name, but his mother's. Both Julián and my aunt were born in San Diego. They were American citizens raised in Tijuana, which is common to many Mexicans on the border. Julián's father, who is my father's brother, had wanted his son to take advantage of his dual citizenship by owning property in both countries. He gave him the house to encourage him to have a family and to start a business in San Diego. Something legitimate, like a grocery-store chain. My uncle had also given Julián a BMW, and a small two-bedroom house near the Hipódromo in Tijuana, which had been Julián's bachelor pad, before he married Eva and moved to the Cays.

We were going to have a light dinner and then go out on the bay in a boat Julián had rented to celebrate the newlyweds. Eva would be our dinner hostess. She gave us a tour of the long one-story house. She was wearing a skimpy black dress and four-inch stilettos, showing a lot of leg and even more cleavage. I always thought Eva was below us, a cheap naca. Her father was a chronic gambler and had gone bankrupt two or three times already. But, fortunately for her, Eva was blessed with a million-dollar body, and, when she threw out her tits, Julián took the bait. Ever since they began dating, Eva and I had always rubbed each other the wrong way. It was a normal thing. She was invading our family, and it was my duty to give her the cold shoulder until she earned my respect, or until she had a baby. Only a child would legitimize her status in our family. Otherwise, she was just a golddigger, verdád?

So, during the tour, Eva acted like she was in control of everything, like she had Julián and this marriage business wrapped around her finger, which I guess she did. "And this is my guest room. As you can see, I've decorated it with my Danielle Gallois collection." I could have strangled her for taking credit for the Gallois pieces. It was really our family that personally knew the artist. The paintings had all been bought for Julián from the time he was a boy. All the cousins had been given several things by Gallois. Danielle Gallois was the most famous painter in Tijuana; she also happened to be a drunken lunatic. Despite this, she was loved by old Tijuana society. Eva's father would have pawned off anything like that for gambling money. Despite my disgust, I kept quiet during the tour and admired the house. It had polished wood floors, a huge red-tile kitchen with marble counters, adobe arches, three bedrooms, a fireplace in the master bedroom, and big windows in the back with a view of San Diego Bay. The house was actually a good compromise between the style of Julián, who liked everything earthy and big, a typical Taurus, and the Gemini, Eva, who had probably cried tears of joy over the tacky fireplace in the master bedroom. She had no doubt bought the tiger-skin rug. The house was a symbol of their success, which we, the young generation of Cascabel cousins, were supposed to take as a hint for us to get our shit together.

At dinner I met a young man named Platón, one of Julián's friends. I didn't know why they called him Platón. He didn't speak

Greek, didn't look Greek. He especially didn't act like a bearded Greek philosopher. But I figure guys like giving each other ridiculous nicknames. For example, it's normal for Mexicans to call a fat guy "Gordo," but they'll also call a skinny guy Gordo as a joke. It's a part of that dream all men have of a secret society where they can play cards, drink beer, have sex with hookers, fart and belch all over the place, and then go home to their wives as if nothing happened. Just another day at the office, honey.

Well, I'm here to tell you that women have the same dream, fíjate. Only it's much dirtier, and much, much more secret. While Platón claimed to be from Tijuana, like the rest of us, and seemed to know everybody we knew, I had never seen him before. Which didn't make much of a difference, at first. I had gone to the party with Rudi, a family friend whom I loved dearly, but who's dead now. There must have been about eight of us total. I remember because later we were cramped in the cabin of the boat that was supposed to comfortably fit eight.

Dinner was boring as usual, with everyone complimenting how beautiful the house was. Julián gave us advice on real estate in Coronado, which was really hot at the time, and we all pretended to be interested. Really boring, actually. Then, sometime after the salmon with capers and asparagus was served, Platón started imitating everyone at the dinner table. Very subtly at first. Until, like a game of telephone, we all got the message and started to notice him imitating how Eva hummed a private song while she chewed; how Julián brooded over his plate like Napoleon, spitting out a rough comment every so often; how my cousin Sergio smacked his gums; how my cousin Veronica became tipsy on one sip of wine, and her friend Gloria pinched her not to drink so much; how I jiggled my leg nervously, and picked at my food, eating very little bites; the way Rudi laughed like he was inhaling helium. I guess it was more entertaining than it was funny. Platón was a regular Charlie Chaplin, whom he resembled in a cute sort of way: the thin crooked nose, the guero skin, big brown eyes, and short curly hair that clung to his forehead. He wore a black suit with a black T-shirt underneath. Once we all got the joke we started talking shit to each other, drunk on wine and laughter.

The fact that everybody knew Platón except me made me more than curious about him. So I asked Rudi, who was my best guy friend, whom I had known since I was seven, and who had never mentioned Platón's name to me before. But Rudi couldn't tell me how long he had known Platón or even exactly where he had first met him.

"Es un chavo de aquí, nomás."

"You mean he's from San Diego?" I asked, while we were still at the house, preparing to leave for the boat.

"No, he's from Tijuana," Rudi said. "He grew up there. I used to see him at Rio Rita's all the time. He lives in San Diego now. That's where he went to high school."

"Which high school did he go to?"

I had gone to high school in San Diego myself. A private, Catholic girls' school. The only boys I knew while I went there were Tijuaneros who went to Saint Augustine, a private, Catholic boys' high school. I hated high school. My mother made me cross the border every day just to be tortured by gringas who thought they were better than me, the ugly ones ready to give any pinche fulano a blow job at the drop of a hat, passing notes about which boy they were going to fuck first. My mother thought that if I was going to be equal to the gringas, then I should go to school with them. I was sure that if Platón had gone to Saints, I would have already known about him. Which would have ruled him out of my love life completely.

"¿Quién sabe?" Rudi said. "One of those pinche public high schools in Chula Vista, I think. ¿Te gusta, verdád que sí?"

"What makes you think I like him? Just because he's cute, funny, and not like all the rest of these Tijuanero fools pretending to be men."

"Hey!"

"You don't count, Rudi. No te quejes."

"Why not?"

"Because you're my best friend. And I don't hang out with fools. That's why."

"Well, try not to make it so obvious, O.K.?"

"Have you ever known me to be obvious about anything?"

"Well, there was—"

"Don't answer that. I don't want anyone to hear. You'll ruin my reputation."

"Just keep your panties dry, Cinderella. And maybe I'll hook you up with him later. I have that talent, you know."

"¡Qué pelado! Don't think I need you to play Cupid, Rudi. I

have my ways of getting what I want."

I know what you're thinking: Little rich girl gets bored with Tijuana social life and wants a taste of the wild side. But I wasn't bored, and I certainly wasn't independently wealthy. Not yet. I had just finished my AA degree at Southwestern Junior College in Chula Vista, and I was looking into starting my own international travel agency. My father had promised to help me start my business as soon as I could find the right space in Tijuana. To tell you the truth, I didn't really want to work in Tijuana. But I let my father believe he was helping me out. So I lied to him every time he found a place for me. I'd say it was too small, or too big, or too noisy, or just not right, and he kept making calls. I will admit that I was always looking for a new adventure. That's the whole reason we're alive. The desire for adventure is as natural as caffeine to coffee. As a businesswoman, I planned to cash in on my generation and take advantage of their desire to flaunt their wealth. Money is the easiest thing to manipulate, if you have the right personality. You have to show people what good things they are missing and then get them to pay for a little bit of fun. That was my business philosophy. It was also the same philosophy I had about men, and, I guess, life in general.

Nevertheless, I had been charmed by Platón, with or without his intention. And the secret to charming a woman—besides being good looking—if you don't know already, is being able to make her laugh. But most women don't like to hear the gross jokes men tell each other in bars; most women are interested in a man who can make them laugh without having to be gross. Unlike a lot of fresas, I can also handle the gross jokes. Because not only have I already heard it all from my father, brothers, and uncles, who are a bunch of groseros, but I'm a person who likes to laugh. Only I don't think of myself as a funny person. Rudi's dirty sarcasm was fun. But any Mexican worth his weight in pintos has always talked in double meaning. In my family, there is a dicho, a saying, for everything. Which goes to show that we are a very literary culture, even if half the nation can't read.

Julián had rented a 40-foot boat and hired a Mexican captain and mate to take us out on the bay. We had passed underneath the lighted bridge, the sails were down, and the motor was in low gear. We sat in the cabin on leather cushions, crowded around a table for four, while my cousin Veronica decided to subject us to a survey of sexual relationships she must have pulled out of a gringa women's magazine. I laughed at her questions about whether it was safe to talk dirty outside the bedroom. Should you stay with a partner you loved, but who couldn't give you an orgasm? When does kinky sex become S&M?

"This is ridiculous," I said. "Why are gringas so obsessed about keeping their man? Why second-guess yourself? I'm instinctual. Si se sienta mal, que se vaya a la chingada. Punto."

"I think this survey is for women who actually have a man, Mara."

"Oh, please. Don't act like you can speak from experience, prima. You don't even know what S&M is."

"That doesn't necessarily mean we haven't had it," Veronica said. "I'm not as innocent as I look."

"All right, Veronica. Tell me everything you know about strap-ons."

"¿Qué-qué?"

"So Mara's the sexpert," Eva said. "How often do you experience multiple orgasm, prima?"

"I could tell you, but then you'd all just be jealous."

"Veronica can't be jealous of what she's never had," Gloria said.

"Mira quien habla. You thought you had an orgasm, until you ran out of Q-tips."

"Even that didn't stop her from humping the pillow."

"You girls are vicious," Platón said.

"I think they're just showing off," Eva said.

"I know Mara is," Rudi said. "And we know for who."

"Tch. Callate, baboso."

"They're Cascabel," Julián said. "Todos somos iguales. Obnoxious runs in the family. It's in the blood, 90 proof."

"Didn't the Surgeon General say being obnoxious causes birth defects?"

"Says right here: Esta botella contiene 35 porciento pendejadas."

"Let me see that. It says: If you're a Cascabel, you need a lobotomy."

"A huevo."

"That's no way to talk about our future children, Julián."

"I predict that in the future all children will be goat children. Hijos del Chupacabras."

"That's enough," Eva said. "I'm not going to let you curse my children."

"Sí, Julián. Ya. We don't need any two-headed babies in the family."

"O.K. O.K. A ver, ¿quién trae?" Julián asked, lowering his dark eyes at Platón.

"Mochate tú, pués," Platón said. "Why're you looking at me?"

"¿Por qué? Porque tu tienes la cois, cabrón."

"Ay, sí. Why don't you tell the rest of the world while you're at it."

"Come on, hombre. We're in the middle of the ocean. No one's going to call the police."

"We're on the bay, pendejo. The ocean's west. And maybe some people here aren't interested."

"Whatever," Julián said, chopping the table with the blade of his hand. "Gimme a line."

It was suddenly silent. I could hear the water lapping against the bow. It sounded like someone swallowing loudly. On deck, the captain and the mate were talking in Spanish. The music on the stereo came through the alternative station, only it was still called New Wave music back then. "Girlfriend in a Coma" was playing. Then someone giggled, and we all started laughing again, like a bunch of giddy girls. I thought that since we were all drunk, no one had taken the sexual jokes seriously. But now everybody was staring at me like they were waiting for me to put on a show.

"¿Qué onda?" I asked.

Then at Platón, who sat opposite me with this look of a cornered animal. Something behind his big eyes started to shift and swell. It was very slight. Like wind blowing clouds over the sky. He was afraid of something. I think I fell in love with him then. That look of vulnerability in a man's face turns me on. I would only see that face in Platón twice more, much later, when I told him I was pregnant, and when the judge sentenced him to prison.

"Everyone here is old enough to say yes or no, carnal," Julián said. "This is what we came out here for, right? To party, ¿verdád que sí? Sacala cois, Platón. I don't want to wait until we get back to the house. She's going to try it sooner or later. I'd rather Mara do it with us. ¿Verdád, prima?"

Julián had always been very demanding. He was used to

telling others what to do. He was the oldest cousin. He did have a bad temper. When he was mad, his thick brow would knot like he was thinking really hard, and he developed dark circles around his eyes. It wasn't pretty. But you could see it coming from a mile away. Luckily, Julián gave you a warning before he did anything. Which was probably his weakness. For the most part, he was happy, fun, and full of energy. And once he got started with anything—drinking, joking, talking, cocaine—it was hard for him to stop. I had an idea from that point on that I was in for something dangerous.

Julián moved the bottles from the center of the table and cleaned it with his handkerchief. Then he handed Platón a Swiss Army knife. Platón pulled out a small plastic baggie from underneath the table, the kind you see at Plaza Bonita and other low-class malls where the cholas buy their cheap earrings and fake jewelry. Inside the baggie was a white rock about the size of a quarter, which Platón pulled out of the bag and laid bare on the table. We all kind of stared at it like it was an alien—or a precious gem. It was the first time I had ever seen cocaine up close. I had always thought drugs were dirty. Stuff that gringos and negros did. It was never glamorous in my experience. So it never occurred to me that Platón was a dealer or part of any drug cartel. I figured the little moonstone was his contribution to the party.

We watched Platón shave white crumbs from the rock. Then he pulled a credit card from his wallet and began to dice up the shavings, making little dotted messages on the table. It was so quiet, I started to get nervous.

Eva, Julián, Rudi, and I watched Platón methodically crush and scrape white lines back and forth across the shiny wood table. Six thick lines were laid out in a row near the middle of the table. If anyone said a word, I didn't hear it. The table became the site of a ritual, which for the others may have been a habit, but for me was a rite of passage. Julián rolled up a $20 bill into a tight cylinder, and Eva was the first one to take a line. She made sure to check her short, slicked-back hair first, before putting the bill to one nostril, while covering the other with her thumb. The fingers on her hands were daintily pinched into threes like a flamenco dancer as she leaned over the table and forcefully inhaled, until the line of cocaine was cleaned up off the table in one quick breath.

Conversation began as soon as everyone had taken their turn.

I was too fascinated to say anything. I liked watching the whole process: the rock that was repeatedly shaved down into white crystals, which decorated the table with a crude pattern of lines that were quickly erased, disappearing up the chute of the $20 bill, zoom, into the nostrils, until nothing was left but the dust that Julián and Eva were eager to collect with a fingertip and clean their teeth with. Veronica and Gloria eventually reappeared from the bathroom and joined in. Of course, it didn't last long. But what a great feeling, that first line! Suddenly, everyone was so interesting, and all I wanted to do was talk, talk, talk, and chain-smoke. What I can still remember about the trip from then on is the heavy numbness in my nose and teeth, and a lot of meaningless chatter and smoke. We never did get on deck to feel the wind off the water and see the sky at night. And whatever desire I had for Platón was completely smothered by the speed of the cocaine, which absolutely crushed my sex drive.

Platón and I did talk several times that night. And what I remember him telling me was that he worked in repossession.

"Really? I loved that movie *Repo Man*."

"Everyone says that," Platón said, looking discouraged. "When I say repossession, they think I'm out sneaking around stealing people's cars. I do research. I look up who owes us money, and basically hand off the information to my supervisor. They take care of claiming the assets. It's like working for a credit firm, a bank, or an insurance company. Except I work on delinquent claims from both sides of the border. I'm like an international agent. Border trader, and all that."

I nodded my head as if I understood.

"NAFTA will make it much easier for us to make money on both sides of the border," I said, repeating what I heard my father say on the phone. "My father has even extended our list of purchasing clients from San Diego all the way to Vancouver, Canada. He thinks the gringos will buy more Mexican products when free trade is signed in."

I never asked Platón the name of his company. It seemed unnecessary at the time. The business of repossession would come up again, however. Like international relations, it seemed like a popular profession many young people were getting into. But like I said before, I was more naïve than innocent. The essence of cocaine, I would learn, like any drug, is a well-orchestrated plot of deception. It exists like another world right in front of our eyes, in every aspect of our lives, and many either don't want to see it, or just haven't learned the correct perspective. Once you've been indoctrinated, though, you learn to use narco vision to see what's going on. Which made coke so exciting and fantastic. Not just consuming it, but dealing coke was a happening underground culture. You were always changing identities, like clothing, for whatever occasion or situation you found yourself in. Because a dealer has to recognize the potential client, the potential to make money off everyone she meets. And then choose the correct mask to wear. You can never present yourself as who you are. You have to forget about whatever person you thought you were before. Because that was the whole reason you got into the drug business to begin with: You're really nobody. But drugs made you feel like somebody.

My reason for using cocaine may have been solely about adventure at first, even leisure, which amounted to little more than forgettable, and, in the end, exhausting conversation. But perhaps given another context, another purpose, another time, the whole experience would have been spiritual, magical, or even practical. Like how the Inca used coca for medicinal purposes, chewing on the leaves to stem hunger, or to give them extra strength. They say the entire Incan empire was built on coca. Imagine a bunch of wired Incans working like ants in fast-forward to construct the great city of Machu Picchu high in the mountains of Peru. As close to God as you could possibly get without having to die. Yet the Inca were unable to defend themselves from the conquistadors. How could that be? Were they so high they couldn't imagine being invaded by anyone other than God? Goes to show you how easy it is for a thief to pass himself off as a supreme being. It comes to the point where you begin to believe your own bullshit, and you start to worship the self that is not you, never admitting that one day these two selves are bound to destroy each other.

LATER THAT SUMMER, I SAW PLATON AGAIN AT A wedding at the Hipódromo, the racetrack, hosted by Los Reyes. Every summer Tijuana was full of bodas. My family was invited to one practically every weekend between June and August. Most of them were just expensive excuses for a party. Everyone knew that weddings were really for the parents. For the most part, the whole traditional family concept was passé, nostalgic even. Mexico may be a Catholic country, but we divorce American-style. Nevertheless, matrimony was still an economic transaction between two families, and, in that sense, probably the last traditional custom the older generation was able to pass down to us. It was definitely the only way you could get any of us into church anymore. My mother would always ask me what I thought of the maridos, and I would rattle off what scandalous rumors I'd heard about the bride and groom. Really, it was about how much money was spent on the wedding, the number of courses in the meal, the quality of the champaña, and how many people attended that made or broke a family's reputation. It was really that simple.

The bride was a freshly frosted blonde/brunette with a bad facial. She went around the ballroom taking photos at everyone's table, forcing twelve people at a time to squeeze together in order to be blinded by the enormous flash of six different photographers, only one of whom had been invited. On a portable bandstand at the opposite end of the room, men dressed in red suits and white cowboy hats played guitars, keyboards, and drums, while the lead singer in a tight little red-sequined outfit sang "Chocolate, Chocolate/de canela, de canela," to a sea of at least 500 middle-aged people badly imitating her in a type of butter-churning dance. If that wasn't bad enough, I already felt like we were in a huge barn. The rafters of the ballroom were so high that even with the colorful lights, silver balloons, and gold tapestries, the bare, white roof gave the room and the wedding reception a hollow, uncomfortable endlessness.

The ballroom had originally been intended to showcase prize-winning horses for the clients of Congressman Bernardo "Bardo" Reyes, CEO of Reyes Industries and owner of the whole complex known as the Hipódromo, which included not only the racetrack, but the neighborhood of residences and small businesses there above Boulevard Aguas Calientes. When the horses stopped running around the track (some say because of a government crackdown on racketeering, others say it was due to the refusal of Los Reyes to pay their debts), they naturally brought in greyhounds to race instead of thoroughbreds, and then turned the showroom into a rentable banquet hall. I mean, who gets married at the racetrack?

The honor—or stupid mistake—was hosted by Los Reyes, an

infamous Chilango father-and-son empire, whose power stretched from Mexico City to Tijuana, from banks in El Paso, Manhattan, the European Union, and beyond. It was assumed by most Mexicans that Los Reyes had a hand in every major decision in Mexico. There were even several Mexican journalists who had been so brave as to suggest that Los Reyes ruled the PRI and handpicked the president. It was a fact, however, that these journalists never published again, if they were lucky to survive writing an negative article about Los Reyes. I was curious to meet one or both of Los Reyes. And if not, at least see what type of people they knew. So far, I wasn't impressed. I gave the couple five regret-filled years, one for every $10,000 blown on the wedding.

Rudi was out on the dance floor getting his groove on with a couple friends. I was sitting at our table with three full bottles of champaña and about five people I did not know, who had no interest in talking to me, either. But rather than try to cross the Red Sea and go visit with my mother and father at their table, I left the reception and went to the bathroom. On my way out, I found Platón talking with an older man in the hall outside the bathroom. I sat down on a marble bench and pretended to be looking for something in my purse, so I could eavesdrop. The older man wore a dark blue suit and had thinning, dyed-brown hair. He spoke Spanish with that condescending Chilango accent, high and nasal. Very annoying. Platón was being scolded for something and was clearly not expected to respond. He stood there in his tailored black suit with his hands in his pockets, his little ass tensely flexing in and out, smoking a cigarette and nodding, while the older man spoke out of the side of his mouth.

"Si quieres ser alguien respectable, tienes que portarte muy atento al quien manda," the viejo Chilango told him. "¿Entiendes? Vemos todo lo que haces. No pienses ni un minuto que no te vemos partiendo nuestros intereses con estos comemierdas adentro del salón. Who do you think you are? No te metas en negocios con nadie. Tu no eres nuestro representante. Eres un peón que entre poco se va encontrar nadando con las peces."

Platón nodded and exhaled smoke as the old man turned his back and walked away, leaving him alone to contemplate whatever mistake he had made. I didn't know whether to wait for him to notice me or to go over and say hello. I was afraid he might be embarrassed that I had just heard him get chewed out, regañado, for butting in on the old man's business. He might be in a bad mood and not want to talk to me. So I coughed.

Platón finally turned around and walked over to stub out his cigarette in one of those silver ashtrays that serve as miniature garbage cans, a few feet from the bench I was sitting on. He smiled when he saw me and bent down to give me a kiss on the cheek.

"Qué bonita esta vestida que llevas, Mara. Red is your color. I can't believe I didn't see you earlier."

"I can't believe it, either. There's only 700 guests. How could you miss me?"

"Right. That explains it. I was wondering when your cousin was going to bring you out with us again."

"What're you talking about? Julián doesn't decide when or where I go. I may not have my own car, but at least I have a choice."

"Of course. I'm sorry. I just meant I don't have your phone number. And...and you must have tripped out last time, hmm? What a night. Wait, how long have you been sitting here?"

"Not long. I just came out of the bathroom and sat down to—"

"Hear me get chewed out?"

"Well—"

"That fucking Chilango."

"Who was he?"

"Who was he? That was Don Bernardo Reyes. The gran-potato."

"And you work for him?"

"I'm supposed to be making sure the wedding guests stay on this floor. Kind of like crowd control."

"I thought you worked for an insurance company. What happened to Repo Man?"

"Pues, sí. I mean, I do. Reyes Industries has many branches, each with its own division of insurance and securities. I work in several different divisions. So, who did you come with?"

"Rudi."

"You go everywhere with Rudi. He's not your boyfriend, is he?"

"No. He's my best friend. I've known him since we used to play hide-and-seek. Rudi's gay."

"O.K. That's what I thought."

"And my parents are here, too."

"Really? They know Los Reyes?"

"No, but we get invited to all the society weddings. Even if we don't know who's getting married. My mother likes to come for the gossip. She makes my father come with her. So he's inside getting drunk as fuck. Mama's being a chismosa. I don't know why I came. Rudi wanted to come. No, I'm lying. I used to date the groom, and I wanted to see the woman he dumped me for."

"¿Y qué te parece la morra?"

"She's a naca, just like I expected."

"Do you want to take a walk with me?"

"Where?"

"Just come on. We'll be back in a minute. Rudi won't miss you. I'm sure he's excited to see all the pretty boys inside."

"You're right. He left me alone at our table. And that's why I came out here."

"You didn't know I was here?"

"No idea. Just bad luck, I guess." I smiled so he knew I was joking and took his arm.

Platón led me down several wide red-tile hallways decorated with baroque art, bronze sculptures of well-toned, half-naked men and headless women, and more marble benches. All of it, the classical museum style, the barn wedding, the racetrack, the Chilangos, was beginning to get on my nerves. My mother says that money can buy you almost anything, but it can't buy you a sense of taste. But it was more than just a lack of taste that made the Hipódromo a really unpleasant place. There was something extremely uncomfortable about the energy I felt there. Like ghosts haunted the halls. I felt like Platón and I were constantly being watched.

We kept walking through unlocked green doors marked Privado. And into rooms where people in white polo shirts and white pants were counting stacks of money and organizing betting cards, writing numbers on chalk boards that listed the daily race schedules. I didn't bet, and I didn't understand what odds meant. The only thing I paid attention to when the dogs or horses ran was what color they were, and who took a crap before the race, because they had the best chance of winning. Platón received the occasional nod as we zigzagged through the rooms. He obviously knew where he was going. Then we came to another green door that was also marked Privado. But unlike the others, this one was actually locked. Platón slid a credit card-type key into a slot underneath the doorknob, a tiny light turned green, and suddenly we were at the end of a long hallway made of glass.

"What do you think?"

"What is this?"

"This is the real interest of Los Reyes," Platón said. "Metaphorically speaking."

We walked slowly down the hall, surrounded by glass on both sides. The hall was humid and quiet. Managed that way on purpose, I figured, because behind the glass walls were green jungle plants with red flowers and vines hanging from trees 20 feet tall. When the vines moved, I stopped and stared at a long brown snake folding itself onto a moss-covered rock. Another snake emerged from underneath the same rock. Only this snake was black with red and yellow rings around its neck, which reminded me of a necklace I had wanted to buy in my favorite antique jewelry store in Old Tijuana. I loved antique jewelry. Carefully cut stones, rubies, garnets, coral, jade, veiny turquoise set in silver dangling around my neck. I thought the two snakes would fight and try to swallow each other, but they only slithered away.

I could hear a faint buzz of electricity all around me as we continued walking. It was humid, like a rain forest. Farther down there were two quetzal birds perched together on a thin branch. Quetzals look like ravens, but bigger, with wings the color of a rainbow. I had only seen pictures of them in books, and stuffed replicas at the big museum of antropology in Mexico City. They are the most protected birds in Mexico, the rarest in the Americas, much more endangered than the bald eagle. Probably less than a hundred in the world. Quetzals are also sacred birds with sleek, long, black bodies; purple, blue, green, yellow, and red feathers. The Aztec kings wore crowns of quetzal feathers to signify royalty and beauty. One of our servants told me that a feather from a quetzal is magical, and especially good for winning a lover or defeating an enemy. When the Spanish defeated the Aztecs, Cortés took Moctezuma's crown of quetzals and gave it to the Spanish queen, who had no idea what to do with it. It was a beautiful crown of feathers, but Isabella had wanted gold. Now Moctezuma's crown of quetzal feathers hangs in a museum somewhere in Europe, where it's been for over 500 years, despite popular demand to return it to Mexico.

Still farther down the glass-encased jungle-zoo we found a

Komodo dragon drinking from a pond. There was a sloth up a tree. Two sea turtles called caguamas, also an extremely endangered species, rested beneath a palm. A white egret. And, finally, an albino tiger.

"What does he eat?"

"It's a she. Her name is Delila," Platón said, frowning. "And she hasn't been eating anything lately. I think she's depressed. But she used to eat small cows, deer, young colts, and even burros."

"I hope you mean the pinche tourist burros painted like zebras. I hope she tears them to shreds."

"No, we have to kill everything for her."

"That's probably why she's depressed, then. Cooped up in here. Look at her. She's going crazy. You can see it in her eyes. I'm sure she's dying to kill something. Why don't you let her kill?"

"She might get hurt. This is Bardo Junior's favorite pet. He stole her from a circus that came through Mexico on tour three years ago."

Delila paced back and forth, panting. She didn't stop pacing back and forth, even though we stood still. She would approach us, blinking her white eyes, and then turn around. I thought of Delila as the sultan's captive princess—you'd have to kill her to have her. Or drug her. She reminded me of the sad wedding, and the ridiculous bride. It was scandalous that the same place would host not only the overblown wedding and the dog races, but also the zoo for endangered species.

"You stole her, and nobody went after you?"

"Los Reyes are extremely powerful people. Even if someone wanted to come after them, they'd probably have to dissolve Congress and rewrite the Constitution."

Platón tapped on the glass, but Delila walked away from him.

"He took her while she was supposed to be breeding in Costa Rica with a Bengal tiger. But Delila tried to kill him."

"I know how she feels. My father's always trying to marry me off to one of his business associates. Some fat-ass pendejo. First, they take your freedom, then they try forcing you to get it on with a stranger. No wonder she tried to kill the other tiger."

"Personally, I think Bardo Junior likes to pretend she's his lover. He plays classical music to calm her down before he tries to feed her. Sometimes he sings her boleros to seduce her into eating. He's driving the poor animal crazy. That's really why she won't eat. But no one has the balls to tell him. Not even the animal psychologist."

"You mean the tiger has a shrink?"

"Yeah. She's actually good. I think it's the closest thing to a friend Delila has."

The sickness of the filthy rich is not only that they must have the rarest possessions, but they must also have rare obsessions. It looked like Bardo Junior had a serious animal fetish. I was finding out more than I needed to know about Los Reyes and asked Platón if we could go.

"We better. I'm starting to sweat."

We walked out and headed back through the hallway maze.

"So this is why Bardo Senior was so pissed off at you, Platón. You're letting all the little people in on what's happening at the Hipódromo. I'm sure they have cameras in there. Aren't you going to get in trouble?"

"This isn't the half of it."

"Then why'd you bring me?"

"Thought it might be interesting. I wanted to see how you'd react."

"I liked the quetzals."

"I knew you would."

"Anything else interesting around here?"

"Maybe."

After a few more minutes of walking, we arrived at a box office with a huge window overlooking the racetrack. Platón had not led me up one staircase or ramp, yet we were at least ten stories above the ground. The stadium lights were on, even though it wasn't quite dark yet. The grass lawn at the center of the track was empty. Around the dirt track, skinny greyhounds hungrily raced after a stuffed white rabbit.

The box office was like a hotel room, complete with a kitchen, bathroom, TV, stereo, intercom, and two leather couches. Platón opened the refrigerator and brought out an unopened bottle of champaña. He grabbed two glasses from the cupboard and set them on a coffee table between the two sofas. I stood at the window, looking out at the golden sunset and, in the distance, at the neighborhood of small houses, one of which my cousin Julián owned. I was looking for Julián's, but I couldn't remember what color his roof might have been.

Platón had opened a bottle and shot the cork into the ceiling. "This is a private reception!" he shouted. "No newlyweds or Chilangos are allowed."

"Fuck the newlyweds! I hate weddings."

"I hate the races, too."

"Fuck the races!" I shouted. "Chinga a los Los Reyes, también! Pero, thanks for the champaña. I never refuse a good drink."

"Never."

Platón filled my glass, then filled and downed his own three times in a row before I had finished half of mine.

"Slow down, Speedy Gonzales. You're gonna get sick."

"Fuck Speedy Gonzales! Fuck getting sick! ¡Arriba! ¡Arriba!"

Platón filled up his glass again, but only downed half this time. Then he grabbed me and planted a wet champaña kiss on my mouth. I pulled away, because he had surprised me. He stood there smiling, while the sweetness of the champaña tingled around my lips. I decided that I liked it. I liked Platón. I wanted him to kiss me again, but he sat down and began chopping up lines on the coffee table.

I sat down next to him, deciding not to wait for him to kiss me again. I was horny and began kissing his neck, his cheeks, his lips, sucking on his ear, while he railed out four lines.

"These fucking Chilangos act like they own the place," Platón said.

"They don't own this place?"

"No, they don't. My father's construction company built this racetrack. He agreed to sell it to Los Reyes. But before anything was signed, they just took it from him. Bardo Senior is a congressman. He told my father that since gambling was illegal in Mexico, the government was claiming it. They paid off my father with pesos. He was so pissed off he moved his business to San Diego. That's what Chilangos do. They cheat everyone. From the campesinos to the banks. They've milked the capital dry. Now they want to suck the blood out of Baja. They're Chupachilangos. Watch. They're going to fuck up all of Tijuana."

Platón rolled up a bill and handed it to me.

"More fucked up than it is already?"

"You haven't seen anything yet, Mara."

"Why are you working for them, then?"

"Money. And a chance to fuck them good."

"You mean before they fuck you, right?"

"Right."

"You're crazy, Platón. But I like that. I like crazy."

We did the lines, drank the champaña, and fooled around some more on the leather couch. After all I had seen, it didn't take much for me to hate Los Reyes. I trusted Platón and sympathized with him for what had happened to his father. Chilangos were always screwing people over. And they always seemed to come out smelling like roses, because they had all the lawyers and government officials behind them, helping them out of trouble.

We got really high, and the next thing I knew my dress was up around my waist, and Platón and I were screwing. Even though I was high and drunk, it still felt good. Platón's mouth and wiry body were all over me, and I held onto him tight while he pushed himself inside of me, getting close to making me come several times. But the coke distracted me just enough that I couldn't climax. I kept thinking there were cameras hidden somewhere, and Platón and I would be broadcast having sex in front of everyone at the wedding. So I faked it. Once Platón came, he let out a breath and sank on top of me. I could feel the frustration lift off him like steam. I stroked his sweaty head and laughed at him for passing out. He woke up a little embarrassed, and we both got up to wash off. We still had to go back to the wedding. At least, I did. Platón was supposed to be working. But he didn't seem to be worried about anything at all. He escorted me back to the reception, where we ran into Rudi.

Rudi was wearing a red straw cowboy hat and holding two balloons in his hand, one green and one red. Behind him was another young man with cropped black hair, thin mustache, and a blue kazoo in his mouth. I looked around and saw that the people surrounding me were also wearing different colored sombreros and blowing on kazoos. I had missed the party favors.

"Where have you been, Mara? We were looking for you." Rudi asked, mischievously shifting his eyes from me to Platón. He was ridiculously drunk and would try to make me feel bad for having been gone so long. It must have been two hours.

"I went to the bathroom. I had to go bad. My stomach was acting up."

"Ah huh. Well, I have this strange feeling that you're all better now. You look, hmm...healthier?"

"You know me so well, Rudi. Nice hat."

"You missed the party favors. Sorry I couldn't save anything for you. I have to think of those people who need me the most."

"Looks like you picked up more than just a new costume."

"This is Simón."

"Ola, Simón."

"¿Qué tal, Mara? Rudi's been looking all over for you. He thought you might have gone out to watch the races."

"No, I hate the races. But I do like to dance." I looked at Platón, who had suddenly gotten serious. He shook his head slightly.

"Well, these balloons are for our table," Rudi said. "I'm going to tie them to the chair for you, Mara. In case you happen to get lost and can't find your way back again. Nos vemos."

Simón blew his kazoo and left with Rudi.

Right then my father appeared with, of all people, Bernardo Reyes, Senior.

Platón stood back as my father, also in a red cowboy hat, with his tie loosened, his suit jacket off, and his belly bulging, entirely drunk, introduced me to the old man.

"Oh, Miranda. I found you. Le presento a Señor Don Bernardo Reyes. Don Bardo, this is our eldest daughter, Miranda Cascabel."

"I'm your only daughter, Papá," I said holding out my hand to Don Bardo. "Mucho gusto."

"Un placer," the old man said, taking my hand and kissing it. "Que bella es. Some day, compadre Cascabel, I would like your daughter to meet my son, Bardo Junior. I think they are from the same generation. He's actually around here somewhere. Anyway, I'm sure he would love to meet your beautiful daughter. Who is not yet married, am I correct?"

"No, not yet," my father said with a drunk frown. "La pobre. Es un poco sangrona, pero once you get to know her, Mara can be a very funny girl. Eh, Mara? Los Reyes are very respectable people. You should be so lucky—"

"I don't think I've ever met your son, Don Bernardo," I said, interrupting my father. I could feel Platón sliding wet down my leg. He was still there somewhere behind me, but I couldn't turn and look for him. "I'm sure we have a lot in common."

"No lo dudo. Bueno, pues, if you'll excuse me, I see an employee here who is not doing his job. It was good to meet you, Señor Cascabel. Un placer, Señorita Miranda. Please, do not hesitate to call on me for any particular thing you may need in the future. I am enamored of the fine families of Tijuana. My door is always open to you."

Bardo Senior bowed his head, turned, and headed through the crowd of tables and chairs, toward the kitchen. Platón followed behind him, and left without saying goodbye.

"Well, what do you know about that?" my father said with a grin. "A fine family from Tijuana. That makes me feel very—"

"Proud?"

"—indispensable. Do you think you'd like to meet Bardo Junior, Mara?"

"He makes me sick."

"Don't be so proud, hija. He is a very remarkable man. Very powerful."

"People are never who they say they are, Papá."

"Are you telling me that wasn't Don Bardo Reyes, el jefe del Hipódromo, the congressman himself?"

"I'm telling you I'm not impressed."

My father shrugged and went back to his table to get another drink. I realized I was alone again, wondering how much pride had to do with it.

Platón and I saw each other a lot after the wedding at the Hipódromo. Once we started dating, I got to know him much better. He had a lot of plans blowing through his mind. Just like an Aquarius. He worried often, mostly about his relationship with Los Reyes. I could tell that he had ideas of somehow getting back at them for how they'd cheated his father. But he was always careful about what he told me. He spent a lot of time with Julián talking about business with Los Reyes. I saw a lot of Julián and Eva while Platón and I were together. He and Julián were a lot closer than I imagined. We'd all spend time at the house in the Coronado Cays drinking and enjoying the view of the bay, watching sailboats race, and drinking champaña. Eva and I hardly said a word to each other. We had the best times going out on El Rio, drinking and dancing in Tijuana at Plaza Fiesta, El Suizo, and Baby Roc. We went to a few concerts at Iguanas and took day trips to Rosarito Beach. Platón, whose real name I learned was Juan Carlos, was always very sweet with me. It didn't matter to me that he wasn't as wealthy as the other guys who asked me out. He never bought me anything other than dinner and drinks, a pair of sunglasses, and, maybe, a blouse or a pair of shoes I don't wear anymore. The good thing was that he always had a lot of energy. We laughed together. But, by the end, I realized I didn't really know him. So I couldn't have loved him.

It only lasted a few months. Plenty of time, however, for me to get pregnant with Alejandra. When I told Platón I was going to have a baby, he got so scared I know he probably considered leaving me right then. He thought that after all the cocaine he'd done, he'd have to be infertile. I hadn't been doing a lot of drugs, and I completely stopped after I became pregnant. Platón didn't run away from me, not exactly—the verdict is still out. Instead, he asked me to marry him. We got engaged, though I never saw a ring, because the very next day he got pulled over in Tijuana and the police found three and a half grams of coke on him and two handguns. Even though possession of both guns and drugs are highly illegal in Mexico, he should have been able to get off, we thought, because he worked for Los Reyes. You would expect that, as corrupt as Mexico is and as powerful as Los Reyes are. They ought to be able to handle anything that happened to one of their own people. Especially something as minor as a possession charge. In fact, Los Reyes did hire a lawyer to defend Platón and paid for all his legal fees. And at one point, it looked like he would get off with a fine. So why was he given ten years in a federal prison? We found out later that the prosecuting and the defense attorney both came from Mexico City and were also both on the Reyes payroll. All of Platón's scheming had come back to bite him como una gran mordida en el pecho.

I wrote him several times over the next three months and even requested a visit. But I stopped writing after I failed to receive a response. I thought if he wasn't getting my letters, then they would have come back. But they never came back. Nothing came back. But I know he received them. I know he has them in his cell now, sitting there unopened, stacked up like bad memories.

I never cried to anyone in my family, though they all knew what happened to Platón. I don't cry very often. I don't like to exhaust myself or waste my emotions on things I can't help. Instead, I just don't talk. I slept a lot. My father would kid me about my choice in men. But everything was a joke for him. My mother said she would die before she let me visit Platón in prison. It was no place for a civilized woman to visit. Or was I planning on joining the cabrón behind bars? What kind of woman was I to be dating a drug dealer? Only Rudi knew I was pregnant at the time and that Platón had proposed to me. Rudi visited me at home, and Julián and Eva would bring me presents, chocolates, and gifts from Nordstrom.

My mother didn't talk to me for months after she found out I was going to have a baby. If there hadn't been so many complications with the pregnancy, I would have moved out. But there was nowhere for me to go, and my baby was breech. At least at home there were servants to bring medicine, check my blood, feed me the right foods.

My mother still hasn't forgiven me. She went on a religious crusade to cleanse the family of scandal. She still takes my daughter to church with her every Sunday to clean the bad karma she thinks Alejandra inherited from Platón and me. I think that's fine. Someone ought to pray for us. Mamá and I never had a great relationship to begin with. I can hear her now: Dime con quien andas, y te diré quien eres. She's tried to teach me lessons about being a woman before. Like how to hide your emotions, how to take advantage of men and get them to provide everything for you, how to pretend you're interested in what other people have to say, how to be polite and lie. But for the most part, I prefer to learn from my own mistakes. It's the only way to really know yourself. I suppose my mother will feel justified once this gets out, like she knew it all along. Even though she never had a clue.

EDGAR TURNED OVER ON HIS SIDE TO LOOK closer at Miranda, facing her back as she lay naked, curled up on the dark green sheets of his futon. Her small, muscular back rose and fell. Edgar scooted closer and poked his nose through her brown hair, into the softness of her neck. He pressed the slippery dampness at the small of her back with his thumbs and wiggled himself farther down while inhaling her sweat, cigarette ashes, and the faint remainder of the aguaflorida she'd bathed in. Always the perfume of liquid flowers on her skin, which he imagined to be the smell of Xochimilco, the flowered river canals of Mexico that

Edgar had only read about in books, but which she had actually visited. Miranda felt loose and limber in his hands, her flesh glazed with dark-orange sweat beneath the electric light of his studio. Edgar lightly fingered her shoulder blades and ran the tip of his tongue down her spine, tasting her salty skin. He had large hands that could encircle Miranda's waist. He pulled himself toward her into spoon position. To test the depth of Miranda's sleep he lowered himself again, this time sliding his tongue between the cheeks of her behind. She shivered, tensed, and moaned, but did not rouse.

Among the many games of attention they played with each other, pretending sleep after sex was one of Miranda's favorites. Almost immediately after Edgar had released her, she would turn away from him and lie still in his bed, while he ended up talking to himself or staring into the ceiling, thinking she was the cruelest woman he'd ever met. He could have accepted that she might be too tired to talk to him, in which case he would have gotten out of bed and begun painting again. But Miranda told him it was uncomfortable to try to sleep when she knew he was awake, working near her. She said it made her feel like she was being spied upon.

"Since when did painting become spying?"

"Come on, Edgar. You said it yourself. You're always trying to reveal something secret about whatever you're painting. You think I'm a fool? I'm not going to be anyone's muse. You'll only see what I want you to see in me."

Edgar supposed a sense of humor would have been the best medicine for the way she controlled him. But he had a hard time accepting her demands not to paint or create any traceable record of his involvement with her. It was for his own safety, she said.

He'd never been told such a thing before and didn't much care for such an imposition. His job was to discover—to push the envelope and paint images that people didn't want to think about. How could he stand to be censored by his own lover?

There was something else about her that Edgar feared, something menacing about her even in a state of vulnerability. Something dangerously insecure. In that case, it really was about him spying on her. Even so, Miranda was a master at manipulating her self-image.

You'll only see what I want you to see in me.

Edgar felt he had to respect Miranda's warnings about his "safety." They were mutually corrupt, one trying to take advantage of the other, and, as long as that was the unspoken rule, then there could be no surprises. It was a barbed-wire relationship—if he gripped too hard he would get hurt.

Edgar thought of his sister, Cristina. She was like Miranda— if Cristina had been a single mother, strung out on cocaine, rich, straight, and Catholic. If she had still been alive. Both were strong women, extremely outspoken. Perhaps Edgar was attracted to the all-or-nothing will of a woman who thought highly of herself and was happy to let you know it. His mother had been like that, surviving a divorce, then raising Edgar and Cristina on her own. Now, in the absence of his sister, Miranda's quirky demands had become something of a home for Edgar. Something about his need for chaotic, doomed relationships with neurotic people like himself. He dreaded being abandoned again. Miranda wasn't the only one who didn't want to sleep alone. So he would stay in bed with her, wide awake, listening to his heartbeat slow in the aftermath of their sex-making, wondering what to do next. How much time did he have?

That afternoon, Miranda had shown up at his studio with a black eye from the beating she'd taken at the hands of Los Reyes. He'd gotten her some ice, while she told him how that morning, after she'd gone to pick up Alejandra from her brother's house, she was followed by a black Grand Marquis that cornered her at a stop sign. They'd pulled Miranda out of the car by her hair, punched and kicked her. Alejandra had witnessed it all. Miranda thought they were going to kill her and her daughter. Just two days before, her childhood friend, Rudi Ballesteros, had been shot 37 times, while waiting to cross the border. She'd known she was next and was prepared. She'd been carrying a gun, and so she shot the two men who'd told her they'd killed Julián. She didn't know how much time she had before Los Reyes came after her again.

Alejandra was now at Miranda's sister-in-law's house in Coronado. Miranda had come to tell Edgar that she and her daughter were taking a long vacation somewhere northwest. Maybe Portland, she'd said. Portland sounded cool to her, angry and grungy, which was what she said her mood demanded.

"There's nothing but rain in Portland," Edgar advised her. "It's depressing. Junkies under every bridge. Suicide's really popular there. That's not the place for you."

"Sounds perfect, if you ask me. Did I ever tell you my father is allergic to the sun? It gives him sunstroke. Could you imagine? I think I'm the same. Anyway, Los Reyes would never think to follow me to Portland."

Edgar did not respond. He sat on the edge of the bed and sucked on a joint. They had been introduced by Tavo, a mutual friend, at one of Edgar's openings. For the last six or seven months, Miranda had been his lover and his part-time drug dealer. She was the first female drug dealer he'd ever met, which made her even more attractive, despite her being the mother of a soon-to-be five-year-old. Now he was feeling confused about his loyalties. He felt betrayed by the seriousness of Miranda's situation, the connection with his dead sister, and guilty that he didn't know what to do about it. There was a large pile of cocaine on a pink plate in Miranda's lap. To kill the pain of decision, he guessed. She bent over and snorted. Edgar declined when she offered the plate to him.

"It's how I am, though, you know?" she continued. "I mean, if I'm pissed off, then everybody else should be, too. Whatever. No one will be looking for a coke dealer in Portland—not if everyone there is doing heroin. Right?"

"You won't find any decent tacos up in Portland," Edgar muttered. "No good carne asada. You'll be starved for home."

"Are you hungry or something?"

"I'm just saying."

"It doesn't have to be Portland. It's a huge country. It could be any small town up north. Somewhere Alejandra and I could see rivers and trees. That's what we need right now. We need peace."

Julián's disappearance had meant the end to their business with Los Reyes. A couple of years ago Julián had discovered the dangerous benefits of double-dealing. Once he found out he could make more money on top of his crossers fee, he had begun to re-cut the coke that belonged to the Reyes cartel and sell to new connections in San Diego. He recruited Miranda, his family, and his close friends. It was a lucrative opportunity the unemployed Miranda did not know how to refuse.

Double-dealing was a common story, but it was only a matter of time before such operations usually fell apart. Edgar didn't ask why Julián, a rich man set to inherit a good portion of his family's supermarket business, would risk dealing drugs. When it came to doing or dealing drugs, the reason why was always the enemy. Getting high on cocaine was a will to power, a pure road with no exit. Now Miranda thought she could escape the consequences. Only in a perfect world, Edgar thought. Only in a perfectly fucked-up world could she be so lucky.

Nevertheless, Edgar did not believe in random causes. He felt there was some reason why these things happened in such a bloody way. He was attracted to it, even. Like a low-class aficionado of gore and horror, he loved to dwell upon these lower instincts as if they revealed something profound—about the human race, about himself, about being Chicano, about being an artist, a lost soul. Perhaps he was just a depraved sicko for whom reality was nothing but pain and abuse. Because sickos attracted sick things like drug addicts and murderers. In adopting their hostile understanding of the world—dog eat dog, an eye for an eye, you get what you deserve, etc., etc.—Edgar wondered if he sounded like a distorted combination of Miranda and Cristina. Unlike Miranda, however, Edgar did not feel he could run far enough away from himself, or the rest of the world, to escape the hostility it held in store for people like him. Perhaps he was deluded, but he was not eager to follow anyone to the grave.

Wasn't there some other way to deal with Los Reyes besides running to Portland? Couldn't she give back the coke and the money? Forgive and forget?

"Are you kidding me? The coke's gone. Your buddy Gabe bought it," she said. "Besides, it's too late for apologies. Those fucking pigs killed my cousin. They killed Rudi. I know Los Reyes well enough. They don't renegotiate contracts. I got lucky today. If I hadn't passed by Nereida's house looking for Julián one last time, if Nereida hadn't given me Julián's gun this morning, I wouldn't be here putting ice on my face. I was just crazy enough to shoot them before they shot me. But they'll kill me the first chance they get."

"You're right," Edgar nodded. "I'm stupid. Fuck them. We need another plan."

"I think you're sweet for trying to help me," Miranda said. She took another line from the plate and got up to look out the window. She must have forgotten that there was nothing to see out the large window at the end of Edgar's studio. It faced another warehouse. Miranda came back toward the bed. She lit one of

Edgar's Camel Lights and sat down.

"I grew up with Rudi. I loved Julián. He was like my brother. More of a brother than my own. But Julián—we gambled on a long shot. Everyone does nowadays."

"You talk about leaving with Alejandra, but what are you going to do? I mean, have you ever worked a day in your life?"

"That has absolutely nothing to do with with it. We have enough money and coke to get us through."

"And why would you think that it's safe to travel with coke?"

"It doesn't matter. I can't wait any longer," Miranda sighed. "I'm sorry, but everyone is nervous and frightened right now, including you. They'll be looking for scapegoats and revenge. Somebody else, someone innocent, is going to get it. Just to set an example. I don't think there's anything you can do to stop this. The only thing for me to do is leave."

Miranda was sure the other hijackers, snitches, and wannabes couldn't be too far off her trail. After Julián disappeared, she was the one left with the stolen goods. Everybody followed the drugs, like smoke to a fire. Let them all eat her shit. They could hound somebody else. She would escape before anyone had another chance to sink their dirty meathooks into her.

What bothered Edgar was that Miranda expected him to do nothing. Again, he was the weak link, just a painter crushed by reality into numb inconsequence. The ineffectual self-indulgent artist. Artists, in the end, did not change the course of events, but merely reported the news of their happening, at best in a new way. His sister had gathered that from some Marxist critic and read it to Edgar while she was still in college, thinking about becoming a writer. Edgar was neither socialist nor spiritualist in any sense. He took it to mean that all art was always an encounter with its deceased subject. Useless metaphysics, ad nauseam. Which was why he took everything so personally.

There was a CD playing on the boom box at the foot of the bed, Maria Callas singing Alfredo Catalani's aria, "La Wally." Edgar lit a Camel Light and handed the joint to Miranda.

"It's like going underground," Miranda told Edgar, quickly pinching the joint. "You know what I mean. Aren't you underground?"

"We're on the third floor," Edgar said, exhaling and touching his hands to his cold, paint-splattered bare feet. "In a warehouse in downtown Chula Vista. There's no underground around here. There's not even a subway."

"But wasn't your sister underground?" Miranda asked, nodding across the studio at the triptych mural of a fetus inside a volcano, a naked and pregnant Cristina gripping a barbed-wire fence, screaming. "Wasn't she political or something?"

"My sister?" Edgar coughed smoke.

"The girl you've been painting. It is your sister, isn't it?" Miranda pounded Edgar's back until he stopped coughing. "Tavo told me how she died. Why don't you ever talk about it?"

"She wasn't underground. She was a lesbian. And now she's dead. So, O.K., yeah, she's under ground."

"You're so fucked up. Is that how you think of it? Like a word game? That's not what I meant by underground."

"Sorry," he said. "It's not my favorite conversation."

"Tell me what was she like, then."

"Well, she left home when she was 17. And she never came back. She was murdered in a drive-by shooting in front of a taco shop. The cops never found out who did it. First, they thought she was a gangbanger, because she dressed like a cholo sometimes. Then they said it was a random mistake. When I told them she was gay, they called it a hate crime and still haven't pursued it."

"Because she was gay?"

"Probably," Edgar shrugged. "Nobody else in my family is gay, at least not openly. She was the first I knew. Shaved head. Dressed like a guy. Always arguing about some gender/class revolution. No one listened to her. My mother couldn't handle it. My sister was like an exile in our family. An outsider. Now that I think of it, it probably made too much sense that Cristina decided to date women instead of—" Edgar stopped when he realized the amount of melodrama in their conversation.

"Ugh! It's a fact," Miranda said, as she leaned back onto the futon. "All of us lead a different, if not totally opposite life from our parents. But underneath we're just like them. Que gacho. We inherit their emotions, their karma. That sucks, doesn't it?"

Edgar nodded. It sounded like the truth. Edgar and Cristina had inherited their parents' inability to understand each other's differences. Their black silences and white rages, the uncertainty of a biracial marriage. All of the arguments and anger lived in Edgar's art and were exaggerated in Edgar's relationships. He carried his parents' war inside him. He was, however, as ambivalent as Miranda when it came to expressing emotions. Art was the one place where anger was creative. On canvas his silences screamed.

For her part, Miranda had had almost no meaningful communication with her father. She was suspicious of those who wanted to be his paternal substitute. She never spoke of her mother. The two times Edgar had sat at Miranda's table with her parents, he had listened to all three of them insult each other with jokes and understatement.

He hadn't spoken to his own mother since Cristina had died a year ago. Who knew where his father was? Edgar tried to forget about his family. Love was oblivion. Life was pain. The anger and hurt kept you from going numb. Gave you something to remember.

"If everything went as you say it did, then maybe you should go to the police," Edgar said. "You've got a justifiable homicide."

"So what?"

"They could put you into witness protection."

"Come on. This isn't something to joke about."

"I'm not. It's true."

"Yeah, right."

"You'd have to tell them everything. Give them everyone." Edgar was imagining how he'd react if he had to tell the truth. But of course, he could lie. So could Miranda.

"Everyone I know?" Mara laughed. "That is ridiculous."

"You'd have to give them Los Reyes. Your cousin. You'd have to name Tavo. Gabe. Even me."

"I wouldn't do that to you, querido."

"You might have to."

"I won't tell them about you. I'll cut you out of the story."

"Thanks. But you'd have to give them someone big."

"Then I'll give them Los Reyes."

"You'd have to go back to Tijuana to set them up."

"That would be like a death sentence."

Edgar had smoked too much pot. He was losing his equilibrium. This happened when he got nervous. Seeing Edgar shake, Miranda hugged him. She leaned him back on the bed, held him and rubbed his arms and shoulders. Even though she was developing a black eye, and the left side of her face was red and swollen like a bruised peach, she was still able to smile at him, the tiny dimple in her thin brown cheek plunging and shining, her thick lips softly puckering as she kissed him.

Something awoke in Edgar—to try to contain Miranda, to keep her closed up in a jar. Why did this idea thrill him so? Edgar also felt the thrill of another idea—to just pick up and leave. Start over somewhere else with something new. Forget the old identity and start from the beginning. Which was again somewhere inside Miranda. So he gripped her tightly, merging his body into hers, remembering, nonetheless, how all illusions were momentary. He told himself not to want her anymore. Not to learn from her anymore. Not to remember her again as anything other than a woman he had fucked. Not to care that she was leaving him, running to Portland, or wherever. Why had she even told him about her plans?

He tried to fuck her as hard as he could, losing his breath, but still trying to sink sharper and deeper into her, through her, to pierce her, nail her to the ground, keep her. She shouted out, half in anger, half in pleasure, and he grunted heavily behind her, on top of her, beneath her, both of them delirious inside the musk of marijuana smoke, cocaine, and sex, high on their own electrified endorphins. Maria Callas continued to sing in nauseating Italian.

Edgar finally got out of bed and grabbed the plate to snort some more of Miranda's good stash. He wanted to wake up before it was time to go. Go where? he wondered. He wasn't sure. But he knew he had to get out of his studio. It was discouraging to live surrounded with images of loss when all the time you'd rather become someone else. Should he go find Tavo, wherever he was? Or go with Miranda, wherever she would let him follow? Everything had happened so quick. He was not quite clear about his own role in the unfolding events. Little was expected of him, other than to paint. And now there was little time for anyone to think about what was actually happening.

Miranda woke up and grabbed for the thin black pullover she'd been wearing.

"I have to go."

"Wait." Edgar held out the razor blade he had been using to chop lines. Now was the time. Before they both forgot each other's pain. Edgar swallowed through a numbed throat, "We need to make an incision."

"What?"

"Here. Take this, please," Edgar held out the razor blade.

"But don't I need the toot?"

"No. You don't."

They both stretched across the bed then, Edgar on his stomach, his legs across the bed, his head hanging over the edge of the futon. He braced his feet against the cement wall and gripped the plate, while Miranda licked the razor clean and rubbed some coke on her gums. She held the razor against the crease of Edgar's right thigh, just below the buttock. When Edgar snorted, Miranda made an inch and a half cut. Then she made another, parallel, and ran her fingers along these red lines.

"You'll have a set of jail bars now," she said. He felt the sting of her salty skin and the numbing of the cocaine.

Miranda ran her finger across the razor. Edgar licked her blood, then dropped his head over the edge of the bed again. He wanted another longer, slower cut this time. Lower on his thigh.

This time he paid attention to the razor being inserted into the back of his thigh. He felt the small point of the blade pop and rip through his hair follicles, tearing open his skin. When Miranda didn't stop, Edgar gasped and tensed, suddenly afraid.

"Bueno," Miranda said, pulling up. "It's nice. It even tails down and to the right, like a hook."

"My turn," Edgar said rising up slowly and carefully.

He searched the floor and bed until he found the blue Bic lighter beneath the sheets. Edgar held it lit for several seconds. Miranda stretched out across the queen-size mattress as Edgar had done. Edgar stroked the back of the thigh he would brand.

"Don't push it in too hard," Miranda said. "I don't want you to cut me."

"I know," Edgar nodded, still pressing down on the flame.

She raised the toot to her nose. Edgar let the flame go down. He pressed the hot metal of the Bic into the smooth, burnt orange flesh just below her buttock. He leaned his head on her ass to watch the lighter sink in. Her skin singed and bubbled slightly.

"Ay! Ay! Ay! Wait!"

Edgar pulled up the lighter and then pressed it into her again, completing a puffy circle of tiny happy-faces that looked like a daisy.

There had only been a series of slices and a few burn scars on the back of Miranda's thigh when she first asked him to add something. Edgar decided to create a bouquet of daisies, with a six-inch stem down the back of her thigh.

"If they found you in Portland, could they trace this?"

"Fuck you." She stood up slowly. Her swollen red flower was now at his eye level. Maybe she would come back to him, after all, he thought. Maybe he had captured her, finally. He pulled her closer to kiss her belly button. He could smell himself around her navel, the musky spot where he had pulled out and come. She laid her hand on his bristling head and pushed him away.

"I have to get out of here."

"Next time, I'll make you a butterfly," he said, passing his hand along her hip, trying to pull her toward him.

"No, thanks," Miranda replied. "Let go. I need a Band-Aid."

She limped over to the picnic table, where Edgar's painting supplies were scattered: dirty cups of water, paint-splattered paper plates, jars and coffee cans full of brushes, putty knives, and nails, smudged sketches, and tubes of paint. Inside a red metal toolbox were a few large Band-Aids, which Miranda brought back and handed to Edgar.

"I miss you already," he said, carefully stretching the patch over the back of her leg. "But you don't want me to go with you, do you?"

"Why would you want to go with me?" she snapped. She reached over him to grab her pants. "You can't be a painter and run from Los Reyes. Don't be so stupid."

Edgar got up from the bed and went over to the cordless phone on top of the metal bookshelves near the door. He brought it back to Miranda.

"I want you to call the police. Tell them what happened."

"What for? Didn't you say the police fucked up your sister's case? You want them to fuck me up, too?"

"No, I'm trying to tell you that it's the only way. You're going to have to do it sooner or later. They can help Alejandra. At least, they can protect you while—"

"While I rat on everybody?"

"—while you're still alive."

"No. I don't have time to play."

"If you don't call them, I will."

"No, you won't. What the fuck is the matter with you? Do you want to see me dead, Edgar? Los Reyes don't care where I'm at."

"Just call them!"

"Call who? Edgar, why are you doing this?"

"Call 911."

"No. I'm just going to leave."

"If you leave, they'll just come after you. Or your family." Edgar gripped the phone tighter. "Or me."

Miranda stared at him. He had a farmer's tan and his chest was smooth and naturally bald. The only hairy part of Edgar's body was his groin. His waist was thick where Miranda could see the first formations of love handles. His penis was at rest, but Miranda noticed that his heart was beating fast, as was her own. She could feel the cocaine numbing her throat as she swallowed.

"Give me the phone," she said.

He handed her the phone and sat down on the bed as Miranda punched in three digits.

"Hello? Yes. I want to report un asesinato."

Edgar wondered how long it would be before Miranda gave the police his own name. He supposed he was prepared to tell his side of the story. He wanted to tell someone why and what for. Edgar figured as soon as Tavo's name came up, his name would follow, as one of Miranda's regular customers.

Inside his imagination, Edgar dialed Tavo's pager and got his voice mail.

"You've reached Tavo with Southwest Repo. I'm either away from the office or out in the field. Please leave a verbal message or punch in your account number, and I'll get back to you at my nearest convenience. Thank you and have a nice day."

In his imagination, Edgar punched in 911#55*2677 and hung up. Tavo had tried to organize himself against easy infiltration. He had four different phone lines, separate ones for family, friends, and clients, and a phony number listed in the phone book for narcs and unwanted solicitors. Fifty-five was Edgar's personal code, and 2677 was the code for COPS. Which meant to get out of the house and across the border as soon as possible. Tavo took the undercover- identity thing seriously, even though he was a small-time dealer, barely able to support his own habit. He didn't have a real job. He lived at home with his parents, who owned maquiladoras in Tijuana. Nevertheless, Tavo was connected to bigger things. And now Edgar had betrayed him.

In all relationships there was that unwritten contract that

guaranteed that at some point you would betray the other person. To prove that the past was real and unforgettable. Because friends just didn't give and take loyalty. They were expected to make bodily sacrifices to the Gods of Trust. That was the way Edgar understood it. Each sacrifice was a betrayed friend, lover, or family member. His father had done it to him when he decided to leave for Denver. Cristina had done it to their mother. Platón had done it to Miranda. And now Edgar would do it to Tavo. Edgar would have done it if he were in Miranda's place. He told himself that if she refused to call, then he was going to call. Because something told him this was a karmic payoff. The gods were hungry.

I WENT THROUGH POSTPARTUM DEPRESSION FOR two months after Alejandra was born. I stayed in bed and developed a very negative attitude. I blamed my daughter for how miserable I felt about myself. Like my future had been stolen from me, my life was over, and I was doomed to be a lonely single mother. I imagined the worst things: that people were making fun of me, saying that I was a puta, a drug addict who would fuck for coke. Platón's bad reputation infected me, until I developed an eight-week cold. Sometimes I even wondered if my baby was diseased and addicted. Because even though I knew I wasn't, who knew what Alejandra might have picked up from Platón's genes? I didn't want to see her. I didn't want to know what she looked like, how she was. I didn't want to care. I even considered suicide, which is against my religion. Until, finally, I convinced myself that I had to leave Tijuana.

Now I realize my mother caused a lot of what I was going through. She hardly spoke to me while I was depressed. In her eyes, I was a failure, a disgrace to the family. I was a symbol of what was wrong with Tijuana. Drugs and promiscuity. Agringada. Americanized. I was the black sheep of the family. I had set a bad example for my younger cousins by having a baby out of wedlock. "Why don't you learn to think about somebody else but yourself?" she told me. On top of that, since Platón was a convicted drug dealer, according to my mother, I was also an addict. Mamá probably thought I needed some sort of quarantine. While I was sick, my father checked in on me every so often, before he went to work and when he got home. I pretended to be asleep to avoid him. My mother, who didn't work, stayed home all day and refused to let anyone visit me.

"Mi hija está muy mal de salúd," I heard her tell people who called for me. "Pray for her. She's really sick." And then, "Have you seen the baby? Yes. My beautiful granddaughter, Alejandra. You have to come see her. Mi nieta es una preciosa, un regalo de diós."

Alejandra was available to receive visitors and gifts as if she were the Immaculate Conception. My mother lavished all her attention on Alejandra. She would fulfill my mother's dreams of perfection, clear her guilty conscience that I had contaminated. Mamá never had a doctor come visit me. There was no one to help me but God. I was only allowed to speak to Padre Ruiz. He came into my room with Mamá after they split a bottle of wine in the kitchen. He asked me to say Ave Maria and the Lord's Prayer with him. I would mumble along, listening to him slur his words.

"We have to pray for forgiveness, Mara," Padre Ruiz said. "You have committed a grave sin against God and your family. Let us pray."

One night I took off in my mother's car and drove down El Rio to Plaza Fiesta. I felt more reckless than ever. I turned the stereo up, honked my horn at drunks on the street, and even circled around the glorieta of Cuahtemoc three times, swerving in and out of lanes, trying to get into an accident. But everyone got out of my way. I knew I'd find everyone with Rudi at El Suizo. I must have drunk five shots in the first ten minutes I was there. It was almost orgasmic. Still, I wanted to cry, I was so angry. Nobody could understand what had happened to me. Rudi had been told I was gravely ill with some contagious disease women get upon having their insides exposed during birth.

"I thought you were in a private hospital in San Diego," Rudi said. "Your mother said you weren't allowed visitors."

"My mother exaggerated. I was sick, but I'm fine now."

"You do look kind of pale," my cousin Veronica said. "Pero, aren't you supposed to be fat after you have a baby? No se te nota ni una gota de peso extra. How'd you work off the extra weight?"

"Time goes really slow when you're pregnant," I said. "It's hard to relax. All you want to do is have the baby, and the birthdate always seems so far away. After Alejandra was born, it all just kind of melted off me."

Whether they believed me or not didn't matter. I had gotten

drunk fast and wanted to catch up on everybody's life. I felt like I had been out of it for years. Eva really wanted to know what it was like to have a baby. She confided in me that she and Julián had been trying to start a family. Unsuccessfully. She told me she thought it was the drugs. She thought Julián had been doing too much cocaine and that he was no longer fertile. And now she was going out and doing cocaine with him, just so she could keep track of what he was up to.

"I think right now a baby could change our lives," Eva told me. "I think it would make Julián focus on our family. It would keep him at home. He's never there for more than a few hours a day now. Sometimes he doesn't come home at all."

I didn't feel a real connection to Eva. She was still the intruder. She was probably jealous I had given birth before her. But I thought about how I would have felt if I had actually planned Alejandra's birth.

"To feel responsible for another human being, your own flesh and blood, with hands like you, eyes like you, is like a gift from God. I know you would be a great mother, Eva."

I was so honest, Eva began to cry.

Rudi leaned over and asked if I wanted a bump.

"A what?"

"Un pase. ¿Quieres?"

"Sure. Why not?"

Rudi rubbed his hands together in front of his chest and said, "Open sesame." He led me outside the bar to the plaza, where I guessed his magic carpet was. I put my glasses on to see in the dark in front of me. Butterflies whirred in my stomach, and the air was syrupy. We walked past the yellow-and-green awning of Mi Barra, where college students spilled over the patio railing, singing, slurring, and shouting beneath six TVs showing concert footage of Queen. I thought it was a waste of time to go to college in Tijuana. The students were boring, so I never hung out at Mi Barra.

Rudi and I went around the concrete path of Plaza Fiesta, between all the other bars, past people sitting outside La Taberna Española Café, past overweight cops waiting until they'd properly digested their gorditas before they decided to arrest anyone for pissing in public, and into Ranas Bar, where all the black-leather-jacket, long-haired roqueros and scruffy punk rock locos were sitting at small wooden tables drinking beer, while a band of shirtless teenagers thrashed on a five-by-five stage. A skinny brown boy with green hair in spikes screamed devil worship and ran to the back of the bar, almost right into us. He jumped onto a table, still screaming in Spanish, strangling the microphone and sticking out his red tongue at me. With his face painted green and his lips black, he looked like a possessed Peter Pan. I smiled back, because I've always had a crush on Peter Pan. I have this thing about adolescent-looking men—the Menudo boys, Chyanne, Johnny Depp, River Phoenix—I like them young and fresh.

It took me a few seconds to realize what he was saying, Aqui mismo vamos a morir. We're going to die right here.

I waved to the young owner, José Luis, behind the bar, whom I had kissed more than once under the influence of many free drinks. He sent an older mesero to show us a table in the back, where it was less chaotic. Rudi and I plunged farther into the 7UP-green walls of Ranas, which means frogs, but is not to be confused with Señor Frog's in Pueblo Amigo. There was a DJ booth upstairs that divided the back room from the front, where the Devil as Peter Pan was still screaming.

"I thought that kid was going to bite me," I said.

"Because you forgot your hairdye and your leather jacket."

Rudi was obviously high. He chewed his bottom lip. He was wearing a stone-washed denim jacket, which he removed carefully and laid in his lap. Then he unfolded a small piece of paper and began to scratch white lines on top of a red flyer for the next punk show at Iguanas. He handed me a rolled-up dollar bill.

"Isn't this a little too obvious?"

"So what? This is a punk bar. Llégale."

We inhaled two thick lines each, and Rudi hid the coke before our drinks came. Before the waiter, who wasn't the waiter, but José Luis, asked us if we had any coke.

"Sorry. Got nothing tonight," Rudi told him. "Call me tomorrow."

"¿Pa'que sirves, entonces, pinche joto?"

"Para negarte las cosas buenas, mijito."

"Ya para de joder."

"Mira," José Luis leaned in toward me and said, "You should come see me upstairs in the DJ booth. I've got some Ecstasy when you want it." He set the drinks down and waited for me to respond. Rudi handed him a wad of pesos, which José Luis refused, keeping his eyes locked on me like he was trying to figure out my combination. The coke was already hitting me, and I felt like my hair was on fire. I had to fight not to bite my lip and give it away.

"It's on the house," José Luis said, lingering over me a while. "What about it, Mara?"

José Luis had this big-mouthed-brat, private-school-boy way of carrying himself. He was typical of Tijuana club owners who only went into the business to be able to pick and choose, on any occasion, whatever mindless slut they wanted to fuck. It was a lucrative business in that sense. But forget about making any money. Clubs in Tijuana generally proved to be money pits. The only way to make money off them was to set up a front or burn them down for insurance.

At that time, I didn't know what Ecstasy was, but I said, "Al rato. Maybe later."

José Luis smiled at me again, and then he left.

Rudi's bony face was flushed from the coke. He hunched over the table, a cigarette dangling from his lips, his thin almond eyes squinting into the smoke. I watched him grip his green bankcard and slide two more white rails.

"Why is José Luis asking you for coke?"

"Things are changing around here, Mara. Everybody's making money fast. Ecstasy is good, but coke is bigger."

"Ya sé, guey. But what are you doing?"

"I'm working with Julián now."

"You mean at the store?"

"No. Forget the store," Rudi said. "Julián is working with Los Reyes, and I'm working for him."

"¿Que-qué? What do you mean Julián's working for Los Reyes? Los Reyes are horrible, fucking, back-stabbing liars. They put Platón in jail. No te metas, cabrón."

"I know. But you see, Mara, Platón was stealing from them. He had a whole separate business going on in San Diego with coke that belonged to Los Reyes. He was double-dealing. It wasn't a lot, but the old man had Platón sent to jail to teach him a lesson. With Julián, they can start all over."

"But Julián and Platón were best friends."

"Exacto. Here. Do another linea."

I was wired and confused, but I did another and watched tiny drops of sweat form under Rudi's eyes. His face was blotchy. I wondered if mine was the same.

"But if Los Reyes knew Platón was connected to Julián, why would they trust Julián now?"

"Because Julián has better business connections. He's a Cascabel. Tijuana loves your family. It's good politics for Los Reyes to get in with Julián. And now he'll be connected to some very powerful people in Mexico City. It's good for everyone."

"Good for what? Everybody knows Los Reyes are crooked as a culo cucho."

"Maybe. But why should that stop you from making money?"

Then something stabbed my thigh underneath the table. I reached below and felt the sharp corner of a bulky manila envelope.

"It's for you. Julián wants you to cross the border with it. And take it to his house in the Cays."

"Cross what?"

It felt like a textbook.

"What do you think?" Rudi said. "You'll get a thousand dollars for crossing it. And two percent of monthly sales. That could add up to a lot of money."

"It's a lot of jail, too. You're fucking crazy. How much coke is this?"

"A kilo. But listen, it's not as difficult as you think."

I knew Rudi wasn't kidding, because it was more coke than I had ever seen. I should have been afraid of accepting it, considering how fast it had all happened. This was the first night I had gone out in months, and WHAM! I'm a dealer, just like that. Rudi told me sometimes it was easier, less suspicious, for a lone woman to pass through customs than a man. But there was an added bonus. Julián had secured a commercial pass from a family friend, a city official in San Diego, which allowed Julián, Rudi, and Miranda to go through U.S. customs, while claiming to be members of the Board of the International Commerce Committee of San Diego. Rudi said the pass was laminated. And it was placed inside the package. All I had to do was drive through customs on the far right of the line, where buses and other commercial vehicles passed through into San Diego, and wave the badge. If I was stopped, I was supposed to have customs call the number of the International Commerce Committee located in the downtown San

Diego Courthouse Building. I was to ask for President Goldwasser.

"You've got to be kidding me," I said. "Uncle Baruch Goldwasser? He went to high school with my father. I thought he was a lawyer."

"Whatever. Now he directs the International Commerce Committee. But he doesn't have anything to do with Los Reyes. Goldwasser thinks this is all about expanding CascaMax and getting an equal share for Mexican business in the American market. We're getting it all right."

Rudi smiled.

"Believe me, the pass works. The pinche migra called Goldwasser on me twice. In five minutes, he was on the phone with Head of Customs at San Ysidro. He reamed the fucking migra so bad, they don't even look at me twice now. I just hold up the badge, and the cabrones wave me on."

"So are you helping Julián, or is it Los Reyes?"

"We're working for Julián. Not Los Reyes. Remember that."

"Does that mean if I get caught, Los Reyes will come after me or Julián?"

"You shouldn't let them scare you. You've got nothing to do with them, other than being related to Julián."

"I don't think I understand."

"You don't have to. Just deliver the package to Julián tomorrow. He'll give you the money. Everything else will be like icing on the cake."

Without an independent income, I was basically broke. My mother thought I was going to provide for my daughter with my own money, but she still gave me money. A little. I needed a job. I had way too many personal expenses and nothing coming in. This was an opportunity to make easy money. It all depended on what perspective you were partial to, what kind of instincts you had, maybe what superstition you subscribed to, whether you were lucky or not.

This was a start. I had been given a break and was free to make my own decision. I could make some fast money without having to thank my mother and father for anything. I started feeling a little more optimistic.

"How much are monthly sales?"

"Right now they're low, because we can't get enough across. If you help, you could make five thousand a month."

I agreed to do it.

"Thanks again, Rudi, for thinking of me."

"To tell you the truth, I didn't think of you. But Julián said he needed more people he could trust. He needed you. But I guess you guys can talk tomorrow. I'll say a prayer to Juan Soldado for your trip."

I nodded and smoked.

"At least this gives me a reason to cross the border now, even if I'm just a moving target."

Rudi stared at me with red spiderwebs in the corners of his eyes. He traced his slender fingers over his thin goatee. He strained to smile when he realized I was waiting for him to say something.

"Ley fuga," he said.

"Ley what?"

"Ley fuga is how they killed Juan Soldado. The capitán told him to run for the U.S. border while he counted to ten, and then the firing squad shot him in the back. If the soldiers had missed, Juan Soldado would have been free, but banished from ever returning home again. But he was killed in the street. A lot of people pray to him before they cross the border illegally. I've been going there before every trip."

"Where?"

"To the First Cemetery. He has a shrine there. I go there a lot." Rudi stood up. "Well, time to fly. I have to make a delivery tonight in Playas."

I nodded. I had never been to the shrine, but I had heard of Juan Soldado.

"Wait, Rudi. Maybe you could show me the shrine."

But Rudi had already walked off. Like it wasn't happening to me. I was watching a long shot of two friends breaking up in one of those grainy, black-and-white silent movies where everybody's movements were mechanically fast. I watched everything happen around me with a numb disbelief—thanks to the coke. I felt so nervous to be given so much that I didn't think about how much Rudi had changed until he was already at the door. I ran after him, ignoring José Luis shouting at me, or maybe it was Peter Pan and his band of possessed panaderos. Whatever. Fuck them. I tried to push through a bunch of neon-colored mohawks jammed together near the front and was told my mother was a shitty whore. Fuck them, too. I called to Rudi, who couldn't hear me over the music—or maybe he could hear me, but didn't want to say anything else. So he left without saying a proper goodbye.

Which is what, really? I stood outside Ranas, wondering how far off a nervous breakdown might be. I told myself to forget about that. Confidence had to be my best friend, if I was going to pull this off.

It was moments like these that should have reminded me that I was a mother, that I had a daughter to be responsible for, and couldn't go hopping off to join every misfit I knew in Tijuana, no matter how long I had known them or how close we were. I had been left hanging, alone, and hadn't accomplished anything that I imagined I would. I was 26 and unmarried. I was still living at home, borrowing my mother's car, and part of me was in denial about Alejandra. Because as long as my mother was at home, and the servants, I knew someone would take care of my daughter. Maybe this was my chance to create something for myself, something independent. So I forgot about Platón and let Rudi go on with his business. I didn't reflect on how quickly things had changed for everyone. Le seguí la corriente. I went with the flow. I wanted to live it up, but I suppose I was cracking up.

THINGS STARTED HAPPENING REAL FAST. I CROSSED one package a week and made $1,000 every time. But I was out almost every night, blowing a lot of money on my own supply of cocaine, until I was doing it everywhere I went, at home, at lunch, at the bars, even while I waited in line to cross the border. I didn't spend as much time with Alejandra as I should have. I let my mother and the maids take care of her while I went out. My mother thought I was working late with Julián in San Diego. She didn't ask what I was doing, only when I was coming home. I don't think she cared where I was. Neither did I.

The connections Julián had in San Diego and Tijuana made for a wired-down operation. Someone from Los Reyes would deliver coke to CascaMax in La Mesa, which was the industrial part of Tijuana, out of the way of everything. Sometimes it would come FedEx, or inside packaged goods like dog food. Then either Rudi or I would pick up the coke and cross the border, waving the NAFTA badge at the customs agent. The NAFTA badge worked with a minimum of joda from la migra. Julián gave me a key to his house in Coronado and told me to leave everything in the refrigerator in the garage. Sometimes Eva was home, and I would hang out with her until Julián showed up. Usually she was out shopping or doing whatever she did during the day, until she finally got pregnant. When Eva got pregnant, she demanded Julián stay home with her until she had the baby. They had plenty of maids, but Eva fired them all to get Julián's attention. I know he was frustrated with her, but she convinced Julián to stay home and cook, clean, and take care of her. So, I started to admire Eva: She didn't take no for an answer, and she knew how to get what she wanted. She fought for every little thing, just like a low-class naca.

There were consequences. At first, Julián swore he would never deal out of his house. Then, when Eva got pregnant, he got behind on distribution. The coke stacked up in the refrigerator, but there was no money coming in. Julián owed money and had to withdraw on his business account to pay back $50,000 to Los Reyes. That's how all the coke became Julián's by default. Instead of selling it and then delivering the money to Los Reyes, he ended up buying it. Once he had set up a network of new customers in San Diego, people were calling all the time. But Julián couldn't leave the house because Eva wouldn't let him. I remember I even had to bring groceries for them on several occasions. Julián would be cooped up in the garage with some workers he'd hired to weigh and cut. But he didn't trust anyone but Rudi to sell it. When I offered to help deliver to his buyers in San Diego, Julián laughed. He said drug dealing was a man's job. A woman would be taken advantage of. Some of his clients were Marines, Filipino gangsters, ex-cons. Mean, rough people who sometimes carried guns, and didn't give a shit about a woman's respect, no matter who she was connected to. It was too dangerous. He didn't want to risk losing money, the drugs, or me.

"They'll think you're nothing but a hooker," Julián told me. "I'll feel responsible for you. And I don't want to have to shoot anybody. It would be bad for business."

We were in the kitchen. Julián was holding his newborn son, Fernando. One of the maids was preparing dinner. We spoke English around the maids so they couldn't understand. But they picked up on some things.

"You're safer just crossing it. Let me and Rudi do the dealing," Julián said, tickling Fernando. "Sí, mijito. ¿Quieres ver a tu Tía Mara? Here, Mara, you hold him while I change. I need to get ready. I've got to pick up some paperwork tonight."

I held Fernando while Julián changed. Fernando was bundled in a pink blanket. He had black hair and black eyes and ears that stuck out like Julián's. Alejandra had the same big black eyes; she was now 14 months. Her first word had been "Quik," the chocolate-milk mix. She said it whenever she wanted something. I thought my mother was spoiling her. But I wasn't ready to be a mommy yet. So I couldn't judge.

Julián reappeared in a black V-neck pullover, black-and-white Adidas sweatpants, and leather sandals. His black hair was slicked back.

"We should talk more about this when I get back, Mara. Los Reyes want me to go to Guadalajara next week."

"What for?"

"To meet with some of their partners. I think Colombians."

"But when will you have the time to sell what's in the garage?"

"When I get back."

"You can lose a lot of customers in two weeks. What if they find new dealers while you're gone? If you let me substitute for you, I could keep them happy while you're on vacation."

"Substitute? Like a teacher?" Julián laughed. "Dealers and buyers are not something you substitute so easily. You spend a lot of time finding and making good customers. They get into a rhythm with you. Like a schedule. You understand? They trust you. You have to treat them like possessions. I either give you my connections, or you take them from me."

"Then give them to me. I probably know most of them. They'd probably rather see a familiar face than some stranger. Besides, I'm better looking. So you and Rudi sell to the nasty gringo sailors and the cholos. And I'll sell to the nice people. That way I can make more money, and you don't lose any. Right?"

I had unknowingly raised my voice, and Fernando started to cry in my arms. He was wet. I handed him to Julián. He handed the baby to the maid, who took him into the living room to change.

"Have you ever shot a gun before?" Julián asked me.

"I don't like guns. Too much macho bullshit."

"I didn't ask you if you liked them, Mara. I asked if you had ever shot one."

"Never."

"O.K." He rubbed his forehead and paced around the kitchen. "I'll give you an easy one. Go to the Coronado Towers. Tower Number 1. Tenth floor. Number 24. Chito owes me $1,500. Come back with the money, and I'll have something ready for you to take to my friend Tavo in Chula Vista."

"You mean right now?" I asked. "Like this?" I was dressed in my professional outfit, black slacks, white nylons, pumps, and a white silk blouse. The way I thought a board member of the International Commerce Committee would dress. Definitely not the look of a drug dealer. I'd left my Gucci and Donna Karan at home.

"You look all business. You can tell Chito you just got off work, and you're on your way to meet me. Tell him you're in a hurry. He's a pain in the ass, and always, always high. But if you pressure him, he'll roll over like a dog. He likes to be told what to do."

I was excited. I scribbled the address on my hand.

"Here. Take my cell phone." Julián handed me the bulky phone. "All you have to do is press FUN and the number 1, and it will page me."

"O.K."

"Take this, too." Julián pulled a small black handgun out from behind his back.

"What's that?"

"It's my .25. This is part of the job. Take it. Everybody has one. You should get used to it."

I got in the car, locked the door, and left Julián in his driveway with the gun still in his hand. Guns weren't my style. I didn't want that kind of action—or responsibility. My instincts would have to be my weapon. Confidence, persuasion, and a sense of humor were all I needed. I could talk shit with anyone, tell a joke, flirt, lie. I was usually nice to people. The key was to make them feel comfortable about giving you a lot of money, and not get killed.

Julián came with me on a few deals to make the proper introductions. Then he left a message on his private voice mail. "Graciás por llamar. This is Julián. I'm away on business for a while. If you need immediate service, please call 619-844-1900. Someone will take care of you right away." They would page, and I would call them back and introduce myself. If I had to, I could drop a hint about who was backing me up. Not everyone knew

Julián was in business with Los Reyes. I didn't say anything to those who didn't know. I had to be careful to avoid saying the wrong thing to the wrong people.

Drug dealing is a boys' club. I was the one girl allowed to play. It made me feel bien macha. Strong and powerful. Like the old naïve and dependent Mara was through.

There was a natural high that came with dealing. Getting in my car and driving all over San Diego was an adventure. I met so many people. I became somebody else, somebody powerful. I felt taller than five foot three. The bottom line was that people had to respect me if they wanted to get high. And I always had to look respectable. Still, there were a few assholes who, when I'd come over to make a deal, would start talking loud and rude to their girlfriends about mensa this and cabrona that, go get me this, give me some money, anything to show me that they didn't take direction from women. They were cowards. The more bullshit I heard, the more I would laugh once they handed over the cash. I never budged, never renegotiated the price, never accepted a front. It could have been their huevos I was holding in those baggies. I told Chito Magallon, the spoiled brat in the Coronado Towers, I told him that if he kept treating his girlfriend like that in front of me, I would not only quit selling to him, I would tell Julián he had molested me. I gave his girlfriend my pager number and told her to call me. But I never heard from her. Chito eventually became Rudi's client. Rudi dealt to most of the Tijuana crowd. Which was actually riskier for him, because Los Reyes had their people almost everywhere he went.

Once I stopped crossing the coke and began to deal it, Julián found other means—other mules, as you call them—of getting the drugs across. Some of them were young society boys, poppis who were up for an adventure. Julián did what everybody does: send seven or eight cars through customs at a time. You might lose one or two packages at customs, but he still made much more than he lost. Sometimes he sent his warehouse workers on delivery to San Diego with the drugs in dog food bags.

There were new customers all the time. Mostly young, rich club kids. Many were from Tijuana and lived in San Diego, Coronado, Chula Vista, Bonita, Eastlake, which was my route. A bunch of them double-dealt the coke they bought from me to their friends—to afford their habit or to boost their reputation as wannabe dealers. I told them that as long as they didn't try to steal my customers, it was all good. And with the rumor of Los Reyes hanging around me, they knew better than to find out what would happen if they tried any funny business.

I guess you could say I learned how to turn a crisis into an opportunity. By having a baby with a convicted drug dealer, I was already more or less an outcast. I guess you could say I used Alejandra for sympathy's sake, for not getting a real job, and for not looking for a husband. In Tijuana, people may have suspected me of being easy or crazy, but none of my mother's friends said anything to me. I'm not sure whether they knew. It was still very convenient for me to live in Tijuana with my parents and deal in San Diego.

"¿Por qué no te encuentras un hombre bueno, Mara?" my father asked me. "What about Bardo Junior? I can call Don Bernardo and set up a dinner party here at our house. He'll remember me from the wedding a few years ago."

I laughed.

"I don't think he'll remember a thing about that night, Papá. That was a long time ago."

My mother would offer her two cents.

"She's right, Cascabel. Don't forget our daughter has a child. She is no longer the type to marry a man like Bardo Reyes, Junior."

I let my parents feel the pressures to marry me off. I had my own life to worry about. Before long I was selling ounces for $1,000 apiece, sometimes half pounds for $10,000. I drove around all day, from the South Bay to La Jolla, Jamul to Carlsbad. I got to know San Diego really well. For instance, I had never paid attention to how many Mexicans there were in Fallbrook, until I read a newspaper article that said there was also a KKK chapter there. I had a customer, an Anglo banker, who lived near Poway in a privately owned community called Fairbanks Ranch. He told me that Janet Jackson had wanted to live in Fairbanks Ranch, but there was a charter that didn't allow black people to live there. I would go to business meetings in bars and restaurants in the Gaslamp Quarter of Downtown. I had lunch with the managers of many upscale Italian and French restaurants in La Jolla. It was very professional. I brought the drugs in a briefcase or a leather tote bag. They would hand me envelopes of money over beef Wellington or my favorite dish, linguini with clam sauce.

Sometimes they wrote a personal check. I would take it all back to Julián, and he would cut me a share that day, so I always had money. I deposited most of it in a Japanese bank in San Ysidro.

I thought I had found the answer to all my problems. I was able to afford new clothes for myself and Alejandra, fine jewelry, two new cars (both stolen by now), trips to Hawaii, Lake Tahoe, Las Vegas, Cabo San Lucas, Mazatlán, Cancún, Miami. I even dated several of my customers. There was Theo from Boce, Alain the French bartender from La Strada, Alex from George's at the Cove, a Mormon lawyer named Chris from La Jolla. All were somewhat simple-minded, but very beautiful. They rarely lasted longer than a few parties and one night in bed. Sometimes I would get really peda, and I don't remember who I ended up sleeping with. I would wake up in some guy's apartment in Mission Valley or Del Mar, feeling like shit. But I didn't care. I didn't want anything emotional with anybody. I was into cocaine and partying. I especially loved it when Julián would rent out a club in Tijuana or downtown San Diego, like Baby Roc or E. Street Alley, and we would have private parties. Over 200 people, mostly clients, eating sushi and drinking champagne, everybody high on coke, dancing, and just going crazy.

I remember one night at Baby Roc in Tijuana when Bardo Junior showed up. We were in a private room upstairs, in front of a huge window where we could see everybody on the dance floor below. I was sitting at a booth with Julián, Eva, Veronica, and Rudi. Julián stood up and smiled when Bardo Junior came in with his entourage of slick-haired, fatass bodyguards. Julián walked over to him, and they sat at a table across the room from us. He pointed over at our table, and I caught Bardo Junior's eye for a minute. Then I saw some people go over to shake hands and kiss Bardo Junior's cheek. He didn't smile or say anything to them. He just sat there, nodding at everyone with no expression on his face, smoking cigarettes. He probably knew everyone was being fake, including Julián. People pretended to like Bardo Junior because they were afraid of him. Tijuaneros idolize power like peasants. I thought Bardo Junior looked depressed because of it. Maybe he was depressed because he was so damn ugly. His hair was long, wavy, and as brown as wet rust. He had a big nose and freckles and was the only person in the VIP room who was growing a beard. His face was pasty. He looked out of shape. Like he spent all of his time inside his private zoo with the animals at the racetrack.

"He looks like a pasty ghost," I said. "And I can tell he has lonjas in that suit."

"He's not very attractive, but supposedly he's kinky as a monkey," Rudi said. "They say he likes men and women. I cannot imagine being that confused."

"I don't know about kinky, but that beard is hideous."

"That's what happens when you are a wanted man," Veronica said. "You walk around with death on your face."

"Don't start freaking yourselves out," Eva said. "We're trying to have a good time. Leave the weirdo alone."

Then, like he had heard every word, Bardo Junior dismissed himself from Julián, and walked over to our table. Even though we had all met him, Bardo Junior introduced himself to everyone. I shook his clammy white hand.

"You are Julián's cousin, right?" he asked me in Spanish. "I keep hearing about you."

"I'm not sure if that's supposed to be good," I said. "Is it?"

"I mean that it's very interesting for someone in your position to be so well known."

"Oh. What is my position?"

While I waited for his answer, I lit up a cigarette and took a big gulp of champaña. I felt uncomfortable that I was getting all of the attention.

"Tienes una hija, verdad?" Bardo Junior asked me. "You are a mother and a businesswoman. Felicidades. That is very rare."

I blew smoke and tried not to change my expression.

"You're right. Almost as rare as an albino tiger," I said. "Maybe even one that listens to Beethoven?"

Bardo Junior laughed. Then he asked me, very soberly, in front of my friends, if he could drink champagne out of my shoe. I was wearing a rayon skirt, a white see-though linen blouse, and black, calf-high boots. My boots were brand new. I didn't know if I had heard him right.

"¿Mande?"

"You remind me of my mother," Bardo Junior told me. "The pictures I have of her when she was young, before she died. Descanza en paz. Era reina, como tu. Y muy bonita también. Por favor, would you let me taste what it is like to be wrapped around your feet?"

"Omigod," Rudi said.

"No, thank you," I said.

I was blushing. I didn't know what it meant to have somebody drink champagne out of your shoe. No one had ever asked me that before, especially not someone as freaky as Bardo Junior. There was no telling what it might lead to. I wasn't sure what I would have to do in exchange if I let him. Besides, I was wearing thick white socks, because my feet rubbed wrong in the new boots. It would be embarrassing if everyone saw those socks.

But Bardo Junior would not take no for an answer. He probably never had. He got on his knees and smiled at me like a mischievous little boy, begging me for a cookie. His teeth were yellow, small, and sharp. Terrifying. I couldn't get out of the booth. I was stuck between Rudi and Bardo Junior. He asked again.

"Come on, Mara," Rudi said. "The man's on his knees."

Who could say no to Los Reyes? Everybody was afraid of them. They were mopping up all the competition. Not just in Tijuana, but in all of Mexico. Dead bodies were piling up. A cardinal in Guadalajara. A presidential candidate in Tijuana. A district attorney in Mexico City. A rival cartel in Juárez. They had a huge army of producers in Colombia, border crossers from everywhere, dealers, and hitmen. Corporate power. International reputations. An incredible regime. All of it backed by their connections in Congress. At least 50 percent of the cocaine that was crossing the Mexican border came through Los Reyes. Es un chingo de lana. A lot of money, and a lot of power.

He had called me a queen, I'll give him that. And to tell you the truth, I thought it was about time. So what the hell? I stuck my left leg out from under the table.

"But don't think I'm going to kiss you afterward."

Bardo Junior held my leg by the calf. He carefully unzipped the boot and pulled it off. My sock didn't seem to surprise him. He pulled it off. He kissed two of his fingers and touched my toes. I giggled and pulled my foot away.

He stood up with my boot in his hand and poured some champagne into it. He held up the boot for everyone to see.

"I propose a toast to the lovely Miranda Cascabel. She is like the mother of us all."

Bardo Junior drank from my boot. He spilled a little on his shirt. He wiped his mouth, handed my boot to a waiter to clean, said thank you to me, and walked away. I was totally confused.

"¿Pos, qué fue eso?"

"Pinche loco."

"What was all that about you being like his mother?" Rudi asked me.

"I don't know. But he scares the hell out of me. I don't think I'll ever wear these boots again."

"They say Bardo Junior's mother was supposed to be so ugly," Eva said, "or beautiful, depending on how you heard it, that when men looked at her in the face, they were turned to pendejos."

"Are you saying that I'm like Medusa?"

"They called her Aguamar, because she was so white. Almost transparent, like a jelly fish."

"Or a ghost."

"But Mara's morenita. She doesn't have light skin."

"But she has the power to turn men to stone."

"Stoned pendejos."

"Como no," Eva said. "But Bardo Junior has been a pendejo for many years."

WHAT IS IT PRECISELY ABOUT A HATE CRIME THAT gets it stigmatized? Why is it different than any other crime? The concept seemed strange to Edgar. Why else would you murder someone—black, brown, gay, straight, whatever—unless you hated them? Was it so horrendous to think that hate drove someone to commit a certain type of crime? Hate for someone who offended your mother or stole your car. For the person who deceived you. Hate for women, hate for white people, hate for life.

Edgar's father was a divorce lawyer who had dutifully made inquiries to local colleagues about Cristina's death. But living somewhere in Colorado with his new family, and rarely in contact with Edgar and Cristina, he had found no one willing to pursue the sticky hate crime case. Edgar's mother also gave up. No one wanted to deal with why Cristina had been killed. Edgar felt that if it were not for the hate, there was hardly a thing left to remember about how Cristina had died.

And he supposed hate was a way to cope with Cristina's death. When he wanted to feel nothing, he did cocaine. Edgar's art was testimony to the self-pitying effects of cocaine, hate, and death. Humberto had sold six of his paintings at the gallery that month. But that gave Edgar no satisfaction. The money was filtered and redistilled into alcohol and drugs, which became blurry watercolor images of one-letter words, a framed hole in the wall his fist had made, a plywood-and-spraypaint architecture of anger and frustrated will.

Anxiety consumed him while he and Miranda rode the elevator up to the third floor, accompanied by a blue-uniformed sergeant. In the past, Edgar had agonized through several failed meetings with the Homicide Division of the Chula Vista Police Department. He felt as if he were visiting Cristina's grave. After no leads had been uncovered and no witnesses had come forth, Edgar and his mother had been told the department might defer Cristina's case to the Hate Crimes Division. However, the Hate Crimes Division had yet to be created; it was still under review by the federal Justice Department. This lack of resolution had thrown his mother into a deep depression.

Edgar knew Cristina would have been disgusted with his drug abuse. Drugs only perpetuated themselves, she would have told him, and led to more violence, more borders, more migra, more hate. Maybe bringing Miranda to the police was one answer, one way to get over his own guilt. It wasn't about Cristina, nor Miranda's fight to save her life. Edgar's reason for suggesting Miranda come down to the police station to save herself was really about his own guilty conscience. He hated the fact that he could do nothing about his sister. So why wasn't hate a worthy cause? Maybe drug dealing could be considered a hate crime. The government couldn't be too far off from lumping drugs and hate together as heinous crimes against humanity. It was already happening in racist states like Arizona and Texas, and all along the Mexican border. Which was nothing more than a glorified line separating and uniting hate and drugs, paranoia and violence.

The sergeant introduced Edgar and Miranda to Detective Dennis. He was not a big man, at least four or five inches shorter than Edgar, and much thinner, but broader in the shoulders. He looked well over 40, and his shiny bald crown was speckled with reddish moles and sunspots. He had a thick, sandy blond mustache, and his sleepless blue eyes burned like coals in a dark cave. He wore a tweed sports coat over a maroon polo shirt. He looked like a serious man, Edgar thought, like a Robert Duvall. But a bullshitter, nonetheless. Detectives were among the best at playing games, not just with suspects, but with everyone.

Detective Dennis stopped on Edgar's last name.

"Revuelta? I remember the name. Your sister was a dealer? No—a gangbanger?"

"She died a year ago in a drive-by. Do you remember now?"

"That's right. You never expect things like that to happen to normal folks."

"Normal folks? And what type of folks do you think we are?"

"Do you work in homicide, also, Detective Dennis?" Miranda interrupted.

"Narcotics," the detective answered. "A lot of drug cases involve homicides. So there's confusion sometimes."

As the detective was about to lead them to his office, Edgar piped up, "What about the Hate Crimes Division? You guys said it would be started to investigate my sister's case. My mother and I are still waiting to hear from someone."

Dennis turned around and nodded.

"Yeah. So are we. The Feds are still trying to define exactly what a hate crime is. In the meantime, we're backed up with a ton of shelved cases."

Dennis led Edgar and Miranda through a windowless maze of cluttered cubicles. There didn't seem to be many people at work this Memorial Day afternoon.

The detective's desk was covered with scattered papers and black-and-white photos in gold frames of the detective and his Mexican wife, two blond boys and a sulky teenaged girl with almond-shaped eyes. Edgar let Miranda have the empty seat in front of the desk, while he sat on a canvas folding chair behind her. The detective took off his jacket and laid it across the back of his chair. He wore a .38 snub-nosed in a camel-colored holster behind his back, clipped onto his brown slacks.

"Now, I understand you want to file a report. Somebody was shot in Tijuana, and you saw it, correct?"

"Technically," Miranda answered.

"Why don't you tell me what you mean."

"My cousin Julián was murdered by narcos. And what I mean is that since the Mexican police are pinche cowards, I was hoping to speak with an American detective who was familiar with Tijuana. Someone who has specifically worked with drugs."

"You mean someone who knows about the Reyes cartel?"

"Yes."

"And you know for sure they killed your cousin?"

"Yes."

"O.K. We're all working overtime to catch these assholes."

He opened a desk drawer and pulled out a manila folder. He handed it to Miranda. Inside were Xeroxed copies of men from Mexico City and Guadalajara WANTED BY THE FBI. Suspected drug dealers and hitmen for Los Reyes. The only photo Miranda recognized was of Bardo Reyes, Junior, who had been in hiding for over a year. No one had been able to pin anything on him or the old man. They had both left Tijuana and supposedly returned to Mexico City. Miranda was relieved to see that there were no photos of herself or her cousin Julián.

"Those are Mexican nationals associated with Los Reyes," Dennis said. "We have a separate file of suspected dealers and buyers from the United States. It's a much bigger collection. Do you recognize anyone in there?"

"Just Bardo Junior."

"You know Bardo Reyes, Junior personally?"

Miranda nodded and took off her sunglasses.

"I met him a few times. He drank champagne out of my shoe once. But I haven't seen him around for a while."

"Right. That's a pretty ugly shiner," Dennis said. He looked from Miranda to Edgar. "Are you involved in this?"

"No, he's just here for support," Miranda said, putting her glasses back on. "He's my boyfriend. I was hoping he could witness my interview with you. We're going to be off the record, right, Detective? You told me on the phone we could just talk, and you would help me with my options. Edgar will help me be aware of those."

"Aware of what?"

"My options."

"Is he a lawyer?"

"No, he's a painter. But I may need help understanding—"

"I'm afraid we don't allow anyone, except lawyers, to witness investigations," Dennis said, tapping his pen on the desk and smiling at Edgar. "But Edgar can stay for a while, if it makes you feel better. Everything will be off the record. For now."

"Thank you."

"So, tell me, Miranda, what exactly you would like to report."

"I would like to report the murder of my cousin, Julián Fernando Cascabel, who has been missing for the last five weeks. I want to report that he has been murdered by Los Reyes. I believe the man who killed him is named Rafael. I'm not sure what his last name is. But he's an assassin for Los Reyes. I didn't see him in your files. I think he's dead, too."

"Rafael killed Julián, and you're telling me the both of them are dead now?"

"Yes."

"Can you tell me how that happened? How they died?"

"Well, Rafael told me he killed Julián, and I...I shot Rafael. I killed him. And his partner, too. This morning."

"Wait a minute. You killed someone? You shot this Rafael?"

"Yes. He was going to shoot me, and my daughter, Alejandra, this morning, but—"

"What is your full name, Miranda?"

"Miranda Sofia Cascabel Sanchez."

The detective began to write.

"Have you ever gone by any other name?"

"My friends call me Mara. Why?"

"Any other names you go by? Nicknames? False names? Code names?"

"Code names? I'm not a spy, Detective Dennis."

"A simple yes or no is fine."

"I already told you. No."

"And what is your status of employment?"

"I am a single mother."

"What do you do for a living?"

"Hmm?"

"Do you have a job? Do you earn money?"

"Yes. Yes, but what does that have to do with anything?"

"How?"

"How what?"

"How do you earn money?"

"I work for Julián. I mean, I did."

"And what do you do for him?"

"Nothing anymore. He's dead."

"Well, what did you used to do for him? Be specific."

"Wait a minute," Miranda raised her hand. "I came here of

my own free will to tell you what happened to my cousin Julián. He is an American citizen. I want the United States to be responsible for him. I want Los Reyes to be arrested for his murder. I am a witness. I'm going to tell you what happened, and then we'll see about where to go from there. Stop interrogating me like I'm a criminal."

"You did just admit to murdering someone."

"That was purely in self-defense."

"If you want me to help you, you're going to have to answer my questions. Understand?"

"Yes, detective."

"O.K. Now please start from the beginning."

JULIAN BECAME VERY CLOSE PARTNERS WITH LOS Reyes. He started to spend a lot of time with Bardo Junior and his bodyguards. Bardo took Julián to Mexico City, Guadalajara, Acapulco. Then Julián would take Bardo Junior to all of the Tijuana society gatherings—bodas, baptisms, graduations, Christmas parties. After every trip Julián came back with more drugs for us to sell. It was 1994, and San Diego was going through a drug boom. Besides cocaine, we were also selling marijuana and Ecstasy, the new club drug, and tons of crystal meth. I didn't feel comfortable with the new menu. What was next, prostitution and gambling? Not that I was suddenly righteous and pure. Pero, ya no valía la pena. I liked having more drugs to party with, especially Ecstasy, but I didn't trust all the new people hanging around Julián.

I couldn't stand the crystal meth tweakers. Crystal costs nothing to make. All these hillbillies in San Diego kept getting arrested for turning their bathrooms into meth labs. When they got busted, they moved the production to Tijuana, and, the next thing you know, we were selling their own drugs right back to them. Some of these people would stay up for weeks on end, and drive themselves loco, twitching, itching, and talking to themselves. I didn't want to have anything to do with them, but Julián kept sending me to meet his new amigos. Before, I was dealing to people in their houses, in their condominiums, at nice office buildings and restaurants. But with the crystal, I hardly had time to meet all my appointments. Everybody wanted it all the time. I had to meet customers in public parking lots and

McDonald's. I felt dirty. When I saw my Mexican friends not caring about themselves anymore, I realized I was adding to the mess. Crystal was definitely not glamorous. Who wants to stay up for days at a time for no reason at all? Then there was the acne and blotchy skin and the drinking whiskey at nine in the morning in some dive bar just to come down. And coming down was like a trip through hell, when you hated everybody and thought they should all burn with you. Then you had to do more just to balance your emotions and make it through the day.

We were making more money than ever. But once I started doing crystal, I didn't like the person I was becoming. Since I never slept, I was often out alone, which depressed me. I hate being alone. I would get desperate for someone to pass the time with. I remember being in Tijuana one night at Frog's at about five in the morning. I had been drinking with some friends and doing lines, and, when they left, I just hung out with the bartender. I went to the bathroom, and, when I came back, they were closing down the bar. I started looking through my cell-phone directory for someone to call. Then I realized how ridiculous I was for needing somebody to talk to at five in the morning. Nobody answered their phones.

So I drove down to Playas and watched the sun come up. The beach is a peaceful place when nobody's on it. I stared out at the ocean, watching the waves rise and fall. I thought it sounded like cars passing on the freeway. Then I thought about where I would be in ten years. One of the nuns in high school had told me that in order to be successful you always had to have goals. I laughed because I didn't know where I was headed. I couldn't imagine my future. I was supposed to marry the right man, raise a family, and get old like my grandparents. That was expected of me, naturally. But now that sounded too much like a pop song. I didn't want my life to be a pop song. I had wanted to start my own business, be an independent travel agent. But I was getting old too fast. I was going to be 30, and here I was alone on a beach watching the sun come up. When people started showing up to walk their dogs, I decided to go.

But I didn't go home. I went to the First Cemetery instead. I went looking for the shrine of Juan Soldado, El Santo del Pueblo de Tijuana, the one Rudi told me about. The cemetery wasn't far from my house. No one in my family was buried there, however.

My grandparents had been buried in the basement of La Iglesia de San Francisco, where they bury young children, orphans, and martyrs. My father bought a special site there so the family could walk to visit the grave.

Outside the faded aqua gates of Cemeterio Número Uno the vendors were setting up their carts. They sold the typical religious fetishes—candles, crosses, saints, amulets, escapularios. Black-and-white Xeroxed photos of Juan Soldado dressed in a soldier's uniform from the twenties were everywhere.

The cemetery was quiet. I was the only one there so far. The shrine itself was a small white room with an entryway of red brick arches. A statue of Juan Soldado was in a glass case. He was leaning on a wooden podium where a crucifix had been placed. He was surrounded by candles and flowers. The off-white walls of the shrine were covered in writing. People wrote their thanks and gave requests for miracles, health, money, and safe passage across the border.

"Juan Soldado, haz que mi mamá trabaje and gane dinero, por favór. Regresare. Angel."

"Gracias Juan Soldado por el milagro consedido."

"Gracias Juan Soldado por consedirme la emigración."

"Juanito Soldado, gracias por haber aliviado a mi niña."

Juan Soldado had been a 19-year-old soldier accused of raping and murdering a twelve-year-old girl who was the daughter of a society woman. The general of the local military ordered ley fuga for Juan Soldado, and as he ran he was killed by a firing squad. After the execution, the general's lover stumbled drunk through the street saying it wasn't Juan Soldado who killed the little girl. Then she went mad. When the general disappeared, Juan Soldado became a martyr; he is now the saint for the wrongly accused.

I kneeled in front of the shrine and emptied my pockets of most of the money I had. Maybe a hundred dollars. Maybe more. I didn't care if someone came in and stole it after I left. I wanted to request my bendición. I wanted to ask for a blessing, but I hadn't prayed in years or gone to confession, and I felt very self-conscious that I was still wired from the crystal. But the tears came anyway. I asked Juan Soldado to protect my daughter if something were to happen to me. I asked him to give me the strength to quit doing drugs. I promised Juan Soldado that if I was able to find a new life, I would return to give more. On my way out of the cemetery I bought a small escapulario of Juan Soldado. I gave it to Alejandra to wear around her neck.

About a month later, I met Edgar. He was a friend of Tavo Treviño, one of Julián's old customers. Tavo was another Tijuanero living across the border in Eastlake. His parents were wealthy and owned maquiladoras in Tijuana and San Ysidro. He had gone to high school with Edgar. Tavo took me to a café in downtown San Diego where Edgar was showing his paintings. Edgar was tall and guapo. He shaved his head and wore black-framed glasses that made him look like an intellectual. He was younger than me. A complete stranger. He didn't know a thing about me or my cousin. He had never even heard of Los Reyes. I liked his paintings. I had dated artists before, but never a gringo. But Edgar didn't think of himself as a gringo, because his mother is Mexican, and he didn't like to be called that. He had gone to college and said he was Chicano. Most Mexicans think Chicanos are nacos, lower-class, pochos sin gracia. They are like people stuck between two cultures, insecure border misfits. But Edgar was interested in learning about the Tijuana beyond Revolution Avenue, drinking and discos, poverty and corruption. I told him there was a lot more, but it wasn't as interesting. Edgar wanted to talk politics. He wanted to learn about the Mexican system from the inside. But politics is not the same in Tijuana as it is in San Diego. There are infinite levels of politics in Tijuana. There are too many political parties, sindicatos, the black market, the taxi-cab mafia, etc. And then there are the narcos and the Catholic church. To me, politics is like a black hole I didn't want to fall into. You have to be in Tijuana on a regular basis to know how fucked up it really is. I told Edgar he had to cross the border every day to feel the difference between Mexico and the U.S. Not just the different economies, but the psychological differences between Mexicans and gringos, also, are like night and day.

Then the differences started to get fuzzy. First of all, Edgar is not Catholic. His mother is, but his father is white and comes from a strict Lutheran family in the Midwest. I don't know anything about Lutherans. But Edgar has an even guiltier conscience than I do. Even though his father is white, he feels like the world is against him because of his race. He said that in the United States, being Chicano was like being black, and that racial oppression causes low self-esteem. That was why he always felt on the defensive. For him, it was the main reason why blacks and Chicanos did drugs. To escape oppression.

"Drugs don't oppress anybody," he said. "People oppress each other. You can use drugs to oppress, or you can use them to escape oppression."

"You have a funny sense of irony," I would tell him. "If everybody thought like you, the world would be a very interesting place."

"I'm not interesting."

"Yes, you are. You're an artist. You don't have to follow anyone's rules, except your own."

"I'm just trying to make money, like you," he said. "I'm not trying to oppress anybody."

"I know."

"What's the difference between selling a kilo and selling a painting, if they both get bought and sold?"

"Well, don't paint me," I said. "Porque te va ir muy mal con Los Reyes or con Julián. If they see me in one of your paintings, they're gonna know I told you everything."

Edgar didn't like me telling him that. He didn't like being told what to do. It was all about freedom for him. But I am unique. And Edgar knew not to piss me off. If he was nice and did what I said, then he knew I would be happy, and then he would get what he wanted. I'm very easy like that. Do what I say, and I'm all yours. Piss me off once, and I'm gone. I didn't have time to argue with people. But Edgar was very patient and sensitive. He let me talk, and he actually listened. He never tried to change me into somebody else. He never tried to control what I did. He let me be who I am, and I appreciated that.

I spent less time with Julián and more time with Edgar. Less time dealing, and more time listening, watching, and sleeping. There were plenty of new people Julián could find to drive around and make the deliveries. Half the time I didn't even know where Julián was. He went on a lot of business trips. He had lied and told Eva he was looking into opening new stores. I didn't understand why he would lie, at first. But then, after a trip to Guadalajara, Julián didn't return on schedule. That's when the rumors started that he was supposedly taking out contracts on people for Los Reyes, that he was a hitman, and the federales had captured him. Which meant that Los Reyes would have to kill him to prevent him from turning them in. It all sounded like a gangster movie. Which was why I never believed it. It wasn't his nature. Julián wasn't violent. He had a big appetite for the things he liked. He did too much sometimes. Worked too much, spent too much, drank too much, snorted too much, smoked too much. Maybe he was just too much for life. But he liked to hang out with people. He was a party animal, not a murderer. Unfortunately, some of the people he partied with, some of the people he trusted, were cold-blooded killers.

Eva went to the papers when Julián disappeared. She felt the press could help her find Julián before the police. You can take your pick over which is more corrupt. Nevertheless, the Mexican papers took the story and ran: "Wife of Tijuana Junior Suspects Mexican Mafia of Kidnapping Husband," "Drug War Invades Tijuana Upper-Class," "Tijuana Juniors Turn Narcotraffickers." It was a gigantic desmadre. Immediately, the family businesses were shut down. All our Mexican bank accounts were frozen.

Then the district attorney rounded us all up for questioning. No one in the family had suspected Julián of being a narco, least of all his parents. My uncle protested to the police and threatened to sue for slander. He was on the verge of contacting Governor Appel, who was a friend of his from college, but once Julián's Bancomer statements had been subpoenaed, they showed wild transactions, which suggested that he had used CascaMax as a front to launder large sums of money. My uncle was crushed, and my family humiliated. The federales shut down all the stores in Tijuana, including my father's stores and Julián's store in La Mesa, which left about 250 workers out of a job.

I didn't have a bank account in Tijuana, and most of my customers were in San Diego, so I kept quiet during the whole thing. After a few weeks of investigation, the police couldn't prove the rest of the family had benefited from Julián's drug dealing and money laundering. As far as I knew, no one else but me was involved. Eventually, the cops left everyone alone. They had no choice but to wait and watch—just like the rest of us.

The gringos weren't as interested in Julián's disappearance. Eva, who was pregnant again, was screaming to the gringo authorities that Julián had been kidnapped by Los Reyes. She pleaded with the FBI to get involved, since Julián was an American citizen and a resident of Coronado. But as far as they were concerned, Julián was from Tijuana, where he had grown up, where he had spent most of his life, where he had befriended Los Reyes. He was a Mexican narco who had freely involved himself in criminal activities. Therefore, it didn't matter where he was born. They would do nothing to help him or Eva. It was a Mexican problem.

My family was devastated by all the negative press and tried to separate themselves as far from Julián and Eva as possible. That was to be expected. As much as Mexicans love scandal, they hate to be involved in one. The word in Tijuana was that there was a high-priced contract on Eva's head, to be claimed as soon as she crossed the border. I heard people were literally signing up to shoot her. So far she has remained at home. She knows not to risk going to Tijuana. There's no protection for her there. At least in San Diego she can call 911.

During the investigation, I was forced to stay home for a couple of weeks. I spent time with my daughter and tried to get to know her better. It was almost as if Alejandra had become a little girl without me. She was four years old. She could tie her own shoes, say her prayers, sing Disney songs in Spanish and English. Her favorite movie was *The Little Mermaid*. I felt like I hardly knew her.

I know I've avoided everyone in Tijuana. I blamed my family for turning me into an outcast, even though it really had nothing to do with them, not my mother, not Alejandra, not Platón, not Julián. Something had happened to me. I didn't care about anyone else but myself, and even that was only a wish. While I watched my daughter play with her Barbie dream castle, naming one of her dolls Mamá Elba, after my mother, I was ashamed that my daughter was so attached to my mother, and I guess I resented them both for it. The only thing I had gotten out of dealing cocaine was a drug habit. All my money disappeared as soon as I made it, except for my savings. Which wasn't much. Now Alejandra is going to be five in August. I want to throw her a nice party. She told me she wants to go to Chuck E. Cheese. I'm not sure what that is, or where, but I'm going to find out.

Rudi was on vacation when Julián disappeared. I hadn't heard from him in over a month, and then this past Saturday night I was at El Suizo again with Tavo and Edgar when Rudi paged me three times in a row. I called him back at a number I didn't recognize.

"Where are you?" he asked me.

There was static and buzzing in the background. It sounded like he was on a cell phone.

"Plaza Fiesta. Where have you been?"

"I can't say."

"What do you mean?"

"Just what I said."

"Did you hear about Julián?"

"Yes. That's why I need to meet you."

"I'm with Tavo and Edgar. Why don't you come have a drink with us? We can talk over here."

"No. Not there. Meet me at Gordo's on El Rio."

I talked Tavo and Edgar into getting some tacos at Gordo's. They weren't hungry, but agreed to chauffeur me. Rudi was waiting for me near the side parking lot when we arrived. We parked across the street in another lot. As soon as he saw me get out of Tavo's 4Runner, Rudi rushed over. He had a new tan, but hadn't shaved. He was wearing a gray silk shirt and black jeans, and he was holding a black backpack. He smelled like he had been doing cocaine for days.

"We need to talk," he said, grabbing me by the arm.

"Good to see you, too, Rudi."

"Qué onda, Rudi," Tavo said extending his hand. "Hace mucho que no te veo."

"Hey, Rudi."

Rudi ignored Tavo and Edgar and asked me if we could be alone. Tavo got the idea and took Edgar to get some food, leaving us his car to use as an office.

Rudi was in the driver's seat and I was in the passenger.

"This is the deal, Mara. I'm leaving Tijuana. Tonight. You should go get Alejandra and do the same. We are no longer popular with Los Reyes."

Rudi was clutching the backpack like it was his newborn son.

"Fuck Los Reyes. We made them popular," I said. "They need us to make them look legitimate. We gave them Tijuana and San Diego."

Rudi was shaking his head.

"They took it."

"Whatever," I said. "Ya no me interesa la droga, ni a los pinche Reyes. What's in the bag?"

"Cocaine."

"What a surprise."

"I'm supposed to sell it for Julián and give him the money so he can take off. He's hiding."

I jumped in my seat.

"Pinche Rudi. You talked to Julián? Eva's been telling the newspapers that Los Reyes kidnapped him."

"No one kidnapped anybody. Not yet. He ran away. From Los Reyes, from Eva. From everyone."

Rudi was shivering even though it was warm outside. I put my hand on his leg and massaged his neck with my other hand. I did this with Edgar when he had anxiety attacks.

"It's O.K., Rudi. Ya calmate. Dime que pasó."

Rudi opened the backpack and stuck his hand in. He pulled out a pinky nail full of coke and lifted it to his nose. He asked me if I wanted one. I looked around for the security guards and saw they weren't watching. I took a bump and told him to finish his story.

"On my way back from vacation in Costa Rica, I stopped in the D.F. to meet some friends. Julián called me and told me Los Reyes found out he was double-dealing. They wanted money, and he thought they were going to kill him. So he left everything in his hotel and took off. Then he saw the articles in the paper and called me. He told me to stay away from Los Reyes. Then he told me where to pick up the rest of his coke. He wants me to sell it and cross the money. He's supposed to call me once he gets back to San Diego. But he didn't tell me when. And I'm not fucking waiting for anyone."

"I didn't know Julián had been double-dealing."

"Well, now you do. So you have to take the coke and sell it for him. He's your cousin. No la quiero. I'm tired of this."

"Que cabrón. You fucking dump this shit on me, and now you're running away? You have to help me. What am I supposed to do?"

"Survive," Rudi said. "I'll call Eva when I get to San Diego and let her know about Julián. You'll hear from me in a week."

"But Julián asked you to do it," I said. "Don't you think if he'd wanted me to take care of it—"

"Do what you want, then."

"Fuck you, Rudi. Pinche pendejo. Fuck you for getting me involved in all of this."

"I'm sorry, Mara."

Then Rudi left me alone. Just like that. Again. Some friend. I wanted to cry, I was so mad, but I had to figure a way out of this, without running into Los Reyes or their people.

When Edgar and Tavo came back to the car, I told them Rudi had left me with the coke. I asked Tavo to cross it for me and told him I would give him a cut of the sale if he could find someone to buy it right away. Tavo wasn't afraid of customs, and he said he could think of someone in Chula Vista who would buy it.

The next morning Veronica called me. She told me Rudi had been shot — 37 times, while trying to cross the border. I didn't believe it. She told me it was even in the newspaper. Rudi had been murdered by three men in a black sedan without license plates.

I didn't think it would take long for everyone in my family to figure out I was involved. There was already a scandal going on about young socialites from Tijuana involved in drug dealing. It was turning into an epidemic. First, Platón went to jail. Then Julián disappeared. Now Rudi was dead. Tijuana was obviously not the place for me to be. But leaving home also meant leaving San Diego. I decided now was the time to go. Alejandra was staying the night at my brother Rodrigo's house in Tijuana, because I still had to meet with Tavo in Chula Vista. So I crossed the border and stayed with Edgar on Sunday night.

Tavo had found someone to buy the rest of the coke for $12,000, which was half the price it was worth. But I didn't want to sell to any of Julián's customers. And I didn't have time to look for another. I just wanted to get rid of it. So Tavo took me to Gabe Aguilar. We met him in the parking lot of Lolita's Taco Shop in Chula Vista. Gabe was this fat cholo with tattoos on his arms. He called me "ruca" and talked like he was black. "You know what I'm sayin'?" The type of guy I never would have had anything to do with if I had been working with Julián. Tavo told me that they had gone to high school together and that Gabe had just gotten out of prison. Gabe was surrounded by his cholo friends near the tailgate of a maroon Toyota truck. They were parked next to a dumpster, which smelled of rotten lettuce and spoiled meat. The whole scene reminded me of how far I had slipped.

Tavo introduced me.

"She's from Tijuana."

There was automatic tension between Gabe and me when I

shook his hand. Then he acted like he was doing me a favor.

"I don't know about TJ," Gabe said referring to me. "My mother always told me there was nothing but trouble down there."

"Your mother must have been born on this side."

"So what if she was?"

"That explains why she doesn't like Tijuana," I said, thinking of Edgar's love-hate relationship with Tijuana. "She probably has low self-esteem. All Chicanas do."

"Tranquilo. Gabe's our connection," Tavo told me, grabbing my arm. He was trying to calm me down. He told me this cholo Gabe was going to buy the coke from us, that we were going to do business with him.

"With him?"

"Yes. Him."

"Well, are we going to give the whole world a free show?"

The parking lot was full of young gringos shouting at each other, running between between the taco shop and their cars.

"I know what I'm paying for, and I know who I'm paying," Gabe said. "And it ain't you."

"It's cool, " Tavo said. "We can handle this inside the truck."

"Better watch your back with this bitch," Gabe said. "Could turn on you any minute."

"That's right," I told him. "Pinche naco. And I've got fangs, too."

Gabe laughed at me, como un loco. He didn't scare me, though, with his bald head and tattoos. He may have been to prison, but underneath those tattoos was a little mama's boy, just like the rest of them.

At first, Gabe only wanted to pay half up front and the other half after he sold it. To tell you the truth, he didn't look like the type who could come up with that much money. I had sold to people who could write a check for $12,000, no problem. But I think Tavo saw an opportunity to take advantage of my situation and went in on the deal with Gabe. Tavo was probably the only one with any real experience with that much cocaine. In any case, they went back to Tavo's truck, and Gabe tasted the coke. Then he handed Tavo the cash. Tavo handed it to me. I counted it, and it was all there. I felt horrible about selling the coke so cheap, but that was the position I was in. I had to give Tavo $2,000, and then I went back to Edgar's house to figure out what to do next. I still had to get Alejandra out of Tijuana.

THIS MORNING EVERYBODY WAS ON THEIR WAY to work, and I was getting impatient with all the traffic on the Boulevard. I have developed a fear of red lights and traffic. I get claustrophobic. I need a clear exit in at least one direction, because I only feel right when I'm constantly moving. You have to be fast and aggressive if you want to get where you need to go. Take every opportunity while you can, but get it quick. Otherwise someone will beat you to it. It was nothing my mother had taught me. Mamá would rather sit like a hen and wait for everything to come to her. I had learned to be aggressive on my own, and I would pass that wisdom to my daughter. I was on my way to pick her up from my brother's house. Rodrigo lived in Chapultepec, in the hills above the Campestre Country Club. It was a little before nine in the morning. I hadn't slept yet. There wasn't any time, and I wanted to beat the traffic. I didn't know where I was going. I just knew I wanted to get out of Mexico.

I started laughing out loud. I don't know why. I had just remembered a dirty joke, or maybe I was laughing at the ugly people in traffic. Or a stupid song on the radio. I remembered Julián was always turning American pop songs into sexual innuendos. Eighties tunes were the worst. "Misherona" became "My Scrotum." Should I stay or should you blow me? I started remembering all these things about Julián. I remembered our Sunday lunches: especiales de asada with fries from Tortas La Vuelta wrapped in a white paper sack, warm in my lap on our way to the bullfights. The ritual was to bring the sandwiches to the bullfights and eat them during the first fight with cold beer. Julián loved the bullfights. He loved to see blood and always rooted for the bull. "¡Que gane el toro!" he would scream. I became a fan of the bullfights, too. I liked to see the toreros in their tight pants. So tight you could see their balls shrivel when they were afraid, and their pitos inflate when they were about to kill. Every season I went with Julián. Sundays had been our days together, either at the bullfights or the dog races at Caliente, followed by drinks and cocaine, discos and mariachis. Everything was on Julián.

I hadn't heard any news about him. I was sure he knew nothing about Rudi being shot. But he had warned Rudi. Maybe Julián had already prepared himself to accept Rudi's death. Maybe he was too busy trying to save his own life, like I was. I could have gone to the Mexican army, the police, a politician, and told them the whole story. But they were either all involved—or didn't want to get involved. We still live by the Napoleonic Code, which says you're guilty until proven innocent, no matter what. Really, Mexico has two types of laws: Corruption and Murder, Inc. Everyone knew ratting on a narco was as bad as ratting on a policeman, if not worse. A Mexican policeman might put you in jail, might rape you, might even kill you. A narco would kill you, too, but only after he had cut off your testicles one by one, squished your brains out in a vice, shot you in each limb and in the stomach, until you begged for your death. Even then they'd find ways to make you suffer more. I didn't want to suffer. I hope Rudi didn't suffer.

I drove past the Chapultepec and, instead of going directly to pick up Alejandra, I headed toward the Hipódromo. Julián's house had already been seized, which meant it was being watched. In the past, I knew that rather than go home to his wife smelling like a party, Julián had sometimes slept off his hangovers at a small pensión behind one of his favorite taco stands across from Caliente Racetrack. He had something for the woman who owned the pensión, a thirty-something widow named Nereida. Supposedly she was a bruja, a witch who had murdered her elderly husband for his life insurance and the ownership of the small bed-and-breakfast. Julián loved chismes. He would bug me to tell him what everyone else said about him and the widow. But no one said anything about Julián's extramarital affairs. No one was that stupid. Nevertheless, there was plenty of talk about la bruja. Nereida had never admitted to anything about how her husband died. Old people just die, she said. That made Julián want her more. He loved a woman with a secret. He told me he liked that I never let on exactly how I felt about anyone or anything. Julián told me that mystery was my weapon. Mystery and secrecy gave a woman the advantage in a male-dominated society.

"Pues, sí. I'll take all the advantages I can get. Who says it's a man's world?"

"Exactly. Now will you kiss me like you did when I was 14?"

"You mean in the park when you attacked me with your tongue?"

"Come on. It wasn't like that. You kissed me back."

"I had no choice. I had to hold myself up. It was either kiss you or hit my head on the rocks."

"You could have closed your mouth," Julián said, his mischievous smile spreading across his face. "Come on, prima. One for old time's sake."

"Ya, Julián. I'm not going to kiss you. Marrano. We're too old to do things like that."

"If you weren't my cousin, you would."

"Unlike you, I am not thrilled by the scandal of seducing my own cousin."

"Mara, you know if you weren't my cousin, I'd—"

"Just be quiet and drive. I don't want to miss the toros."

I don't know why he talked like that. He had this contempt for family values. Julián tried to put himself above everything. As if he was an astronaut and everyone else was trapped in the petty Mexican society. I thought if only his mother hadn't spoiled him, maybe I wouldn't still be searching for him.

I took the Cadillac up toward the racetrack and noticed that the oil gauge had started to dip. I thought that maybe it was because I was going uphill. When the road flattened out by the racetrack parking lot, I saw that the gauge had evened out again. That's when I noticed a black Grand Marquis that had made the last turn with me. It was a few car lengths behind me as I turned past the taco stand. I couldn't tell who was in it; there was a glare off its windshield. I decided to turn back toward the taco stand and get out as if I was going to order tacos. I guess I should have realized the taco stand would be closed at nine in the morning. But I stopped anyway. The Grand Marquis didn't make the U-turn with me. I parked and watched it drive down the street and out of sight.

I kicked a dusty dog that tried to sniff my leg when I reached the office of the pensión. I rang four times, but nobody answered. The door was open so I went inside.

The office was small, with hardwood floors, a couch and a coffee table. Opposite the door was a large wooden desk with a bouquet of flowers and an empty coffee-maker. The walls were light pink and decorated with black-and-white photos of people enjoying the bullring, the Campestre Country Club, the playas, and the casino during the thirties. The one color picture was of a horse with pink bridle and a jockey. There was a bell next to the coffee-maker that I did not press. Instead, I went around the other side of the desk, looking for anything to do with Julián. Inside the top drawer on the left, beneath tissue paper, a calculator, and other office supplies, I found a snapshot of Nereida and Julián at the beach. It was a recent photo. Nereida had her red hair covered in a light blue scarf. She wore a baby blue bikini top and a blue-and-white leopard print wrap around her waist. She was guera. Her breasts were small, and her body was thin and white con pecas. Julián wore sunglasses and a white plastic visor. His dark hair was cropped short. He held a bottle of beer in his left hand. His lean body was tan, a gold chain gleamed from his hairy chest.

I held onto the picture while I searched the other drawers. The center drawer was locked. On the right, there were mostly papers, manila envelopes, receipts, files, and more office junk. I opened the bottom right drawer, and on top of a stack of papers I found Julián's black .25.

"Well, you've found the mementos I have of Julián."

I jumped and squeezed the trigger of the gun, but its safety was locked. There was Nereida standing in the doorway. She wore a long yellow sundress with her trademark light blue scarf over her hair. She had a striking freckled face with a straight nose, high cheekbones, a wide mouth, and blood red lips. She looked Irish.

"Discuple, Nereida. I'm sorry," I said. "Nobody answered when I rang the bell. I thought maybe he might—that you might know where Julián was."

"Here?" Nereida shook her head. "Believe it or not, you're just the second person to have come looking for him in a month. I was sure with all the gossip somebody would come looking for him here." Nereida walked over and touched the picture. "But it's just you. It almost makes me think we didn't exist. Except—"

"Except what?" I was still holding the .25. It had been too small for Julián, but it fit perfectly in my hand. I remembered when Julián had tried to give it to me to take on deliveries. I didn't think I'd ever need it. Now I pushed the pin to unlock the safety.

"You like that gun?" Nereida asked.

"It was Julián's," I said.

"Yes, he made me keep it here just in case. I never wanted to keep it loaded, but he would bring bullets and load it. I don't even know how to shoot it. You look good with it, though. All black. Like a fashion statement. I thought I was going to need it for protection once he'd disappeared. But I only feel neglected. Why don't you take it with you on your way out? Or were you planning on renting a room?"

"No, no. I'm sorry I bothered you." I tried to smile at Nereida. It was all very awkward and wrong. "I thought that somebody who loved him ought to be looking for him, too."

"Whether he's alive or dead, I believe that some people just don't want to be found," Nereida said. She reached over and unlocked the middle drawer of the desk, pulling out a pack of Marlboro Lites and a large manila envelope. She offered me a cigarette, but I didn't feel like smoking.

"I think I may have been followed here. I'm not sure who it was, but maybe you should keep the gun."

"Please," Nereida said. "If you were followed, perhaps you'll find a purpose for it."

I hadn't brought my purse inside the office, so I shoved the gun into the back pocket of my jeans. It fit snugly against my ass, but it wasn't uncomfortable.

"I'm sorry if I seem rude," Nereida said. "I'm sure you've heard what they say about me. But I swear it's just a case of bad luck. Would you like some coffee, Miranda?"

"Graciás, pero no. You said someone else came by for him?"

"Her lawyer," Nereida said. "A gringo from Coronado. He came yesterday to serve divorce papers." She waved the envelope in the air in front of her. "Maybe you would like to take those, too?"

If the lawyers couldn't even get to Julián, what chance did I have of surviving Los Reyes? Maybe some people didn't want to be found. Julián would have hated to go through a divorce. That would be a dangerous exposure of his private life, his books and expenses. But Julián was too full of himself, too full of desire and rage, to fake his own death. When he was younger, he had wanted to be an artist, an actor. Tijuana was no cultural paradise back then, so he had to find other ways to satisfy his ego. When Julián realized that he could get what he wanted from Los Reyes, he turned the border into his stage. Maybe he had gotten too big for his own good. Maybe some people were just dead, with different pieces of their body buried in different places, never to be put back together again.

On my way to the Chapultepec, I kept checking the rearview mirror for the Grand Marquis. I rushed through the winding maze uphill, running stop signs, thumping over speed bumps. I can't stand the flamboyant attitude of the Chapu. Each house had a different color, structure, and design. No neighborhood organization. The random architecture is as tacky as a pair of dyed-gold pumps. The only things each minimansion had in common with the others were stuccoed security walls patrolled by guards from Oaxaca and Chiapas.

When I reached Rodrigo's house, my sister-in-law, Patricia, was feeding the children breakfast. Rodrigo was at work. Alejandra was eating pancakes and bacon.

"Mamá, I'm the Little Mermaid."

"Sí, chiquita. You're my little mermaid. Did you go swimming yesterday?"

"Sí, Mamá. They tried to drown me," Alejandra pointed at her two cousins across the table who squealed at the accusation. Alejandra had maple syrup all over her hands, which stuck to my neck while she hugged me. Everyone, except the maid, Elisa, was still in their pajamas. Patricia wore dark purple silk with matching slippers. She had a bob in her brunette hair that brought out her round cheeks. She loved to play the quintessential mother and always allowed Alejandra to stay at her house when my mother couldn't babysit.

Alejandra said she wanted to go swimming again.

"No, mija. Mami has lots of errands to do. ¿Estás lista?"

Alejandra shook her head.

"Por favór, Elisa, puedes recojer a las cosas de Alejandra? Ya nos tenemos que ir."

"Sí, como no."

"Ay. You've got all day, Mara," Patricia said, smiling and patting the placemat next to her. "Sit down and let Elisa bring you some pancakes and coffee. Tell me about your errands."

Patricia was guiri-guiri and could talk all day. She told me she wanted to move the family to San Diego. "I don't like having to live with security guards, Mara. Me siento cautiva. It's not good for the children to grow up with guards everywhere. I think maybe they'll become paranoid when they grow up. But we need security here. ¿Quién sabe que nos pueda pasar sin alguna proteción? De todos modos, ¿que piensas si nos cambiamos de casa a San Diego? Me gusta la casa de Julián. ¿Qué te parece Coronado, Mara?"

"I think you'll be fine right here," I said. "You're completely removed from what's happening downtown. You have nothing to worry about. That's what security guards are for. And Coronado is really boring. Full of gringos."

"Ay sí. Pero, rich gringos are different from tourists, ¿qué no? Bueno. No sé. I was reading in the paper this morning that this young man was shot last night. Rudi Ballesteros del centro de Tijuana. ¿No es un amigo tuyo? It said he was in line trying to cross the border, and they shot him 37 times. Qué bárbaro. Dicen que fue por droga. Te digo, Mara, que tengo miedo."

I had to keep Patricia busy, occupied with something other than questions for me to answer.

"You know, Patricia, if you don't mind, maybe I'll have some breakfast while Alejandra is getting dressed."

"Claro," Patricia said, getting up from the table.

"Is there any orange juice?"

"Claro que sí, hermana. Todo lo que quieras."

"Graciás, Pati."

While Patricia went through the swinging door and into the kitchen, I smiled at my niece and nephew and ran upstairs. I grabbed Alejandra's things from Elisa and dragged my daughter out to the Cadillac.

"Thanks for opening the gate, Elisa."

At the stop sign halfway down the Chapultepec, where the road forked into two paths, a black sedan was idling. Maybe it was because I had just run out of Pati's house with my daughter dangling by the wrist—maybe it was denial—I did not realize the car in front of me was the Grand Marquis from earlier until I was directly behind it, honking my horn at the pendejo driving it. When I stopped honking and threw the Cadillac into reverse, a yellow Mercedes angled in behind me, closing off the left side, leaving the unprotected edge of the canyon drop for an escape route to the right. I looked down the hill guessing I would flip if I tried to take the Cadillac into the ravine below.

In my rearview mirror, I saw two men get out of the yellow Mercedes. One fat and one skinny. Both dressed in suits. Like Bardo Junior's bodyguards. They walked quickly toward the Cadillac. That's when I threw the car into reverse and aimed for them. They jumped out of the way, and I rammed the Mercedes.

"¡Hijo de puta!"

I threw the car back into drive. But the Grand Marquis had already backed into the Cadillac, locking me in.

"¡Chinga su pinche madre!"

"Mamá, ¿que pasa? ¿Mamá?" Alejandra was crying.

Then I decided to try to run. But instead of unlocking the power locks, I was so scared that I locked them and left the windows down.

"No!" I screamed, fighting with the handle of the door and the switch to roll up the window at the same time.

A black shape plunged through my open window and grabbed me by the hair. He slammed my head against the side of the door. An electric shock went through me. For a second I couldn't hear or see. There were two hands on my face as I was pulled out of the window. I was screaming at whoever had a hold of me, until he punched me in the mouth. While I was being pulled out the window, I tried to reach into my back pocket. But they kept punching my head and face, and I had to try to protect myself. My left eye felt as if I had swallowed it.

"Ahora sí, pinche culebra. Now you're moving like the snake you are."

I didn't recognize the voice. It was high-pitched, a Chilango accent. He was definitely one of Los Reyes. They had probably murdered Rudi. He would murder me, too. I tried to open my eyes, but I couldn't see anything, and my ears were ringing. I felt the vibration of feet walking around, engines idling, two voices talking loudly. Then I heard myself crying.

"Where are you going, Mara?" a man's voice said. "Maybe if you tell me what the fuck you're up to, I won't kill you slow, eh? Come on. Where is it? Miguel, go search the car."

They kicked me again, and somebody laughed. I turned onto my side, away from the guy on top of me, and tried to curl up into a ball.

"Alejandra," I said. But it came out like a groan. I could smell cologne, which made me sick. I threw up. Then I felt someone near my face, breathing hot in my ear. He grabbed my hand and began to stroke my palm. He was leaning on me. I could feel something hard against my thigh. At first I thought it was a gun, then I realized he had an erection.

"I've been looking for you for so long, amorcito," he said in a low voice. "Were you with that gringo painter and his faggot friend in San Diego again? Why do you date gringos, Mara? Do you think he is going to save you? Tch-tch-tch. That's awful selfish of you, mi amor, putting him in danger like that. Shouldn't we just keep this between the two of us? We don't need any more complications than we already have. You tell me what you did with the coke Rudi gave you, and I'll see if we can work out a deal."

I tried to open my eyes, but I could only see out of one. The other was throbbing and heavy. I told myself I could take it. I could take the pain. I had to.

"Tell me, Miranda," he said. "How can you make me do this to you? Do you like to be hurt? Is that it? Do you like getting punched and kicked? Come on, tell me where it is, pinche puta."

I turned over, searching for the .25.

"I hear you have a daughter, Mara," he hissed. I could see his face now. He had long curly hair, a pig nose, and crooked teeth. "Why didn't you ever get married, querida? Is it because you're a lying, two-faced, stuck-up little puta?"

He was laying right on top of me, now, licking the cuts on my face, grinding his erection into my stomach, and feeling me between my legs. My hand was pinned beneath me, and so was the .25. I didn't know how they were going to kill me, but I hoped it would be fast.

"You know something," he said. I could feel him get off me. "I'm feeling sympathetic for you, mamacita. I think you deserve a chance to think of your daughter for once. Even though you're a puta, I'm going to give you this chance I didn't give Rudi. Or Julián. If you meet me, Rafael, later tonight at the racetrack—"

The gun exploded into his neck. The recoil jumped back through my shoulder. Rafael fell away. Through my good eye, I saw the fat one who had beaten me. He stood less than five feet away, in sunglasses, a shirt and tie. The folds of skin under his chin tripled as he stared at the splattered blood on his white shirt and yellow tie. He was frozen in shock. I shot him in the stomach three times. The fat man sat down next to Rafael. Something clacked and ignited behind me. It was the Grand Marquis starting up. I pushed myself up on one elbow and pointed the gun at the car. I fired twice more, but the car peeled out in a U-turn, went through the stop sign, toward the Boulevard, and was gone.

I could smell gunpowder and burnt rubber. I heard dogs barking. The fat man moaned for help. I heard him cough and spit up blood. I started crying. I was ashamed, humiliated, and angry. This was what I had feared the most. This was hell. Alejandra would see me beat up and bloody. She would remember this forever. There seemed nothing left to do but cry. But I hurt too much. I would have to cry later. There wasn't any time now. I was alive. They were dead.

I pulled myself up, holding onto the rear fender of the Cadillac. I thought about putting a bullet into the fat man's head to keep him from suffering. But his suffering didn't matter. Alejandra was all that mattered now. Getting out was all that mattered.

I could see that people had come into the street. I could hear their voices calling to each other, to me, the dead men.

"Oiga. Oiga, señorita."

My ears were ringing, but I didn't feel like hearing anything. I crawled into the car. An old man came to the window. He asked what happened. Why had I been attacked? Did I need the police? Who were the dead men on the street? But I heard nothing.

I tried to focus my good eye on the road in front of me and started the car. I still had to get Alejandra across the border. I still had to face Customs and Immigration. The ride wasn't over. I had to see Edgar. I put on my sunglasses and felt the pressure of the frame against my swollen eye. I looked at the crowd gathered in the street. They were looking at me. There was blood everywhere.

III. Two Birds, One Stone

Con dinero baila el perro
(Any dog dances for money)

Mexican saying

At the same time, Mexican Americans' success for generating such new bases for solidarity went a long way toward guaranteeing the survival and growth of a distinct, if syncretic variant of Mexican culture in what had become part of the United States. This was the last thing the proponents of Manifest Destiny had in mind when they had predicted the fading away of the region's ethnic Mexican problem.

David G. Gutierrez
Walls and Mirrors

*A*lfredo rode in the rear of the Bronco, handcuffed, with Gil in the seat in front of him. The radio echoed through the cab, announcing coded messages as the driver answered back in a low voice. They were headed down the 5, toward the last U.S. exit in San Ysidro, and the border. Alfredo and Gil had already been informed that they would be taken to the Customs and Immigration complex to begin a "procedural investigation." Being captured by the Border Patrol meant Alfredo would probably be put in an immigrant detainment cell. A patriot in a cage of rats, he thought. This nightmarish thought frightened him. Assaulting his memory were the men who had come by the apartment Alfredo and his mother had shared when he was a boy, before she'd married Shawn. Rough men in cowboy hats, boots, and sometimes in cheap suits, who showed up at the apartment with his mother after work, a bottle of tequila or a six-pack of Tecate under their arms, groping Dora before she even had a chance to change out of her Coco's uniform. Men slurring in Spanish and making sucking sounds at his mother. The mustachioed men reaching out and pinching Dora's ass in front of Alfredo. His mother's wheezing; the bedsprings in the room next to his own. Gruff voices moaning while Alfredo wondered where his real father might be.

Alfredo had been to the Detention Center before, six years ago, with his mother, after two of her cousins had been picked up. Dora had found them jobs in the kitchen at Coco's. One afternoon, instead of having to hassle with firing half the kitchen staff, the manager had simply made a call to the INS. An hour later, Oscar and Ramón were hauled away in a green-and-white van, much like the one Alfredo now rode in. Dora followed them down to the Customs Office in San Ysidro. She brought Alfredo with her. When he first saw the uniformed soldiers guarding the Secondary Inspection, he asked if they would shoot his cousins. "Ramón told me the migra shoot Mexicans. He told me they shoot them out in the canyon like dogs."

"No, mijo. They won't shoot them, but you stay away from the canyon," Dora scolded. "That's where the polleros fight to rob the others' clientes. Remember that coyotes son todos bandidos. What Ramón meant was that, when la migra comes to break up the fighting, they can't always tell the pollos from the coyotes. Sometimes the migra shoot the wrong people. Sometimes good people get killed. I'm telling you this so you'll know better than to go hanging around the canyon. ¿Me oistes? No te vayas por el cañón. I don't want you to get hurt."

One of the Border Patrol agents was arguing with Gil, who wanted to go back to the elementary school so he could pick up his identification, which he'd left inside his car.

"Just sit tight, son. We'll take you down to San Ysidro and sort this out."

"Excuse me," Gil went on. "I'm an American citizen. You have no authority to detain me. You're not the police—"

"On the border we are, Bubba," the driver said. "And you were busted in our territory. For now, it's our case."

"Are you the ranking official?" Gil asked.

"What?"

"Are-you-the-ranking-official?"

"Yes, I am. Captain Aguilar. At your service. This is my assistant, Agent Terranza. We're happy to do whatever we can for you."

"My name is Gilberto Garcia. All we need to do is go back to Loma Verde Elementary School, and I'll get you my driver's license. Do you want me to tell you my driver's license number? It's A74—"

"Shut up!" The agent in the passenger seat banged his hand on the lime-green steel web that separated the driver's seat from the back.

"The captain already told you we'd handle it when we get to San Ysidro. Mr. Burns—if that's his real name—is the only guy with ID. And all of you have been apprehended with firearms and no gun license. You're in some pretty big trouble."

"I told you," Gil whined. "We were just hunting rabbits and coyotes."

"At three-thirty in the morning? Just shut up till we get to San Ysidro, all right? Why don't you take it like your friend? Very well behaved back there, son. So do me a favor and calle la boca. This is my boss, all right? I need to make a good impression."

"I'm sorry," Gil said dramatically, "I don't speak Spanish. I'm Filipino. And if you're being official, you should speak English to Alfredo and me. I shouldn't have to remind you that English is the official language of the United States."

"Is this your friend, Alfredo?" Captain Aguilar asked, leaning his head back from the steering wheel and raising his voice over the radio so that it bellowed through the Bronco.

Alfredo struggled in his seat, wanting to thump Gil on the head and knock him out.

"Do yourself a favor and shut up," Alfredo whispered. "You're making us look bad."

"Please, Captain Aguilar," Gil continued, "if you could just call my mother."

"There'll be plenty of time for that once we get inside," Captain Aguilar answered.

Alfredo continued to look out the back window as they passed the last U.S. exit sign. He felt exhausted, like the victim of a mutiny, a prisoner of war entering a concentration camp. He wondered if he had enough strength to make it through these next hours. This would be a test of his will: Was he who he said he was?

ALFREDO STARED AT HIS BARE FEET, AT THE MARKS left by the tongue of his boots. He was naked. His fatigues had been tossed to the left, next to his boots, and sat in a pile on the white tile floor of Captain Aguilar's office. The customs inspector asked him to bend over and cough. Another agent stood at a wooden table examining each article of his clothing with an electronic wand, while the detective took notes.

The customs inspector touched Alfredo on his lower back with latex gloves and then pulled him upright. A bust of President Clinton looked on from Captain Aguilar's desk.

"What do you usually do—give him a bunch of Ex-Lax?" the

detective asked.

"No, we have a generic that works quicker."

"What if his body has a bad reaction?" the detective asked. "I read that you guys were having problems with a pregnant woman who miscarried because of an abnormal dose."

"Most laxatives don't have that much effect. They say she may have been just too old to have a baby."

The inspector gave Alfredo two red pills.

"Thank you for cooperating, Alfredo," the inspector said. "I believe you'll be using the restroom in about five minutes. We'll be back to check with you."

The detective and inspectors left, taking Alfredo's clothes.

"I spoke with your mother, Alfredo," the captain said. "I thought she might want to know where you were."

Alfredo tried to imagine his mother waiting out in the car, while Shawn came in to talk with Captain Aguilar. He knew Shawn wouldn't be afraid to talk to the police. Alfredo only wondered if he would be sober enough after the party. Either way, Dora wouldn't revisit this place asking for favors. Alfredo knew she wouldn't set one naturalized foot inside the Immigration office ever again—citizenship or not—if she could help it. And especially not alone.

"Do I get to go home now?"

"No. We're still waiting on the ballistics report."

Alfredo wondered what Gil and the others had told the police. It had been hours, and Alfredo feared they had cracked under pressure.

"Where is the rest of my company?" Alfredo asked.

"Your friends are at the Chula Vista police station," Captain Aguilar said. "Their weapons were reported stolen several months ago."

Alfredo snorted and shook his head.

"Is there anything you want to tell me about that?" Captain Aguilar asked.

"Then why are you holding me here? I'm not illegal."

"No, but I've decided to keep you here. I thought you would prefer my office to a jail cell."

"Great. In the meantime, they're going to dissect my crap."

The captain uncorked a silver thermos and poured coffee into the cap. He drank, and Alfredo saw the gold band on Captain

Aguilar's left hand.

"I'm interested to know how they got the nightscopes," the captain said.

"I have no idea," Alfredo replied, although he had a vague idea that Jesse had gotten the guns from his older brother, Tavo.

"Your mother said she let you take the rifle," the captain said. "She said she let you take it out for your birthday. Is it your birthday today?"

Alfredo didn't answer. He imagined his mother stuttering the lie into a shot of vodka. At least her timing was right. He doubted she would have remembered if it hadn't fallen on Memorial Day.

"So the rifle's like the car, or something?" Captain Aguilar laughed. "Your parents let you take it on a joy ride, is that it? Is your mother crazy?"

Alfredo shivered again, but didn't respond.

Captain Aguilar sipped out of the silver thermos cap and frowned. He wiped his mustache with his bare wrist, left his desk, and offered Alfredo the silver cap of coffee. Alfredo shook his head. His body ached from spending four, five, six—he wasn't sure how many hours he'd been waiting.

Captain Aguilar put his arm around Alfredo, and they both sat on the vinyl sofa together.

"Do you want to put my jacket on?"

Alfredo rolled his eyes and thought if he'd had the strength, he'd have thrown Captain Aguilar's arms off of him. Every time some strange guy wanted to play daddy, he had to hang on Alfredo and smother him. Like he didn't know it was extortion.

"Or is it the air conditioner? The whole building has a regulated temperature. I don't think I can fix that."

Alfredo grunted.

"What if your friends said you got them the guns, Alfredo?"

Alfredo felt as if he'd been struck on the head. His face went numb; his whole body begin to cramp. He swallowed twice and took rapid breaths. He tried not to panic. His tongue was pasty. He tried to swallow again, but couldn't. It felt like his tongue was swelling.

"Are you and your friends coyotes? Is that what you were doing out in the canyon? Were you smuggling illegals?"

Alfredo gagged.

Captain Aguilar guessed the laxative was working.

"Is that it?"

Alfredo shook his head furiously, fighting the need to shit. He couldn't swallow. He couldn't clear his throat. Aching at the back of his tongue, his tonsils burned as if he had been shouting. From the back of his head darkness began to circle toward his eyes like a curtain. He bit his tongue, hoping the pain would keep him conscious and divert his attention from his bowels. He wanted to take a deep breath, but he couldn't breathe. He opened his eyes wider. He imagined he looked very ugly and frightening, clenching his teeth and fists, his neck straining against the pain in his bowels.

"Alfredo?" The captain called to him. "Are you O.K.? Do you need to go to the bathroom now?"

While the captain repeated his name, Alfredo tried to draw the strength to stand up and walk to the bathroom door. He took one step and straightened up. Then it all came.

THE DARKLY TINTED HATCHBACK WINDOW OF the truck's maroon shell was open, and the thumping bass of rap music escaped. *Coming up as a nigga in the cash game, living in the fast lane, I'm for real.* Gabe bobbed his head with the beat as he lit a Marlboro Light. Three of his homeboys stood around the truck parked to the side of Lolita's Taco Shop, near the fenced-in dumpster, drinking and eating, listening to the music. A lamppost flickered above Chino as he stood near a pay phone. He was rapping with a beer in one hand and a burrito in his other.

Forgive me, I'm a rider. Still I'm just a simple man. All I want is money. Fuck the fame.

"How you know this dude, Gabe?" Shane asked. "I don't remember no Tavo from Donovan."

"Tavo's a friend from high school," Gabe said. "I been knowin' him for a long time. Just look for a short guy wearing a shiny cowboy shirt with curly hair and a goatee."

"Cowboy shirt? What kind of shit is that?" Mico asked. His Cardinals cap was pulled to the side.

Gabe shook his head.

"His dad owns a couple of factories down in TJ," he said. "Folks got money. He don't bang."

"What about my money?" Chino asked. "You still got it?"

"Did you think I went and bought something with it?"

"Why do we have to wait all night, then?" Mico asked.

"If there's anything in your life worth waiting for, Mico, it's a deal like we got with Tavo. Making money takes time."

Despite what he may have told his friends, however, it made Gabe nervous standing around holding so much cash. He was still on probation and still unemployed. Ironically, he wondered if this was what it was like to be rich. Rich people must always worry about losing their money. He guessed that's why they were always stashing it in banks. So somebody else could worry about it. Gabe had never had a bank account. Whatever cash he'd come across he'd always carried on him, like now. But it had never been this much.

A dark blue Toyota minitruck pulled into the parking lot. The wide wheels spit up loose gravel and then stopped in front of the taco shop. The three passengers in the front were all looking at Gabe and his friends. They cut their lights while the motor was still running.

"What those fucking wetbacks looking at?" Mico said.

"Forget the scraps. I've got to check on some business inside," Gabe said. "Come get me if Tavo arrives. He knows what my truck looks like."

Gabe walked toward the blue truck. He could hear the passengers speaking Spanish. One smiled at Gabe, flashing two silver front teeth.

"A la verga, puto."

"Don't smile at me, vato."

The Sureños laughed at Gabe, who kept walking toward the restaurant. He wasn't wearing gang colors tonight. The large 14 tattooed on his left bicep was covered by his triple-extra-large polo shirt. But the letter N, in Old English on his forearm and neck, was hard to ignore. In the pen, he had joined the Norteño side and fought with the Sureños many times. Gabe had had to join a gang, or he wouldn't have survived. He had seen the Sureños get shanked, raped, and killed in the pen. But Gabe knew he had to try to forget about the prison wars. He had to if he wanted to make it on the outside. Now money was the foundation of his loyalty. Now he focused only on money and success. Tonight was a big night, a money-making night, and Gabe needed everything to go his way.

Lolita's was busy. It was a teenage crowd standing outside.

High schoolers and the recently graduated. Gabe didn't recognize anyone. He supposed none of these folks would remember him from when he was in school. He was barely 18 when he went to prison, and now he was looking at a whole new generation. He thought he hadn't missed much. Everyone was treating it like Saturday night, even though it was Sunday. He overheard people on their way to Tijuana, which had become the cool place for local teenagers to party. Gabe had had his share of times in TJ. He'd been kicked out of bars, and he had kicked people, too. He had fought somebody different almost every trip down there. Sometimes more than once a night. TJ was a mess, and he'd been a mess back then.

Lately, he had seen Tavo around the taco shop. They had given each other their separate stories. Tavo told Gabe he was in the repossession business. He worked with a girl from Tijuana. They had come across a lot of cocaine during one of their jobs. Did Gabe know anyone interested in it? Gabe didn't think twice. Last night he had contacted Shane, who had contacted Chino and Mico and told them to come up with twenty-five hundred each, and meet at Lolita's. They would split the profits four ways. There had been no action for the longest time, and now the coke would put Gabe where he needed to be.

As he entered the restaurant, the aroma of tortillas, Mexican rice, frijoles, and liquid bleach reminded Gabe of his mother. The young Mexican, Mexican American, Anglo, and Filipino customers, dressed in their casual beach clothes, baseball caps, and T-shirts, chatted and flirted with each other across the small orange dining tables. The register at the opposite end beeped numbers and spit out receipts, while the cashier shouted special orders in Spanish to the kitchen staff. They wore white T-shirts with their sleeves rolled up. When Gabe reached a table near the register, he found three teenagers in camouflage fatigues and buzz cuts hunched over styrofoam cups. Their faces were painted black and green. They looked like they were planning a battle.

One of the Commandos stood up when he saw Gabe.

"You don't have to get up, G.I. Joe. Just pretend I'm here to take your order."

Gabe looked down at the young soldiers and sat next to a kid with the name Garcia, G., stamped bold above his left breast pocket. He looked across the table at the scrawny soldier with the name Treviño, J., printed on his uniform. He nodded at Tavo's little brother, but he sensed there might be something wrong with this picture. He looked around, but no one seemed to be taking notice. Perhaps these kids were just playing war games. Gabe knew about paintball. But they were wearing face paint in public and trying to buy real weapons.

Next to Jesse was a pudgy-faced, blue-eyed girl in a camo cap, her short fingernails painted green.

"Who are you?" Gabe asked.

"Erica."

The kid next to her impatiently demanded three Remington hunting rifles with nightscopes, or one of their friends would be in trouble.

"—extreme crisis. This isn't a joke. We've been waiting all night. Where's our product?"

"Why don't you ask your duck-hunting daddy?" Gabe said, irritated with people pressuring him. "Do you know what a pato is, Top Gun? That's a bird who don't fly straight."

A puzzled look came over their faces as Gabe smiled. Quoting Al Pacino in *Scarface* had been a favorite thing to do when Gabe was wasting time with friends, getting high, scheming for money. The Commandos may have been too young to appreciate the reference.

"My brother said we were supposed to meet you here at midnight," said Jesse. His frail features and green sunglasses made him look like a frog. "We've been waiting for an hour. We were supposed to be somewhere. That's why Gil's upset."

"I don't punch a clock," Gabe said. "But I just about had to go through the fucking CIA to get a hold of those damn nightscopes."

"Don't give me that," Garcia said. The green paint around his eyes and mouth wrinkled as he frowned. "You can send away for them in *Soldier of Fortune*. The only reason we didn't do it that way is because Tavo said you're supposed to be able to get them quicker. That's why we're paying you more."

"Are you guys on your way to Montana or something?" Gabe asked. "It's not like there's any deer in Chula Vista. Why do you want hunting rifles?"

"That's classified," Jesse said. "We just want to do business with you."

Gabe nodded.

"A 12-gauge is a much better bang for your buck, if you know what I mean," he advised. "I can hook you up with a shotgun, and probably a .45 right now."

"We don't need shotguns," Garcia said. "And if we did, we would need three, not one."

Gabe felt someone behind him. Shane bent over and whispered into his ear. A brown van had pulled up outside.

The Commandos began to lay twenties, fifties, and hundreds on the table.

"You said three thousand for everything including the scopes, right?"

"Put that shit away," Gabe hissed.

"But isn't it time to—"

"Just wait for me outside. My truck is parked next to the dumpster. Don't leave the restaurant until I'm outside. I don't want anything to be more obvious than your uniforms."

Gabe watched the brown van head toward the Canyon Club, at the end of the strip mall. He asked Shane to follow the van and tell the driver to turn around. Then he walked back to his truck. All the movement was beginning to tire him. He'd expected Tavo and the girl from Tijuana to show up with the cocaine first. But this was actually better. He could give Tavo the money he owed for the coke out of what he earned off the guns.

Mico and Chino were still standing around Gabe's truck.

"Mico, get inside the truck and close the hatch window."

"Fuck you, nigga. I ain't no bitch."

"You got my back, or what?" Gabe said. He thumbed back toward the van. "I need you in there for surprise. Keep your eyes on me and the dude in the van."

"Oh. O.K."

He turned to Chino.

"You go stand in front of Lolita's and look for Tavo in a silver 4Runner. Tell him to wait for me inside."

"I thought we were waiting for Tavo right here?"

"We are. But you're going to wait for him over there."

"Awright. But when do I get paid?"

"Nigga, shut up."

Shane came over to Gabe's truck, his tree-trunk mass bouncing as he jogged.

"The dude in the van is wearing a Hawaiian shirt."

"I know. His name is Bruce. And he's an ex-Navy SEAL. So don't fuck with him."

Shane shook his head, confused. Gabe realized maybe he should have told Shane that he was trying to kill two birds with one stone. He would need Shane in case the deal went bad. But it was too late now.

"What's going on, Gabe?" Mico asked from inside the truck bed.

"Just stay in the truck, Mico. And keep your eyes open. Here he comes."

The van pulled up in front of Gabe's truck. The driver leaned over to the passenger window and rolled it down.

"Everything's in the back," Bruce said. "I'm going to pull up next to your truck."

Gabe walked around his truck. Shane followed and stood by the passenger door as Gabe climbed inside the van. Bruce didn't smile and kept his eyes on Gabe's hands. He nodded at Shane behind him.

"How you doing, bro?" Gabe said. Bruce lowered the volume on his stereo, reached back, and opened a black curtain that led to the back.

"Go ahead."

"All right. Thanks."

Gabe squeezed between the two front seats. The rear of the van was dark as a cave. Gabe hunched over, waiting for a light to be switched on. But no light came. Gabe thought that must mean he was supposed to find the guns by himself.

"Is there a flashlight or anything back here?"

"They're toward the very back. By the door, in the right hand corner. In the duffel bag."

The floor of the van was a damp carpet of sand. Gabe could smell gasoline, oil, sweat, and cocoa butter. He extended his hand out toward something that shined to a point. He touched hard plastic: a surfboard. His foot clunked against something hard. He reached down and felt a long wooden handle. A pickax. Gabe reached up to the wall of the van and touched a rake. He had forgotten that Bruce worked as a lawn custodian for the rich folks in Coronado.

They had met only one time before, a couple weeks back at

a party. Besides one uptight black guy in khakis and blue oxford, Gabe had been the only one wearing a collared shirt. Bruce had lit up a joint on the back porch, and Gabe asked to join. Once they began talking, Bruce described his experiences as a SEAL. Then he mentioned his gun collection, which included high-tech weapons from all over the world. When Tavo asked Gabe to find the guns and scopes for his little brother in exchange for a good price on some coke, the connection was only two phone calls away.

Gabe was starting to get frustrated with the dark. His eyes wouldn't adjust. He'd always hated the dark. He remembered how dark his cell became after the lights went out at nine o'clock. He could hear other inmates talking shit to each other, singing, moaning, crying, reciting Scriptures, rapping. Gabe would fall asleep to their voices. When he woke up, he would go over and over how he'd gotten himself into jail. He'd been on his way to a party, high on crystal meth and a bottle of RUSH. Edgar had waited for him in the car as Gabe went inside a liquor store to steal some beer. He was running out with two twelve-packs, when the young Filipino clerk hopped the counter and tried to stop him. Gabe smashed the clerk with a twelve-pack, busting open his nose, knocking him out. It had all happened in seconds. But instead of running out to the car, Gabe got greedy and decided to reach for the register. The video taped him pulling out $214. Four weeks later, the clerk picked him out of a lineup. He was sentenced for armed robbery and aggravated assault.

The dampness of the van gave him claustrophobia. He couldn't find any duffel bag. Why hadn't Bruce made it easier and just opened the back doors for him? Gabe decided to turn back. He set down his right hand on something dry, like canvas, behind him. He pushed down farther and felt, through the bag, the long handle of a rifle. The bag had probably moved during the trip. It was wedged beneath the surfboard and the tools. Gabe yanked until the bag came free, spilling the metal head of the shovel onto the surfboard in a loud clang. The noise frightened Gabe.

"Fuck!"

"Hey, man. Don't ding my board."

"Sorry."

Gabe made it to the front of the van. He sat down and caught his breath.

"I've got one piece of advice for you," he said.

"What's that?"

"Next time we should think about doing business in a real office. With some motherfucking light."

"No, I'd rather operate out of my car. I like being mobile."

"Well, get a fucking light back there. I felt like I was in a horror movie."

Inside the bag were three fully assembled hunting rifles mounted with bulky silver scopes. Gabe handed the money over, lifted the bag onto his lap, and reached to unlock the passenger door. He climbed down, shut the door, and the van drove away.

Outside, Shane was talking with the three Commandos. Gabe gathered himself, went to the back of his truck, and opened the hatch.

"I couldn't see shit after you went inside the van," Mico said. "What happened?"

"Come on out, Mico. It's all good." Gabe set the bag of guns inside the truck bed. Mico climbed out, and the Commandos appeared at the back of the truck.

"Now who the fuck are you?" Mico demanded.

"It's all right, Mico. They're here to do some business with me."

"Oh, yeah?" Mico said, stroking his baseball cap. "How much am I in on that for?"

"Your loot is with Tavo," Gabe said. "This is my business right here. My truck. My business."

Gabe unzipped the long aqua blue canvas bag with the name O'Neill in black cursive on it. The Commandos peeked into the truck bed.

"Those will do," Jesse said.

"All right," Gabe said. "I hope you understand that I did not provide you with anything. You were never at the taco shop, and you don't know who I am."

"Fine."

Money changed hands once more, and the Commandos were on their way with the blue surfboard bag.

"What the fuck was that all about, Gabe?" Shane asked.

"I was doing a favor for someone. You guys had my back. Thanks."

Shane looked at him suspiciously.

"What about the money that just came through?" he asked. "You got us for that?"

"I told you. Tavo's got your money."

"You been saying that all night. But I'm still waiting for you to come through."

"Don't worry, bro. I ain't forgot about you."

Tavo showed up shortly afterward with the girl from Tijuana and Edgar Revuelta. Gabe hadn't expected to see Edgar; there was an awkward hello, but Gabe didn't say anything about how he had kept his mouth shut about Edgar driving the car six years ago when they did the beer run. He had already put it all behind him. He hugged his old friend and laughed. They had grown up in the same neighborhood, and now Edgar was a famous painter. He told Gabe he'd been written up in the dailies.

"As long as they didn't publish your picture with WANTED underneath, I'd say you did good, bro. Congratulations."

"We used to wonder how you were doing inside, Gabe," Tavo said. "But Edgar didn't know how to get a hold of you."

"I survived."

"Did you hear anything about Cristina?" Edgar asked.

"Cristina?"

"My sister. You remember her."

"Of course, but I didn't hear anything about her."

Gabe remembered Edgar's sister as a loudmouth tomboy. He shook his head when Edgar told him she had been killed because she was a lesbian.

"Fuck, man. I didn't expect to hear that. I'm sorry." Gabe shook his head. "Do you know who did it?"

"Cops said it was a hate crime. They don't know who did it."

Tavo introduced Miranda to Gabe as a friend from Tijuana.

"I don't know about TJ," Gabe said. "My mother always told me to stay away from there. Better watch your back with this chick, Edgar. She could turn on you any minute."

Miranda smirked. "Your mother must have been born on this side," she said.

"So what if she was?"

"Chicanas are typically low in self-esteem. That's why you're so paranoid."

"Come on, Mara," Tavo said. "We still have to do business with him."

"Well, I'm waiting," Mara said. "Or are we going to give the whole pinche world a free show?"

"THEY MUST THINK I'M JUST SOME TOKEN ARTS administrator with a Mexican connection," Humberto said, tapping his pen on the desk to "The Girl From Ipanema" playing over the gallery speakers. The downtown San Diego gallery he owned was called Mesa Blanca. Humberto checked his voice mail and continued on about how he had spent time in Los Angeles and New York during the early eighties, and he knew a wily art agent when he heard one.

"None of these people know how long I've been at this, how hard I've worked to put unknown artists like you on the map."

Edgar jammed his hands inside his jeans-jacket pockets. Mesa Blanca was open on Memorial Day, as it had been since it started four years ago. But it was also empty, except for Edgar and Humberto, who had promised to settle accounts.

Humberto hung up. Edgar noticed that his ponytail had so much gray in its fuzzy tangle that it hung from his head like the tail of a raccoon-skin cap. His cleanly pressed, peach-colored guayabera, however, was quite another attraction. Humberto proudly referred to his multipocketed daily attire as the "tuxedo of Latin America." He had been born in Tijuana when it had still been a small town, and he preferred that people see him as a brown boy from el pueblo de Tijuana, even though he was well into his forties.

"Then when they finally pay attention to what you have to say, they demean you with references to 'I knew him when—' Or, 'I always knew the kid had talent.' But tell me something, Edgar, if they knew all along you were so talented, why didn't they offer to do anything about it?"

"Who are you talking about, Humberto?"

"Never mind."

Humberto walked across to the small bar where he'd left his bottle of Bohemia between a stack of brochures and a pile of Xeroxes of reviews of the Sights on the Border exhibition. All six of Edgar's paintings in the show had sold.

"This is groundbreaking for us, Edgar. We're not sitting around waiting for anyone to come to us anymore. We're taking this show on the road. Are you ready for Chicago?"

"Chicago? I thought you had a check for me. I came to get paid, Humberto."

"I expected you at two. It's almost six now. You were supposed to work today in the gallery, remember? You should be here to greet people. Inform them about your work."

"But it's sold already."

"You don't understand. You can't just live from show to show. You have to think about the future. The next ten shows. That is how you build your reputation. Without continual production of new work, people distrust you as an artist. And since you're Chicano, people distrust you even more. They want to chalk up any success to the exotic nature of your ethnicity. Believe me, I was around in the sixties, when we started thinking like this. That's why you have to speak to your audience personally. All of them—strangers, friends, old ladies, white people, revolucionarios, Raza, even kids. Kids are the most important. Kids will look to you as a role model. Do you know what it's like to be a role model, Edgar?"

"No. I only know what it's like to be broke. And I know broke artists are never anyone's role models. They're just plain broke. And I want to get paid."

Humberto laughed.

"So where were you?"

"The police station."

"What? What the hell for?" Humberto began rummaging through the drawers within the white table that served as the front desk, until he pulled out a pen. "Sit down. Do you want a beer? I have to write out the check still. Tell me what happened."

Edgar decided not to sit down. He also decided not to tell Humberto why he had been at the police station. If he had needed help, however, Edgar would have called Humberto.

"Don't treat it like gold, Edgar," Humberto said, handing him a check for $8,000. "There'll be plenty more where that came from. And with the press you'll earn the gallery, we'll all be one big happy familia."

Edgar shrugged. He supposed that as long as he listened, the money, via Humberto, would keep talking, willfully leading the way. The thrill of his new success gave him a strange tickling sensation at the back of his throat, like he was ready to cough up a hair. He was excited to hear such news, but unsure how to control the wave of confusion that came with it. Edgar wondered if it hadn't come too fast. He was 26. Was he prepared to be a success? Was he even prepared for a road trip? Who were the strange people calling for him?

"Did the people who called leave their names?" Edgar asked. He had always been a private person, preferring his studio to the nightclub. But since dating Miranda, Edgar was even more cautious of strangers.

"I can't remember their names," Humberto said. "It doesn't matter. You don't need an art agent. You've got me. From now on, Edgar, we don't settle for American cheese. No way, baby. From now on we want queso manchego."

Edgar had sold paintings before. He'd hung a show in a small downtown bar nearby, while he was still in college. Three pieces had sold, earning a grand total of $625. It had cost him more than a month's pay busing tables at the Charthouse Restaurant to produce the whole show. He had actually lost money. No matter. He blew half the money on dinner, cocaine, and one night of drinking at the Elephant Bar in La Jolla. And that night a girl named Sarah told him she was indeed pregnant. Since Edgar had insisted on "not wearing any fucking condoms," the last of the money earned from the show was spent on her abortion.

"What about some outreach for the next project?" Edgar asked. "I'd like to do some work with kids in Chula Vista or National City. A high school in Logan Heights. What about a mural project outside the gallery or a tribute to Chicano Park?"

"We can do all that, " Humberto said cautiously. "Another day. Right now we have to stay one step ahead of the hype. We have to build our credibility and our national resumes. If we're going to make it, we've got to take advantage of the publicity right now. Besides, there's absolutely no money in outreach. Really, you should start thinking about your next show."

"Does it look like I have dollar signs in my eyes?"

Humberto stroked his thin black mustache, as he always did when he was about to get serious. "Don't get me wrong, Edgar. I want what's best for you. You can do all the community service you want. But it's like I always say: There's nothing more pitiful than an underpaid artist."

The phone rang.

"For you," Humberto said, covering the cordless receiver with his hand. "He wouldn't give me his name. Sounds like one of the guys on my voice mail. I don't think you should talk to him. I'll take a message."

Edgar grabbed the phone.

"¿Qué onda? It's Tavo."

"Why are you whispering?"

"You're fucked, that's why."

"Who?"

"You, motherfucker. Me, Miranda, you. Fucking us, man. We're fucked." Tavo spoke in a raspy voice, grinding his teeth between sentences. "The migra caught Jesse shooting at people in the canyon last night. They called the police when they found out his ROTC friends were all carrying stolen guns. The ones he got from Gabe. Now the police have him and they're asking him all kinds of questions about last night."

"Oh, Jesus," Edgar mumbled. His testicles jumped up inside him; butterflies began to beat inside his stomach. Did Tavo suspect that Miranda had gone to the police already?

"They're not stupid enough to give you up, are they?" Edgar asked.

"The cops already called my mom," Tavo said. "If my brother gave me up, I'll kill him."

"Where are you?"

"At Gabe's. He's having a party, remember? We were about to eat, and my mother paged me. She's afraid to go to the police station. She wants me to go get my brother before they beat him up."

"Did you tell Gabe the police caught your brother with the guns?"

"No puedo. I don't know how to tell him. I'm afraid of what he'll do."

Silence.

"Where's Mara?" Tavo asked.

"I'm not sure," Edgar began to sweat.

"What do you think we should do?"

"You got a lot of nerve asking me that."

"Why?"

"Why? Because you deserve to get fucked for your little two-birds-with-one-stone idea," Edgar hissed. Then he winced. It was as much his doing as anyone else's.

"Don't pretend like I don't know what you're saying," Tavo said. "If you think I'm going to wait for the police to bring me down—man, you don't know me at all. I'll fucking take off, with or without you. Without Mara. Without telling Gabe. And don't think I'll go down quietly, cabroncito. If they get me, ya estuvo, guey. For all of us."

"Just wait."

"For what?"

Edgar bit his lip.

"Don't do anything yet."

"Don't do nothing?"

"Nothing."

"That advice sucks, Edgar. I'm going to split."

"Just wait and see what happens with your brother, O.K.? Stay with Gabe until I get over there. I'm going to see Miranda right now. Then I'll page you. We'll talk later."

Edgar hung up and handed the phone to Humberto.

"I'm sorry, Edgar, I'm sorry I sound like an asshole today. This show has put a lot of pressure on me. I just want us to succeed. We have to be a team, you know?"

"I understand."

"I gave you the job, the residency, and the show, not because I felt bad about your sister, but because I believed in you. You have to understand that."

"I know. Thank you. I know I owe you a lot. Thank you."

Edgar hugged Humberto, feeling an unpredictable pendulum swinging him back and forth. The size of the shock to come made Edgar wince in Humberto's arms.

"You're like my son, you know?" Humberto said. "You and my crazy nephew, Alfredo. You're like my sons. I love you."

Humberto's nephew, Alfredo, had worn fatigues once while visiting the gallery, when Edgar had organized a panel about Prop 187. In the discussion, Alfredo had talked as if Mexicans would flood the border and take over California. It was strange to hear that from Alfredo, because what Edgar remembered Humberto telling him, Humberto himself had crossed mojado. His whole family had come illegally. They had all been pollos. Was it so repulsive that they now had to destroy their own history?

The phone rang again. Humberto answered, and quickly turned and walked away.

Edgar pulled out his check again. He was getting paid to paint! If only Cristina could have shared his success. Humberto had let her organize gallery events in the early days. The gallery had been associated with the radical gay movement then. Dances and poetry events were her pet projects. But the downtown community didn't attend. So Cristina tried to get more Chicanos involved. There were none in Hillcrest, so she'd gone back home to Chula Vista looking to recruit.

Humberto returned to the bar in a hurry, looking for his keys and cursing under his breath. He pulled out a bottle of Herradura tequila and a shot glass.

"What's the matter? Why're you in such a hurry to get borracho?"

"That was my sister, Dora, on the phone," Humberto said, pouring a shot. "Alfredo's in trouble. He had a seizure this afternoon. He's at Kaiser in Chula Vista. Dora needs me."

"I didn't know Alfredo was epileptic."

"He's not," Humberto said. "At least, I don't think so. Dora said the migra caught Alfredo and some friends last night firing rounds in the canyon with unregistered guns. They searched them for drugs, and then the fuckers gave Alfredo a laxative. It had a negative effect and sent him into a seizure."

"What the fuck? A laxative?"

Humberto downed his shot and offered one to Edgar, who refused.

"Can you believe it? A fecal exam to look for internally smuggled drugs."

Then it finally hit Edgar: Alfredo was tied to Jesse and Tavo and Gabe.

Humberto found his keys behind the coffee mug.

"I've got to go. Every time we have a family problem, I'm the one who has to deal with the authorities."

THE JEEP RAN SMOOTHLY AT 75 MPH IN THE SAFE lane. I-5 was not crowded this evening. Edgar passed Pacific Beach on the left and used the jeep's electric lighter to spark his second joint of the day. The combination of highway speed and marijuana had kept him in a dreamlike state all day long. The reaction took him outside his body. No wonder there were so many accidents on the wide southern California freeways. Where you were going was all that mattered. The paradox was that the mind moved only toward what had just been passed. All memory was constructed within these dissolving landscapes, a glimpse of the already depleting image. Nothing was fixed. Not even the concrete of intersecting overpasses which divided the sunlight, and which earthquakes broke apart. He felt like he was traveling a road built on air; below was a chasmed nothingness.

Edgar knew by the way his skin crawled with the drop in temperature and the dry canyon landscape that he was heading westd and was nearing La Jolla Shores. He could smell the burnt embers of beach bonfires and taste salty grounds of sand on his teeth. He was going to meet Miranda above Black's Beach. Miranda had wanted to meet at the cliffs one last time. She didn't think they would see each other while Julián's murder was being investigated.

A few cars were parked along the edge. Miranda was hunched on a rock facing the water. A small figure in white cuddled next to her. Inside a white Taurus, a lone man in sunglasses observed Edgar as he got out of his jeep. There was a slight evening breeze.

Edgar waved at Alejandra, who looked up at her mother. But Miranda did not move.

"Ola, Alejandra. ¿Cómo estás?"

Alejandra looked at him, but didn't answer.

"¿Qué bonita la playa, verdád? ¿Te gusta nadar?"

Alejandra nodded.

"I'm the Little Mermaid."

"Oh, yeah?"

Alejandra turned to point at a yellow hangglider floating 20 yards in front of them. "Quiero volar así."

"Me too, baby," Miranda said.

"¿Vamos a volar así, mami?"

"Si, chiquita. We'll fly just like that."

"¿Cuándo?"

"Soon, niña. Very soon."

When Edgar bent over to kiss Miranda, he saw the swollen cheekbone below her left eye. There were other deep red marks on her face, and a red scratch near the part in her hair.

Miranda helped Alejandra to her feet. "It's time to go. Say goodbye to Edgar. Andale, niña. Say goodbye."

"Bye-bye."

Edgar smiled at Alejandra, but did not say goodbye to her. He had something else in mind.

"Now wait for me in the car," Miranda ordered her daughter. "I'll be right there. I have to say goodbye to Edgar."

Alejandra looked out at the hanggliders once more. She turned away, spread her arms out, and jumped off the rock. She circled the Cadillac with her arms spread out.

"She's afraid to be alone in the car?" Edgar asked.

"She's been through a lot today."

"So are you going to tell me what happened?"

Miranda turned back to look at the white Taurus. "That's Officer Sehorn over there," she said. "I'm not sure if he's my bodyguard or parole officer. Anyway, they're investigating, and they want to make sure they know where I am at all times. I think they want me to set something up with Los Reyes. But I can't."

Miranda tucked her chin into her chest. She began crying, softly at first. Edgar wrapped her in his long arms.

"Don't get upset about this anymore, Mara," he said. "At least you're safe. You've got someone to protect you. After your case closes, maybe we can get out of here for a while. Humberto says he might take the show to Chicago."

Miranda only cried harder.

"I want you to come with me, Mara. We can rent a place together in Chicago until this whole mess blows over."

Miranda pulled away. "What are you talking about? This mess isn't going to ever blow over. Even if they do catch Los Reyes. That won't change anything. Things will only get worse for me. I'll have to watch my back for the rest of my life."

"What if I'm there to help watch it?"

Miranda removed her glasses and looked at Edgar. He saw how disfigured her face was.

"Does it look like I'm ready for a gallery tour?" Miranda shouted into the wind. "Do you think Los Reyes won't follow you around once I've disappeared?"

Edgar reached out to hold her, to keep her from denying everything he'd wanted with her. But she stepped away.

"I can't go with you. I might as well put a target on both our foreheads right now. I've got no home, Edgar. No family, no friends. I need to get out of here before it's too late for me, for Alejandra."

"I won't see you again?"

"I'm sorry," Miranda said.

In the long silence, Edgar began: "When my sister left home, it was after a fight she'd had with my father, who'd shown up, out of the blue, after ten years of not seeing my mother, nor either one of us. That day he brought letters for Cristina and me to read. Letters he'd written to us while he was away at law school, but had never sent. He made Cristina and me read them in the living room, while he waited on the couch."

Edgar didn't know why this story had jumped out of his mouth. He remembered his mother sitting in her easy chair while he and his sister read the letters.

"Before Cristina had even finished the letters, she blew up. She attacked my father. She tried to beat him up, but he was too big for her to even land a punch on his face. So Cristina pounded his chest and kicked his shins. Until I pulled her off. She called him a coward, an egotistic, talking-head, no-balls motherfucker."

"What did the letters say?"

"It was full of my father's advice about how to survive in the real world. We were poor, you see, and he was trying to justify his having abandoned us by showing us how he'd learned to survive on his own. He was going to enlighten us about the struggles he'd overcome. Divorcing my mother, he tried to claim, was a necessary step on his way to becoming a lawyer.

"He told us he had made it in the real world because he hadn't needed to depend on anybody. No psychological or moral crutches, like religion or even family, for that matter.

"His parents had been strict Evangelists and had tried to control every aspect of his life by threatening him with God's wrath. My father was essentially telling us that he had only become a man once he'd left us. Along with the responsibility to his family, he'd also thrown away a false God. And become a real man."

"And so your sister tried to kill him because he was an atheist?"

"No. She tried to kill him because he was so wrapped up in his own bullshit."

"He was a hypocrite. Another fucking hypocrite."

"When my mother didn't say anything in defense of her own children being assaulted with bullshit, Cristina said we were all hypocrites. Then she took off. She moved in with some women from Hillcrest, who turned out to be lesbians."

"Why didn't you stand up with her against your father?"

"I was just trying to calm her down," Edgar said. He remembered how he had pulled Cristina off, how she'd hyperventilated and almost passed out. Edgar had carried her back to her room, massaged her shoulders, back, and legs. He'd whispered to her that they could help each other. They didn't need their mother or father. But the next day Cristina was gone.

"You see, I don't have anything left, either." Edgar looked at Miranda. "I'm just as lost as you."

"At least you'll never be considered a hypocrite. When you start a family, you can take pride in knowing that."

Miranda put her hand to Edgar's cheek and smiled at him.

"Maybe if I had tried, like you said, to help Cristina kick my father's ass, she might not have left. She might even be alive today."

"I don't think that would have saved her life. We all have to live with the decisions we make, good or bad."

"Why can't we figure something out, Mara, together? Can't we help each other?"

"Look, you don't have to leave. You're American. You have the law on your side. They would be so fucked if they messed with you. But I do. You don't know because you've never—"

"Never what?"

"You just have to watch your back."

Miranda put her arms around Edgar and kissed his lips and cheek. Her mouth was salty, her lips stained with tears and sand.

Edgar tightened his embrace until Miranda winced.

"Did I bother one of your wounds?"

"It's O.K." She wiped tears from her face and put her glasses back on. "It reminds me that I've got to get moving. And so do you."

CAPTAIN AGUILAR LOOKED DOWN AND SAW THAT his own barrel-chested body could just as easily pass through the dirt tunnel as crawl into his own bed. He could feel the warm breeze coming though the opening on the other side, bringing with it the acrid scent of Tijuana. There were no smog- reduction systems in Tijuana. It was his sixteenth hour on the job, and he hadn't had any coffee in three hours. He knew a sleepy Border Patrol agent was about as good as a dead one. Nevertheless, he had begun to compare everything to his need for sleep.

There were too many holes like these beneath the border wall, which had built out of metal scrap from World War II airplane hangars. The wall lined almost ten miles of the border between

San Diego and Tijuana, and there were plans to extend it the whole 60 miles of the California-Mexico border. Captain Aguilar stood up to his waist in the sandy hole and kicked a dirt clod through the opening. Some fence, he thought. He turned around to face north, the canyon, its blond hills, gray plateaus, I-5 on his left. There were footprints in the sand near the body and in all directions. There were no drag marks. The man must have been dumped—or shot where he stood in front of the wall, execution style.

Which was not what the captain planned to memorialize today. He had taken a graveyard shift so as not to miss Gabe's visit. He had decided that today was going to be the day he would speak honestly with his youngest son, who had come home from Donovan. During the five years Gabe had been locked up, Captain Aguilar worked overtime, as if to compensate for his son's crimes. Last night he'd caught four teenaged Rambos running through the canyon with high-powered rifles, each with a nightscope. One of them in particular, Alfredo Burns, had gone into some sort of seizure. It had shaken the captain up. But, as usual, he had little time to be emotional. A few minutes after the ambulance arrived to take the boy to the hospital, Captain Aguilar was called into the field to investigate the body.

"You need a hand, Captain?" one of his men asked.

The captain kept slipping on what looked like a solid rock, but which crumbled when he tried to step on it and lift himself out of the hole.

"I can make it."

"There's no need to struggle, sir, when you've got able-bodied men around willing to help," Agent Terranza said, patting dust from the captain's shoulder.

"I'm more able-bodied than any of you chicken necks," the captain retorted. He also regretted missing the baseball game.

"Does anybody know the score?" he asked.

The other agents, once Captain Aguilar approached, flicked their Winstons and went back to picking through the sand and bushes.

"Who knows the score of the Padres game?" the captain repeated. "Anybody?"

"Last we heard, it was five to three, Reds. Right?" Agent Terranza responded, looking around at the other men, all of whom knew to keep up on the San Diego Padres if they wanted to stay on the captain's good side.

"I think that was in the seventh," Agent Lopez said. "It should be over by now."

"Bunch of losers," Sergeant Walters said. Walters was new to San Diego and hadn't yet learned not to argue baseball with the captain. It didn't matter that the Padres were perennial losers. All the agents knew the captain had a soft spot in his heart for the underdog, and that he would explain any loss his team suffered by shifting the blame to reasons other than the Padres's lack of talent.

"It's that damn AstroTurf in Cincinnati," Captain Aguilar said. "We can't win on turf. San Diego is a natural-grass team. They should outlaw that stuff and burn it in a bonfire. I would honest to God celebrate that."

"Maybe we should lay some concrete and artificial turf around here," Sergeant Walters said. "To patch up all these holes. It might just work, you know?"

A couple of agents snickered in agreement. Captain Aguilar didn't pay attention to the ridiculous comments his sergeant made. Walters was a young cowboy from Arizona. He may have known horses and the range, but he obviously didn't know how resourceful hungry Mexicans were.

Captain Aguilar stared at the dead body, the swollen, blackened face. It looked nothing like the typical dark-skinned, mestizo or the indigenous Mexican faces he frequently found dead in the canyon. This guy was different. This one was a blanco, a wealthy, white Mexican, or Mexican American. He had been shot in both shoulders, both thighs, and in the head once—the five points of a star. An assassination. His dark, thick hair appeared to have been expensively styled, and there was a two-day growth of hair on his face. He wore a bloodstained white long-sleeved shirt with the initials JC sewn into the cuffs, along with a pair of beltless mouse-gray slacks. There was a tan line around his left wrist and around his left ring finger. His shoes and socks were missing, and, although his feet were swollen, they were not callused or cut from walking barefoot. In fact, it looked as if he had recently been given a pedicure. The captain guessed he might have been murdered within the last 24 hours. He knew that the coyotes in the canyon wouldn't take longer than 48 to smell the blood and tear the corpse to shreds.

But why dump the body here, the captain thought, directly in front of the fence?

Somebody tapped Captain Aguilar on the shoulder.

"Captain?" Agent Terranza asked. "We were just discussing whether we should contact the PD, or maybe the Federales. It looks like this guy had some money and might have been important. You know, like a kidnap victim who was trying to escape, or something."

"Naw. Probably a drug dealer."

"Or a stool pigeon."

"Captain?"

"Maybe it's Cascabel," Sergeant Walters said. "The one who disappeared a few weeks back. The guy Los Reyes are after."

"Looks like they got him."

"Los Reyes would have buried him," Agent Terranza said. "They wouldn't just leave him out in the sun."

"Unless they wanted him found," Lopez said.

The captain listened to his men speculate and to the crisp leaves of the juniper trees sounding like wind chimes. What would he have said to Gabe, if he had shown up for the barbecue? He'd stiffed his father before. Many times. Captain Aguilar supposed he'd been the one to blame, being at work all those years while Gabe was growing up into a foolish hoodlum. The problem was his son didn't pay attention to the big picture. He saw himself as just another young, brown-skinned hood, resentful of his Mexican American heritage. My example wasn't good enough, Captain Aguilar thought.

"Terranza," he said, "get on the horn to the PD. Tell them we've got a body that looks like Cascabel. Tell them to get somebody down here from forensics ASAP."

"Yes, sir."

The agents began to chatter loudly.

"Listen up," the captain ordered. "While I'm gone, I want the rest of you to start scanning a 50-yard radius in each direction. Make that 100 x 200 yards. Look closely for other tunnels, shoes, socks, shells, bullet lodgings, holes in the fence, bloody clothing—whatever looks unnatural. There's got to be more out here."

"But Captain," Walters protested, "everything in this canyon is unnatural, including the smell from that goddamn sewer on the other side of the fence. The pollos are throwing shit over the wall

all the time. Tires, drawers, linens—"

"I don't care," Captain Aguilar said, walking briskly toward his white Bronco. "I want us to find something. Call Brown Field and get the metal detectors out here if you need them. Take notes on everything you find. I've got to make a visit to the hospital."

"Do you mean that kid who had a seizure?" Walters asked the captain. "You think he killed Cascabel, sir?"

"Did I say that?"

The idea of the border being a war zone was not popular with the Border Patrol. The captain did not agree with the new militarization of the area. His job was increasingly more dangerous and violent with the government authorizing military tests of new high-tech weaponry in the name of the war on drugs. He felt the army, the infrared lasers, the electric cattle fence, the armed helicopters only increased the occurrences of violence and death— not just for immigrants, but for Border Patrol agents as well. In the past year, seven of his men had been wounded in random shoot-outs with coyotes, drug dealers, vigilantes, and other psychos who roamed the canyon looking for nameless victims like outlaws of the old West. Border vigilante groups, ranchers, and aggressive landowners took trespassing laws into their own hands. Some had taken to hunting illegal immigrants in the same way they used to go after coyotes who threatened livestock. They were even encouraged to do this by a boneheaded ex-mayor of San Diego, an AM radio host named Roger Hedgecock. The more people talked about the border being a barbaric frontier, the more Captain Aguilar had to accept the fact that being a Border Patrol agent was like being a soldier on a tour of duty.

The captain would be 47 in June. With his seniority, he should have had a different position: Advisor, Director, or at least Assistant Director in some department of Customs. But the captain knew the cushy jobs went to guys with degrees. Years ago, when he was still ambitious, he'd ridden horses through the canyon imagining himself a Texas Ranger tracking outlaws. He was proud that he was guarding the same territory where he'd grown up. He knew it as well as anyone, and he took his responsibilities seriously. By the time he'd turned 21, while his friends were still drinking cheap wine and experimenting with bad drugs, he had a job, with benefits, security, and, most of all, an opportunity to stay home and raise his family. Something his own father had spent his whole life trying to accomplish with three jobs, an eighth-grade Mexican education, and limited English. Though the captain's father had immigrated illegally in the forties, he'd encouraged Jorge to be patriotic. He even suggested joining the Navy or working with the Border Patrol, so that young Jorge would never be treated with disrespect. Jorge Sr. told his son that authority is power, and power is as good as gold.

But behind every fortune there's a crime, Captain Aguilar thought. And he had lost touch with his sons because of his long hours on patrol. Gabe had been failing in school, and his older son, Lalo, had been getting into fights. When the captain tried to explain to his sons the need for discipline and self-control, they just mutely nodded and looked away. One night, he came home to find out that Gabe had been arrested for armed robbery and attempted murder. Gabe was sent to Donovan State Prison, not five miles from where Captain Aguilar worked in San Ysidro. The captain had felt embarrassed, cheated, his pride and overtime taken for granted. He had thought about quitting the Border Patrol and moving to Riverside, but it was hard to walk away after he had put in so much. It was even harder to speak to his son. He had not even been able to bring himself to visit Gabe in prison.

By the time he reached Kaiser Hospital, the captain was sure he had figured out what Alfredo and his buddies had been shooting at. The only people who used such holes were illegals and drug traffickers. However, the hole the captain had found earlier was too small for major drug cargo. It had probably been used for the sole purpose of human traffic. The captain thought Alfredo and the boys had been shooting at whatever was coming out of the hole—most likely, illegals. And, in the process, they had assassinated Cascabel. Perhaps they had tortured him and then finally executed him. Of course, the captain would keep his opinion to himself. He would have to wait for the story from ballistics before he knew the whole truth. But he was confident his conclusion would be proved right.

The only question that remained concerned Cascabel. If, in fact, it was Julián Cascabel, the junior narco from Tijuana who had been reported missing for several weeks, what had he been doing there? Why would Cascabel be trying to cross the border like an illegal when the newspapers said he was born in the U.S.?

Captain Aguilar was greeted by Narcotics Detective Dennis,

who had also been at the customs complex.

"Good to see you, Captain. We got the news about Cascabel over the radio," the dectective said, firmly gripping the captain's hand. "Everybody's working overtime on this one."

The captain smiled.

"Well, at least I'm not the only one."

The detective took a deep breath and tucked his shirt deeper into his pants as they walked toward Alfredo's room. Dennis was blond, wore a tan blazer, and was taller and thinner than Captain Aguilar. They were both about the same age. Both had lost most of their hair. They'd known each other since Dennis had investigated Gabe's case several years back. In an act of sympathy, he had thrown out the narcotics-possession charge Gabe had been hit with when they finally picked him up with three and half grams of cocaine several weeks after the robbery.

"Listen, Captain," the detective said, "why don't we go down the hall where we can talk and have a cup of coffee."

"Sure. Let me just go in and see how Alfredo's doing."

"Don't bother. The doctor's in there. Besides, I think he's still unconscious."

"I feel really bad about that, you know. I had no idea he was—"

"You shouldn't worry about that right now," the detective advised. "Let the doctors do their job. Alfredo will pull through."

"I wanted to be the first to talk to him, is all," the captain said. "I kind of know the boy. And his mother. He's going to wake up to some not-so-good-news."

"I'll see what I can do for you, Jorge," Detective Dennis said. "I'm sure everything will work out for both of us."

They walked down the busy emergency room hall and turned into a closet with some machines. Detective Dennis dropped a few quarters into a coffee machine and waited for the first full styrofoam cup. The machine whirred as they both watched the white cup fill with black liquid.

"Everything cool, Detective?" Captain Aguilar asked.

"Sure. Black, right?"

"Thanks."

The captain sipped the hot coffee and remembered the last cup he'd had, just before Alfredo had gone into seizure. He'd called the ambulance, and, as soon they'd taken Alfredo away, he'd gotten radioed back out into the field. It had been a long day. Maybe he was just tired, and only imagining that the detective was patronizing him. It felt as if he was about to be accused of something.

"You pull a lot of overtime, Detective Dennis?" the captain asked.

"I'm always on call," the detective said, tapping the beeper clipped to his waist. "Family can't stand it."

"That's what I thought. How long you been with the force?"

"Listen, Captain, this may sound rude, but I've asked you over here to talk about more serious matters. I'm sorry there isn't more time for small talk."

The captain held a gulp of coffee in his mouth, swallowed, and nodded.

"Well, now that you mention it, I've got an idea—"

"Please let me explain, Captain," the detective said, raising his hand to his chest, halting Captain Aguilar's words.

"Go ahead, Detective."

"Thank you, Jorge. About two hours ago, we got a confession out of one of the boys you took in last night. The boy's name is Jesús, or Jesse, Treviño. He told us how the rest of these kids were able to acquire their rifles."

"I bet they were hot as skillets."

"They are. The Treviño boy gave us a name. We know who sold the boys the firearms."

"Oh, yeah?" the captain said, his face lighting up. "That's great. Who'd he name?"

The detective took a deep breath. "He named your son. In fact, they all named Gabe Aguilar as the person who sold them their weapons last night at Lolita's Taco Shop on Telegraph Avenue."

The captain felt as if he was under water. The pressure in his ears began to build.

"Are you sure they said Gabe *Aguilar?* I mean, did they really say his last name?"

"I'm afraid so. The Treviño kid told us his brother, Gustavo Treviño, got them in touch with Gabe."

"Tavo was involved in this? I know that boy, too."

"We've already got an APB out on him. Do you know where Gabe might be?"

"He just got out of prison. They had him staying in a group home downtown. I don't know where. He's on probation, for Christ's sake."

The captain began rubbing sweat from his forehead. Panic surged through his entire body as he realized the consequences of the Cascabel shooting. If one of the boys was found responsible for Julián's death, and Gabe had indeed sold them the stolen guns, he could be linked to a first-degree murder charge.

"Maybe they gave you Gabe because they knew he was my son," the captain said. "After all, I was the one who brought them in last night. You know how kids will say anything to get out of trouble."

"That's a possibility," the detective said. "There are several others. But we still need to bring Gabe in. We need to get a statement from him right away."

The captain stared blankly at the silvery coffee dispenser. He had a vision of his son on the varsity wrestling team, the only match the captain had ever seen, the first and only time he'd seen his son compete. In a violent flash, Gabe had turned the other boy on his back and pinned him in the middle of the second period. It had been so amazing to see his son struggle through the arms of the heavier boy, and to quickly go from bottom to top. Gabe had stood up and smiled widely at his father.

After the match, Captain Aguilar was convinced that his youngest boy had a bright future. He had gone back to work proud, telling all his men that his son was a champion.

"I know this is difficult, Captain. It could be that Treviño falsely gave us Gabe, like you said."

The detective paused and pulled out a small green notebook. He flipped it open to the notes he had taken earlier.

"You have any kids, Dennis?"

"Two boys and a girl. Why?" The detective frowned. He was being sidetracked, which meant he was losing time.

"You keep in good contact with them?"

"Sure. They're at home with their mother."

"Good," the captain said. "The family is all we have, the only thing we can trust."

"Captain, do you think you can tell me where Gabe is, so we can at least try to help him out of this mess?"

The captain felt the stubble of his beard growing like a

thousand needles pushing out of his face. His job now was to give the police the whereabouts of his son so they could take him to jail again. His duty now was to deliberately break apart what he had worked so many years with the Border Patrol to protect and provide for. But that was his downfall. He had always been working.

"I know where my son is," Captain Aguilar said. "He's a good kid. I know where he is."

ALFREDO AWOKE TO HIS MOTHER'S VOICE TELLING someone there was absolutely no hereditary disease in her family. Alfredo would certainly have liked to believe that, except there were too many fetal-alcohol cousins, clubfooted nieces, and hare-lipped uncles; too many disfigured relatives among an infinitely split family tree for Dora to be exactly sure what fate her genes carried. In any case, she had a knack for forgetting some of the most important things in Alfredo's life. She contradicted herself a lot. He couldn't even trust her to remember his birthday.

Alfredo heard the flush of water slapping and gurgling against a toilet. And he realized the television was on. Then Dora's voice broke through.

"It's O.K. now, mijo. It's O.K. You can wake up."

She helped Alfredo take off the oxygen mask. She held his head up and wiped sleep from his eyes. He could smell the perfume on her silk blouse. Alfredo felt the soft warmth of his mother's skin and was momentarily comforted. He almost believed he was a child again. Dora rocked him, her hair falling on his face, covering him with darkness.

Dora sat up, searching her jeans' pocket for something to wipe her face. Alfredo fell back against his pillow wondering about the others. He now realized it had been his biggest mistake to include them. He'd thought he could control them by example. He knew they weren't brave enough to admit to murder, no matter what the cause, but they could blame him, just to bargain their way with the police. They still had to face the wrath of their parents. And they had to try to save their military future. They wanted to be officers and travel the world. Alfredo had also wanted that dream, but was unsure how much had been jeopardized by the confusion of the last 24 hours.

He had to get out of the hospital. He tried to say something, but his throat was tight and dry. He could pronounce nothing more than "muh."

"Don't try to speak, mijo," Dora answered. "I'll get you some water."

Alfredo wondered how long he had been unconscious. Dora held a styrofoam cup of water to his lips. He drank with difficulty. He could not breathe with his mother leaning on him. Alfredo coughed and tried to move into a comfortable position, but the sheets also constricted his movement.

"What is it?" Dora asked.

"The sheets. Can't breathe."

Dora began stripping the sheets. She reached under the blankets to straighten Alfredo's hospital gown and pulled it back down around his legs. She poured more water from a purple jug and gave the cup to Alfredo to drink. He finished the cup and regained his regular breathing. There was no pain and he felt able to speak.

"What time is it? How long have I been here?"

"It's about six o'clock," his mother said. He could tell she had been crying. "You had me so worried, Alfredo. I didn't know where you had gone last night. And then Captain Aguilar called to tell me he had you in San Ysidro. Ay, you know how I hate Immigration, mijo. Then before I got there, you had already been rushed to the hospital. You've been asleep for a couple hours. I didn't know when you were going to come out of it."

"What about the rest of them?" Alfredo asked. "What happened to Gil, Erica, and Jesse? Did they go home yet?"

Dora stood at the side of the bed with her arms crossed, biting her lip. When she did not respond, Alfredo tried to sit up, but Dora tenderly held his right shoulder down. Alfredo was weak and exhausted. He laid his head back upon the pillow. Dora then leaned over to grab the automatic control to adjust the bed. Alfredo felt the bed rise behind his head.

"I don't know where your friends are," Dora said. "The police came an hour ago to tell me about this desmadre. Why would you be out in the middle of the night shooting guns?"

Alfredo did not feel like arguing with his mother. He didn't have the strength, and this was neither the time nor the place.

"Did the police say I was under arrest? Am I a suspect?"

"They didn't find any drugs. Whatever the hell made them suspect that you were a narco, Alfredo?" Dora faced the door, as if to accuse whoever stood on the other side. "You could have died, and the pinche migra would have been happy. We're going to sue them for endangering your life. Humberto will help us figure out how to do it. He knows about suing people."

"He's an artist. Not a lawyer."

"He went to college. He knows about these things."

"What about my friends?"

"The other boys influenced you, didn't they, mijo?" Dora crossed her arms. "I mean, they were the ones caught with stolen guns. You didn't tell them to go buy them, did you? I don't believe that just because you're older you would be their leader."

"I am the ROTC leader. What did Captain Aguilar say?"

Dora wrote something on the floor with her foot. "Your friends confessed that it was Captain Aguilar's son, Gabe, that sold them the guns. Did you know him?"

Alfredo shook his head.

"He just got out of jail, and now the police are looking for him. Humberto is outside talking to the captain right now, trying to work something out for you. Your uncle is a good man. You should give him more respect."

"He's just a hippie freak, Mom. Don't get your hopes up."

So Gabe was the son of Captain Aguilar; Alfredo had heard the other boys mention the name, but he had no idea what Gabe looked like. He could never have pointed him out. Gabe was supposedly a friend of Jesse's brother, Tavo, the greasy cokehead. No wonder they had been late. Alfredo wanted nothing to do with people like that. He should have arranged his own individual plan. Now he was linked to drug addicts and ex-convicts.

"Why are you hanging around with criminals, Alfredo?"

"I'm not. I didn't have anything to do with how they got their guns. They're just people from ROTC class. We're training to be soldiers. We're supposed to have guns. It's part of our training."

"Is it typical, then, to shoot at people while you train? I don't think so. But you tell me what you were doing out there in the canyon. I want to know now. Before the police and Captain Aguilar come back in here. I'm your mother and I have a right to know. So you tell me. Because they seriously think you killed somebody, Alfredo. You better believe it. They found a dead body and they are waiting right now to find out if you and your friends did it."

She had no right to question him about anything, Alfredo thought, because she spent half her time in a drunken stupor, busying herself with wine and romance novels.

"Well?" his mother asked. "Are you going to tell me?"

"Who did they find?"

"A dead body. Somebody who had been shot several times."

"A woman or man?"

"What does it matter? Somebody was murdered and they want to blame you. Doesn't that frighten you? "

"I'm not afraid of anything."

"Well, you better be."

"Was it a Mexican?"

"Who?"

"The dead body. Was it American or Mexican?"

"You're a very strange boy, Alfredo. How many gringos do you think they find dead in the canyon? What did I tell you about the canyon? To stay away from there. Pero no. Tú te creés hombre. You're not afraid of anything. Did I raise you to be a fool?"

"I'm not a fool," Alfredo shouted. "I have my own reasons for what I did, and you have no right to demand anything of me. You're just a drunk. You're nothing."

Dora quickly walked to the side of the bed and slapped Alfredo in the face.

"You can't talk to me like that." She tried to slap him again. He screamed while trying to catch her hands. As he struggled with his mother, Alfredo's IV was yanked out of his arm, and the EKG wires were pulled from his chest. He screamed again in pain. There was a loud beeping. When Dora heard this alarm, she let go and stepped away.

The door opened and Humberto hurried in, followed by a thin nurse with glasses and a short, balding doctor.

"Is everything all right?" the doctor asked. "What's happened in here? How long has Alfredo been conscious? Joanie, please reattach Mr. Burns's IV and check the EKG."

The nurse reinserted the IV and began taking Alfredo's blood pressure, while the doctor asked Dora questions about how Alfredo had regained consciousness.

Humberto smiled and shook Alfredo's foot. "I told you he

would be fine. He's a strong man. Runs in the family, I guess."

He asked the doctor if there was a private place he could discuss Alfredo's medical history. The doctor hesitated and agreed, dismissing the nurse to another call. They left Dora alone with her son, who lay back flushed, winded, and lightheaded.

Then Captain Aguilar came in. "I hope you don't mind, Mrs. Burns. But I'd like to talk to your son for a few minutes. About what I mentioned earlier."

"Listen and answer the captain clearly, Alfredo," Dora instructed. "So he doesn't have to stay any longer than is necessary."

"Thank you, Mrs. Burns, for that vote of confidence."

Alfredo looked away from his mother. Did she hate him now as much as he hated her? Or was she thinking of his father? Did he remind her of him? He probably reminded her of how they fought and argued, how they hated each other. How did they make up? Alfredo wondered. What did my father do to convince her that he loved her? There was nothing but a picture Alfredo could recall, the photograph he had blurred into fantastic memories. No one could take that desire for his father away from Alfredo, neither his mother, his uncle, the doctors, nor Captain Aguilar. He would fight until it happened.

The captain looked Alfredo up and down, almost measuring him while he lay in bed. Alfredo held his chin up as if being inspected by his superior.

"Alfredo, we found a dead body in the canyon near the border wall this afternoon," Captain Aguilar began. "A man appeared to have been shot several times from fairly close range. The police are checking ballistics to see if the shots match your gun or any of your partners'. An autopsy has been requested by the victim's family and will be done soon."

"Are you accusing me?"

"Not necessarily."

"Well, who was he?"

"I'm not able to say that right now, but I can tell you he had recently been murdered. I wanted to ask if you might have known anything about it, since you were out in the canyon last night. Did you see anything or anybody near the fence last night?"

Alfredo was silent, sure he was being asked to help only in order to confess. He was on to the game.

"Tell him you didn't shoot anyone, Alfredo," Dora demanded. "That's what the captain needs to hear. Tell him so he can go."

"Please, Mrs. Burns," Captain Aguilar said. "Believe it or not, other than an attorney, I'm the most qualified person to help you right now. I'm the one who has asked the detective to lay off so I can help you, all right? I want to help. Please give me a chance."

Alfredo began to breathe faster. His throat tightened. He turned to his right to reach for the jug of water. Captain Aguilar came around the side of the bed and poured him a cup. When he had drunk, Alfredo turned to face the captain and saw the exhaustion streaking his blood-shot eyes, the salt-and-pepper stubble developing around his tan cheeks. Alfredo wondered at the amount of coffee he had consumed just to stay on top of this case.

"I saw plenty of things last night, Captain."

"Good. What you can tell me about last night can affect the lives of many people, including your parents. Do you understand what I mean? Depending on the outcome of your case, you have the potential to link many people to a very serious crime, including your own family. Do you understand that?"

Alfredo sat up and pulled his legs closer to his stomach.

"So am I also responsible for your son's crime, Captain?"

"That depends," Captain Aguilar said, taking a deep breath.

"Depends on what?"

"That depends on you. On what you can tell me."

Alfredo realized he had to stop hoping that the inquisition would stop. He needed to accept the fact that he would never get answers of his own. He had indeed opened Pandora's box. But what about his right to know about his father? Why didn't anybody else see a connection between his operation in the canyon and the fact his father was a Vietnam vet, missing in action?

Alfredo knew he had gotten off at least ten rounds last night, before the others arrived like a pack of hyenas. But he had been prevented from confirming the body count.\All he had to go on was the guarded accusations of the captain.

"I've seen dead bodies out there before," Alfredo admitted. "Drug dealers. Coyotes. Illegal immigrants—dead two or three days. So what? People die out there all the time. My mother was the one who first told me that. You'll find whatever you want out there, Captain. But no one will ever find my father."

"Your father?"

"Your father, Alfredo?" Dora repeated. "Where—out in the canyon?"

"What exactly are you referring to?" the captain asked.

Alfredo slid off the bed and stood on the cold tile floor. The IV extended like a plastic rope between the aluminum stand and his arm.

"My father is a POW/MIA in Vietnam," Alfredo said, staring at the captain. "I haven't heard a word about where he might be, or who is holding him, or his condition. I don't even know what he looks like now. Or if he knows that I'm his son. I don't even know if he's alive."

"I'm sorry, Alfredo," the captain said. "I know that must be hard on you, but, really, we aren't talking about—"

"What do you know, Captain?" Alfredo accused. "You don't know anything about me. You're just harassing me and my family."

"Now listen, Alfredo—"

"No, you listen. For Memorial Day I wanted to do something for my father. Something no one else could have done. I wanted something in exchange for his memory. I wanted to bring his memory back to the canyon, near the border. That's where the war is now. The border is our war, like your generation's was Vietnam. My father was a patriot. But his name isn't on any memorial wall. I checked. He's not even listed under the official POW/MIA registry. But he deserves a memorial, too. So I gave him one the only way I saw fit."

"Stop being ridiculous, Alfredo," Dora said nervously. "This isn't any of Captain Aguilar's business. Quit talking about your father now and answer the questions."

"Thank you, Mrs. Burns. You're right. This is going way off the track." The captain looked deep into Alfredo's eye. "What exactly did you do for your father?"

"Wait a minute. Don't you want to know more about me? You've been torturing me for the last 24 hours. You want to know what I was doing last night? I was fighting a war. I was stalking the enemy, cleaning up the canyon. Helping you do your job.

"Do something for me now, Captain. Marine Corporal Gerald Scott Peterson is my father's name. I have a picture of him at home I can lend you. I'll tell you exactly what happened last night if you exercise your connections and get me in contact with someone in Vietnam where my father—"

"That's enough, Alfredo!" Dora yelled. She stood just behind the captain, gripping the bar at the foot of the bed, shaking as she spoke. "You don't know what you're talking about. That's not his name. There is no Marine Corporal Gerald Peterson. I made that name up!"

"You made what up?" Alfredo asked.

"No, no, no," Captain Aguilar said, waving his arms in front of him in an attempt to refocus the statement Alfredo had begun to make. "We need to continue our confess— our conversation, Mrs. Burns. Alfredo, please."

"What did you make up?" Alfredo asked his mother again.

"I made the whole damn thing up," Dora said. "Everything I've told you about your father is a lie. Pura mentira. You're never going to find out anything about your father, because there is no Corporal Peterson. Ni siquiera existe, ¿me entiendes? I made it up so you wouldn't have to regret being born the child of a drunk gringo sailor who followed me to the bathroom one night at the Arrow Club and raped me in the bathroom.

"Are you satisfied now that you have the truth? That's your father, Alfredo. A rapist. Now stop being foolish and answer the captain's goddamn questions. Because I can't stand this any longer."

Alfredo could tell by her high-pitched voice that his mother was delirious. She rarely cried when she was sad, but, whenever she was enraged, tears burst forth like they did now. Her eyes were pinned on Alfredo, and, although she tried to laugh through the shock, the lines on her forehead thickened into ripples of worry. This was the face that loved him, but Alfredo could not see it. Instead, he saw futility, weakness, and vulnerability. He saw an uncertainty that was like his own; he could not sympathize with it any longer. She had tried to steal his moment with a confession of her own.

What did it matter now whether he admitted to contributing to the whole mess? Alfredo didn't care anymore what they found out in the canyon. It was a gold mine of illegal activity. Death, violence, murder, and mystery were scattered all over its sand and trees. They would pave over the canyon soon enough, put up more tract houses, strip malls, and parking lots, and cover it all in asphalt.

Detective Dennis entered the room, with another uniformed policeman. Humberto and the doctor followed.

Captain Aguilar shook his head. "I'm not sure what's going

on here," he said to Dora. "But it looks like you've got some things to work out with your son. I think it would be best if Detective Dennis took over from here. Excuse me."

Alfredo tried to recover from his mother's blow. He felt his need for violence had not been satisfied with the shots at the border. He wanted to return to the canyon and finish his work. He did not have to fear who he was in the canyon. There he was the gatekeeper with knowledge of who, what, when, where, and how new things entered his world. Alfredo could manipulate time there, between past and future, as if it waited for him to change direction with a bullet or a bomb.

He had been ashamed of his difference before, his Mexicanness, his color, his mother. The solitude it brought him he had thought was a sign of weakness. He had struck out to break his difference, to destroy the mirror reflecting his own face, leaving only the blue eyes blinking like two bright stars in the black night. Despite all that had happened, all the lies his mother had told him, all the different authorities wishing to assault his freedom, despite the same body that failed his will, Alfredo vowed to return to the canyon and put the picture back together.

But whose face would it be then?

Alfredo didn't believe it was true that Dora had been raped by an anonymous sailor and that he was the consequence. It was her way of shutting him up. She had arbitrarily changed the facts of his life to maintain control over it. Just like the police did when they wanted to get you to confess. They played mind games. Alfredo knew he was being given the squeeze on all sides. Perhaps it had worked, for now. But he would not give in so easily.

The detective explained the case against him. Alfredo listened carefully, yet he could not remember what his rights were once they had been stated.

His mother sat silently in a chair next to his bed, bouncing her leg softly off her knee. He supposed she wouldn't cry. For some reason, Alfredo had expected her to shout and deny the charges against him. But Dora had not said a word.

Traces of gun powder recovered from Alfredo's fatigues had matched his rifle. What was left to be identified was whether the rounds found on Alfredo matched the bullets excavated from Cascabel's body. Humberto had said something about an attorney and told Alfredo not to say a word from here on.

Alfredo went limp. He had failed. He now felt that his mother had had nothing to do with it.

So now, perhaps, he was off to jail, like his father. A patriot in a cage of rats. Alfredo assumed "hate" might have had something to do with it. However, he wasn't exactly sure anymore who it was that he hated. He had desired something to satisfy a void. But it was not hate that satisfied him. Destruction was an immediate gratification, but the thrill was gone, and Alfredo was not satisfied. There was the throbbing, however, somewhere deep inside his brain. He hadn't remembered this feeling from the last time he recovered from a seizure. He had lied to the doctors when he told them he'd never had a seizure. There had actually been many seizures in the last year. After the tests the doctors would run on him, he wasn't sure whether this fact would show up. Nevertheless, after the tests, he assumed he would be medicated before being transferred downtown.

Perhaps it had all been a simple lack of medication—the right medication. A question of sustainability. Everyone had their own requirements. Everybody was an individual when it came to pain. The plan for the Memorial Day assault on the border had been a year in the making, a year without medication, a year of seizures, a year and one dead drug dealer. Another year, and what?

"Do you think before I go to jail someone can bring me my copy of *Heart of Darkness?* I have a paper due by Wednesday."

"Alfredo, be quiet until the detectives leave," Humberto said. He was calling an attorney on the phone. "Yes, is Jon Farkas available? Thank you."

"But I graduate on Friday. Do you think I can still graduate?"

"I don't know."

Then Dora looked at Alfredo in confusion. Was it really that important? How could he have done this if he'd wanted to graduate from high school? How could he be a killer and graduate at the same time? Graduate to what? He was about to go to jail. What did a diploma have to do with it?

Alfredo saw nothing ridiculous about his desire to graduate. In fact, he was set on accomplishing that goal. He was not afraid of his mother's questions. And he thought that a jury might think differently of Alfredo's crime, given the facts still left to be introduced. There was a whole story to be told. Given the right audience and the right product at the right time....

IV. DARK ENERGY

An angry man opens his mouth and closes his eyes.

fortune cookie

*T*he video was shaking and zooming in and out in amateur fashion: A man in front of his house was firing a gun at the police; cut to a news reporter talking about a shooting in Chula Vista earlier that night. Miranda had been at the hotel for almost three hours. She'd been given the option of staying with Julián's wife, Eva, in Coronado under police surveillance, but thought it too dangerous. Detective Dennis told Miranda that the police would pay for her stay as long as she cooperated.

She muted the TV, got up, and shut off the air conditioner. She dialed Edgar's number. It rang four times before his machine came on. She hung up halfway through the greeting. Maybe now was a good time to talk to Eva. She had neglected to mention to Eva her meeting with Nereida earlier, when she'd been shown the divorce papers. She hadn't told her about the shooting in Tijuana that morning, either. Nor did she say how Rafael had killed Julián. Miranda didn't know how to tell Eva without feeling like she was stabbing her in the back.

Eva answered coldly and was surprised to hear Miranda. She said the police had found Julián, and they wanted Eva to go downtown to the morgue.

"But I'm not going down there, a ese infierno ¿qué te crees?" She sounded insulted.

"How will you know it's him then, Eva?"

"They asked me to describe him over the phone," Eva said. "I told them where his birthmark was, what size shoe he wore, how much he weighed, what he was wearing the last time I saw him. His blood type. Todo ese rollo. It all matched. I told them to have his mother identify him, because I didn't want to see him."

"I understand," Miranda said, imagining Julián's blue body on a cold metal slab. She hadn't wanted to see Rudi like that, either. "Are you O.K., Eva?"

"I guess." She paused. "Where are you?"

"I'm...I'm at Edgar's house," Miranda lied.

"Where's Alejandra?"

"She's with me. She's asleep. Pobrecita."

"Your mother called me," Eva said. Miranda could hear her lighting a cigarette. "She said you had packed your things. That you took Alejandra this morning and left. Is that true?"

Miranda was silent.

"Are you leaving Tijuana, Mara?"

"I don't know. I haven't decided what I'm going to do yet."

"Well, I don't want to stay here anymore, either, fíjate," Eva said. "I don't want to stay in this house. It gives me the creeps now that Julián is —"

"Did my mother sound upset?"

"No, but she was worried. She wanted to talk to you. Will you call her?"

Miranda said she would call her mother tomorrow. She wanted to tell Eva how she felt manipulated and bitter. "I spoke to the police earlier today. I told them...everything."

"¿Qué-que?"

"I told them about Julián, about Platón, about me, and you. About Los Reyes. About the refrigerator. About the dealing."

Eva was silent.

"I couldn't think anymore," Miranda said. "I didn't know what to do. I mean, they tried to kill me today. And Alejandra was in the car with me."

"Who did? What are you talking about?"

"Rafael. Bardo Junior's bodyguard. They came after me this morning after I left Rodrigo's house in the Chapu. They attacked me in the middle of the day. I didn't know how to tell you. I was hiding my face. My eye is swollen and black, but you couldn't see, because I had sunglasses on. But they shot Rudi. They killed Julián, too. They beat me up and...and I shot them."

"Miranda, you're scaring me. Stop joking around. I'm going to throw up."

"I'm serious, Eva. Los Reyes killed Julián. I told the police everything. I told them about Julián." Miranda waited to hear if

Eva would get angry. "If I testify against Los Reyes they'll—"

Click.

"Eva?"

That was it. She had been cut off from everything. She had forgotten who she was. Who was this person betraying everyone? Why had she agreed to testify in a gringo court? Miranda doubted the FBI, the DEA, or even the Mexican army could bring Los Reyes to court. And even if they did manage to arrest Bardo Junior, they would never be able to touch his father, the congressman. Even if they got Bardo Junior behind bars, it wouldn't bring Julián back to life. It wouldn't bring Rudi back to life. It wouldn't heal her family's reputation. It wouldn't settle the score for anyone. Because even if the court forgave Miranda for her crimes, Los Reyes wouldn't. Whether Bardo Junior went to jail or not, they would kill Miranda the first chance they had.

Miranda watched Alejandra sleeping, her ponytail streaming across the pillow. Miranda went to the door, opened it, and peeked down the orange hallway. It was empty and quiet. She thought she could smell cigarette smoke. Maybe the detective who was guarding her had gone out to smoke. But she couldn't remember if he smoked or not.

Miranda closed the door and picked up the phone, but couldn't remember who she wanted to call. She hung up and went over to the bed. She grabbed one of the ends of the brown comforter and rolled it over Alejandra, wrapping her up, and then picked her up in her arms. A heavy bundle. Once she had Alejandra firmly in her grasp, Miranda left the room and headed down the stairs. She went out the back door and then onto the street. She remembered that Edgar's gallery, Mesa Blanca, was only a few blocks away. She thought to go by and look for him, but decided against it. She hated asking for any more help. She couldn't trust him. She didn't trust anyone. Especially not the police.

She headed into the Concourse parking structure. She took the elevator to the top. Once the door opened, she could see the dark blue Cadillac, the only car on the top floor. She walked toward it, keeping her eye out in case anyone might be following her.

From the top floor she could see the Coronado Bridge like a blue bow through the air. She could smell the saltwater. Halfway across the empty lot, she heard voices shouting one floor below. She began jogging toward the car as the voices grew louder, echoing up the ramp. She reached the Cadillac, unlocked the doors, and laid Alejandra inside the back seat. She climbed into the driver's seat, inserted her keys, and started the car. She reversed quickly and headed toward the exit.

Coming up the ramp in front of her were six skateboarders. A couple of them clutched their boards at their sides while they walked up the center of the ramp. Others were riding their boards, kicking back and forth, zigzagging toward her. One of the young men at the front had long blond dreadlocks and smiled at Miranda as she approached. She didn't expect that the Concourse would be a place for skateboarders to hang out. But they might remember her face. Miranda floored it, screeching past the skateboarders, causing them to jump out of the way, abandoning their boards. It reminded her of the drunks on Avenida Revolución when it was crowded; how they stumbled out onto the street, but managed to scramble back onto the sidewalk before they were hit. The skateboarders shouted at her as she passed, cursing and giving her the finger.

Miranda turned right out of the garage down a one-way street. She made another right and drove until she found the blue signs directing her to the 5. She had a choice of north or south. South had always meant home. What did north mean to her? She looked in her rearview mirror to see if anyone was following, but the street was deserted. Warehouses lined the left side of the block, ice plant the right. She was near City College. The police station wasn't far away. It wouldn't take long before Detective Sehorn discovered she had fled the hotel. He would be looking for her.

She turned to look at Alejandra. She did not know how to be a mother. She doubted she even knew what was the right thing to do most of the time. She only knew how to follow her instincts. Leaving the hotel had been an instinct. Killing Rafael had been an instinct. Her instincts had saved her so far. Maybe that was the wrong way to look at it, because they had also gotten her into trouble. Edgar had told her that instincts had their own logic. That she was thinking, even when she acted spontaneously. But Edgar was a philosopher, and Miranda was not. Thinking about herself meant thinking about the past. Miranda had no past. She preferred to always risk new territory. The past was over. The past was boring and nostalgic. The past was south.

She remembered that Rudi had a rancho somewhere near the

coast in Baja, where they grew figs and Brussels sprouts. But they had never gotten around to going. Rudi said he hated the rancho. He was bored there. All you could do was eat and think. You could ride horses, but it was so dusty that you just got dirtier the more you rode. The last trip Miranda had taken was this past New Year's. She'd gone somewhere with Julián and Eva and gotten really drunk for three days. She couldn't remember where it was. Somewhere near the beach. Mazatlán? Rosarito? One of those places. It didn't matter. It was like going to a bar: the same wherever she went. It's just the same people doing the same thing as always, because there was nothing else to do. It was no wonder she'd gotten into so much trouble.

The light was red. Miranda became angry with her indecision. She was disgusted with Tijuana, but she wanted to return. Platón had hated Los Reyes so much for forcing his father out of Tijuana after they had stolen the racetrack from him. She was being forced out, too. But what was she really leaving behind? Nothing but a story. Tijuana was her home, but it wasn't her life. Her daughter would certainly be humiliated if the whole world knew her mother had been killed, or thrown in jail, even if Platón was already in jail. Pinche Platón. Pinche vato. Pinche guey, cabrón. She couldn't remember what it was about him that she had loved, except his anger.

"Mami," Alejandra whined. She sat up in the back seat. "Mami, are we going home now?"

"Sí, hija. We're going home."

"Quiero Quik, mami. Will abuelita give me some Quik when we get home?"

"Yes, you'll get whatever you want when we get home. Now go back to sleep. We have a long road to drive. And if you talk too much, Mami will get distracted and lost."

North meant escape. But Miranda was tired of running. It seemed she had spent her whole life in a car driving, or waiting in traffic, or parked. Who was to say she wouldn't always be driving from one place to the next? Like a moving target.

I BELIEVE SOME PEOPLE SHOULD BE PUNISHED FOR their crimes. Like it says in the Bible, though, let the one who has not sinned cast the first stone. When I was 18, the judge sentenced me to prison to rehabilitate me. I'm not sure what that means exactly. A lot of cons get raped inside. Not just physically, but psychologically, too. If you want to call that rehabilitation, then maybe you can see why so many go crazy. It's the unwritten part of your sentence to be sodomized, humiliated, and mentally destroyed. Don't matter if you're guilty or not. When you spend enough time with prisoners, there is no such thing as guilty or innocent. There is only survival. That's why the gangs inside are so powerful. The numbers don't lie. There is power in them, for sure. And that's also why the state is so powerful. But the lawyers, the police, the politicians, the migra, and the judges are the real vampires. And that's what they try to turn you into when they send you to prison. They want to rehabilitate you into a fucking vampire.

People want to deny that this happens. It's like they carry around a guilty conscience. I remember thinking that if I made it out, I was eventually going to have to go back into the world. And vampires hate the world. Because they don't want to interact with people other than to try and eat them. You follow me? Other people remind them of their own selves, which they hate. So they just kill them, or try to convert them. That's why there was a lot of religion in prison. The chaplain was always trying to preach to us in the yard, and then he'd try to bribe us with sentence reduction if we came to Bible study. I went a few times. But it was all about repent this, forsake that, and confess you did it. Then you would be saved. But nobody was about to confess shit to no one. Besides, there was no one to confess to. Even the priest was a vampire. Otherwise, why else would he have been in prison?

The truth is, the pen is just another name for concentration camp. Inside, I read about how Hitler blamed the Jews for all the problems in Germany and then gassed them. They were supposedly criminals who had stolen the pride of the Germans by controlling the markets. Today, the black and Mexican folks get rounded up by the police for selling a rock or trying to scheme a dollar. They tell you that you're going on vacation for a little while, metaphorically speaking. So you hand in your clothes and valuables—I didn't have any gold watch, then—and they walk you naked to the showers to spray you with rehabilitation. They call that the law. I call it the lie.

You get to think a lot inside. The majority of your time is

spent inside your cell, in your bunk. Nobody really wants to talk to anyone, because they're too busy thinking their own thoughts. It's like even your mind becomes a cell. And the same questions repeat themselves every day in the same routine. Usually it's, How did I get here? What am I going to have to do to survive? When am I going to get out? Who am I, anyway?

After a while you start to split into two different people: the person you were and the person you are becoming. These are two completely separate identities, two totally different sets of memories, and they don't like each other. In fact, they hate each other. And when the hacks come to let you into the yard, it's like letting out a bunch of crazed dogs. That's when the hate gets taken out on somebody else. All of a sudden the battle in your mind becomes the battle outside, and vice versa. It's what you call a vicious circle.

See, I know a lot about trying to learn from my mistakes. You try to discipline yourself to recognize when you're about to make a mistake. That's why I surround myself with familiar things. Familiar folks. Familiar places. I am a creature of habit. Everything must be put into routine in order to understand it. Like a machine. It makes me feel like I got control over the situation. If you know what's going on around you, then chances are you can't be stabbed in the back. So I keep my friends close and my enemies even closer. Still, I don't feel safe. I feel like there's this tainted blood inside. Vampire blood. My father is the migra. A fucking vampire like all the rest. I guess that explains my predicament.

You can think of me as a dream waiting to happen. A nightmare. You can think of me as an old friend you haven't seen for a while. Someone you may have forgotten about while you went on with your everyday life, your petty struggles, your boring job, your irritating relationships, your experiments with danger. I don't mean that you haven't experienced pain. I know everybody suffers. Imagine if your suffering spoke to you like I am right now. Would you listen? Probably not. But that's O.K. because if you want to find out how this story ends, you're going to have to listen to me sooner or later.

It's like this. My mother cooked up a carne asada for me and my friends to hang out and eat—to celebrate my homecoming. Yeah, I been out six months, but I ain't really spent much time with my family. I was too busy trying to make the adjustment back to normal society—meeting with my job counselor, pretending to be looking for a career in machinery. I'm good with cars. But that don't mean I like working with my hands. My mother kept calling me at the group home and asking me to come visit. But I didn't go on account of I don't get along with my dad. But today he was working, I guess, like always. So I decided to go once my mom said she would barbecue for me and my friends.

My brother, Lalo, was downtown serving time for beating up his girlfriend and another homeboy who she was cheating on him with. I talked to Lalo on the phone earlier, and he told me he was going to marry her when he gets out. He told me she was pregnant. Sylvia is her name, and she was there, too. My mother invited her so she wouldn't be the only woman at the party. So she'd have someone to talk to when I wasn't around. Shane, Mico, and Chino were there. Tavo had already left. He'd only been there a second before he got a call and then took off. Then Edgar showed up.

We were in the living room watching TV, drinking Tecate and lime. The Padres game was over, and I was in the La-Z-Boy kicking back. My mom was in the kitchen talking with Sylvia. I liked this time of the year, when it stays light until almost eight. You always feel like you've got plenty of time to do whatever you want. And we still had beer to drink and that coke to cut. We had to start selling it tonight. Everybody was supposed to have at least two contacts. Everyone except Edgar, whom I invited for personal reasons. He knew a lot of folks that could help me out. We would need a lot of contacts. Especially after Shane and I cut the half key into a whole one. We were planning on getting rich, and everyone was feeling good.

"I want a mansion somewhere in La Jolla," Mico said, with a big smile on his face. "A big one up on a hill where you can see me from the road." He raised his can of Tecate up over his bald head. "I want everyone to know I'm a high rolla."

"When I get a hundred gees, I'm going to Hawaii," Chino said. "I'm going to live out there with my peoples, hook up with a topless Hawaiian chick, and get laid."

"Why you always pretending you're Hawaiian?" Shane asked.

"I am. So what?" Chino said. "My father is Korean. My mother is half Hawaiian, half white."

"So why don't you go to Korea and hook up with a Korean

girl and get laid?"

"'Cause I don't want to go to Korea. I want to go to Hawaii."

"I feel you, Chino," I said. "I don't want to go to Mexico with mine, either. I'm about to head to Australia or some shit far away like that. Somewhere nobody knows me. I'm gonna chill in seclusion. Ain't no one gonna be able to find me."

"What about if we got a new deal?" Chino asked. "We gotta keep this crew together if we're gonna make any real money."

"I'll send ya'll some coded messages. I'll be all about some international espionage."

"What? Why you talking all these big words, nigga?" Chino said. "Your fantasy is too complicated for me."

The others laughed.

Then Mico heard something behind him, and he turned on the couch to look out the front window.

"Fuck, man. Check it out. The cops are here. A lot of them."

"What?"

Flashing lights filled the living room, blinking off the walls.

"Mico, close the curtains."

Mico started to look for the string to close the curtains. Shane went to the front door to peep through the eye-hole. He started waving back at us.

"Get the fuck down," he said.

Mico hit the floor, leaving the window uncovered in the middle. Both Chino and Edgar crouched into a catcher's stance. Mico had this nervous grin on his face. Edgar looked like he had just shit his pants.

"Who is it?" Edgar asked.

"Gabe, your old man's out there," Shane said. "He's talking to the cops."

He's the reason they would be here, I thought. I crawled across the living room until I reached the yellow linoleum of the kitchen. My mother was drinking coffee like she always did after a meal. I got up and brushed off my Dickies.

"The police are here, Mamá," I said, trying to be as calm as possible. My mother's hair was tied back and she was wearing turquoise earrings that hung down like a rockslide. She has this indented, round face—kind of like a sandstone plate with two brown beady eyes. She claimed her family was Hopi from New Mexico, even though she was born in San Diego. She was sitting at the kitchen table with Sylvia.

"What are the police doing here, Gabriél?"

"I don't know, Mamá. Dad's outside right now talking to them."

"Your father? He's outside right now?" she repeated. I nodded. She always repeated things when she was nervous. She wasn't slow, just a little sensitive. If you had two sons in jail and a husband who was out all the time trying to catch pollos, you would either be hard and cruel, or fragile. My mom was always over-protective of us. She was always worried about me and my brother being hit by a car or kidnapped from school. We couldn't even go trick-or-treating without her. But when I started smoking pot and getting Fs in school, or when Lalo got arrested the first time for hitting his girlfriend, she didn't know what to do. She just worried.

"What are you going to do?" Sylvia asked me.

I didn't like Sylvia, so I looked down at the red plastic tortilla container with a picture of two ears of corn crossed together, and waited for her to leave. Sylvia went to the living room. I heard someone turn off the TV. Then everything was quiet. I could hear the clock above the oven on the left tick-tock, and then I could hear my mother start to breathe quicker. That's scary when you can hear someone change their breathing.

I went to get a drink of water.

"Is your father coming inside?" My mother got up and began to walk toward the door.

"Mamá, don't go over there," I said. "Please."

"But I want to know why the police are here."

"Don't open the door."

They could have been there for anything. Shane was also on parole. Who knew what shit the rest of my friends might have gotten into. But she kept going. So I shouted.

"¡Mamá! Get away from the fucking door!"

I grabbed her by the wrist. She tried to yank loose, but I got my body in front of hers and locked the front door behind me. I pushed her down the hall into her bedroom. She yelled at me to leave her alone. But I wouldn't be able to concentrate on what was happening, if I had to worry about her.

"What did you do this time, Gabriél? Why do you insist on making it hard for our family?"

"I'm not making it hard for the family. You invited me over."

It was dark in the hallway. There used to be photos there, while I was locked up, of me and my brother dressed up like cowboys. One of me in a light blue blanket—underneath was written the name Boo-Boo, which was what my mother called me when I was a baby.

"I want peace, Gabe. Do you know what that means?"

"What do you want me to tell you? That I robbed someone? Fuck no. I didn't do anything. I don't know what they want."

"Don't cuss at me."

"Sorry."

The phone rang. My mother and I looked at each other.

It rang again.

"Are you going to answer it?" she asked.

"Go ahead."

My mother picked up and sat near the foot of the bed, which had an embroidered white cover like a shawl. There were lots of black-and-white family photos on the stained-wood dresser, and on her white vanity and night table. My mother was obsessed with family. On top of that she was a clean freak. She had never had a regular job while she was married to my father. She was always around the house. When we went to our relatives' homes for dinner, she would pick up their trash and wash their dishes. It was embarrassing.

"Yes. Yes, he is," she said. "Can I ask who's calling?"

She hung up the phone.

"Who was it?"

"I don't know. They asked if you were here and then hung up. I'm going to talk to your father."

"Mamá, wait."

I walked down the hall. My dad was standing in the living room. His hat was off, and the crown of his bald head was shiny with sweat. There were dark stains under his arms. I noticed how the forest green of his uniform matched the color of the couch and the curtains. He had dark circles under his eyes. He smelled like dust and exhaust. Like sulfur. Like the border.

We were looking at each other, but not saying anything. Then my mother walked up next to him. They were both staring at my hand.

I realized I was holding Shane's nine-millimeter. I'd had it on me since last night. My father took a step back, watching the gun. I peeked my head around to the left to see if the front door was open. But it was closed.

"Put the gun down, Gabe," my dad said. "We have to talk."

I could hear someone in the kitchen. It must have been Sylvia talking on the phone.

"What are the cops doing here?"

My father's face sagged as if the skin had been hung on a hanger.

"They would have found you sooner or later, Gabe. At least this way I can help you out."

"Help me out? How do you expect to help me out by bringing the cops over? You're always pulling some bullshit like this. I'm your son, and you're about to have me arrested?"

"Please, Gabe. Put the gun away."

My mother was holding out her hands. "He's not trying to hurt you. He wants to help."

"The police think you sold some guns to a couple of kids last night," my dad said. "The same kids we caught in the canyon shooting at illegals. They told the police you sold them the weapons. The police want to know if that's true. I told them you would cooperate. Don't make me look like a fool."

"You are a fool," I said. "Especially if you think I'm about to go talk to some pigs. That shit wasn't even mine. I just connected some folks together."

"It's true," I heard Edgar say behind me. "Gabe was only the middleman, Captain Aguilar. He didn't —"

"Shut the fuck up, Edgar," I said.

"I'll shut him up, Gabe." Shane said. I could see him preparing himself to handle Edgar. I shook my head no.

"My men also found a dead body last night. Near where we arrested the boys who say they got their guns from you. Do you know what that means if the ballistics match?"

I had felt bad that I hadn't included my friends on that deal with Bruce, but now it seemed better that I hadn't. They wouldn't get blamed for being accomplices.

"That means if the boys killed someone with the guns you sold them, you could be convicted of conspiracy to murder."

"I didn't kill anybody. I didn't know what the stupid kids were going to do with them. How should I know they were freaks?"

"We should talk to Detective Dennis about it."

"The narc?"

"He's outside waiting for you."

"But he's a narcotics detective—"

My father nodded his head. I realized he wasn't going to tell me everything he knew in front of my friends. I guess they realized that. At least, Shane did. I saw him slip behind my father. He turned and went out the back door. Mico and Chino followed.

I started to head toward the back yard myself. Sylvia was on the phone in the kitchen talking to someone in Spanish. My mother kept calling my name, but I just wanted to see where my friends were going. I looked out the sliding glass door and saw them running up the hill of iceplant. When they reached the top, Shane hopped the short wooden fence into the neighbor's yard. He'd have to hop another fence, beyond that the canyon began. I thought about running, too. Then the neighbor's dog started to bark, and so did mine. Soon about five dogs were barking at Shane, Mico, and Chino.

"Come on, Gabe," my father said. "If you take it easy, no one's going to hurt you."

Sylvia had hung up. I stood there in the kitchen staring at my dad in disbelief.

"Man, fuck that. You think I'm stupid? You think I came here just to get thrown back in jail? Man, I got plans."

"I understand, son. Maybe you can go through with them once we get everything cleared."

I looked at my father's hands as he held them open at his sides, the dark meaty hands with spidery black hairs on the back. They were mine, also. I had also inherited my father's thick chest. His short stature. His slumped shoulders. My father was good with his hands. I remembered when he rebuilt the engine in the '66 El Camino for Lalo right before he got his license. He would be doing all kinds of wrenching, ratcheting, banging, welding, and painting from morning to night. He spent all his free time on the car. But Lalo didn't appreciate the Camino, which made my dad secretly pissed. He took his disappointment out by ignoring us. My mother's got the Camino now, and I got Lalo's truck.

"Even if you don't believe me, I...we want to help," my father said. "We can help you. I can help. I love you, Gabe. But what's best for you right now is to turn yourself in."

I could hear the police on a bullhorn. I couldn't understand what they were saying, but they were probably checking on my dad. Or warning me that they were coming in. Then everything got loud inside my head. I could hear the voices of those cons inside jiving to each other, the older guys talking about how many years they'd pulled. Some dudes were trying to get AIDS, happy that they would live the rest of their life in a hospital rather than a cell. Others were banging on the bars, screaming gibberish trying to get thrown in the mental hospital. Anything to get out of there.

"I'm not turning myself in for shit," I said. "You're going to have to make me go."

My father stepped close to me and deliberately grabbed for my gun. I shook my head at him and stepped back. I was watching to see if he would draw his gun. The button strap over the handle of his .45 was undone, but he didn't go for it. I wished he did.

"I had planned all these things I wanted to talk to you about today, Gabe," my father said. "I spent the whole day thinking about what I had done wrong in the past. I know I work too much. That it seems like I don't care. But I do. And I wanted—and now that you were out of jail, I wanted us to start all over. We can still do this. Please let me in, Gabe. If you come peacefully, the judge will appreciate that."

"What judge? What are you talking about, Dad? YOU ARE ABSOLUTELY INSANE IF YOU THINK I'M LETTING YOU TAKE ME BACK TO PRISON. I AIN'T TURNING MYSELF IN. SO FUCK THAT. FUCK YOUR GUILTY CONSCIENCE."

I bucked my father to the side and rushed to the front door. There were at least six squad cars parked in front. Lights were flashing through the tree branches. Out of the corner of my eye, I saw people standing in their doorways and on their lawns. The cops were just standing around. No one had their guns drawn. I raised my gun and saw one cop motion with his arm. He shouted something, and the cops started ducking. I started shooting, pulling the trigger as fast as I could. My hand was jerking. I felt like my wrist would break, or my eardrums would explode. The shots echoed off the stucco walls of the cul de sac. I couldn't tell if I had shot anyone. I didn't care. I was trying to reach out and touch the whole blob of blue-and-white in my front yard. I had almost emptied the clip when they started shooting back. I could see the bullets zip by me. Finally, one hit my left shoulder. I staggered. I got hit in the stomach, and the leg. I fell down in the doorway. My whole body began to hurt. I was tired. I curled up in a ball and waited.

THE LIGHT WAS DIZZINGLY BRIGHT IN THE kitchen. Edgar stood in front of the sink, answering questions for a young detective who scribbled into his note pad.

"He was my friend. I've known him since we were kids. We grew up in this neighborhood."

"And do you know whether Gabe said anything about a kilo of cocaine he bought last night?"

"What? No."

"Did you hear Shane or any other of his friends talking about a kilo of cocaine they bought off of Miranda Cascabel last night?"

"No."

The detective waited a minute for Edgar to continue. But he didn't.

"Aren't you Miranda Cascabel's boyfriend?"

"Yes. No. I mean, we were dating. But that's personal. I don't want to talk about that."

"Weren't you with her last night at Lolita's Taco Shop when Gabe bought the drugs off her?"

"What does this have to do with what just happened?"

Edgar was irritated and in shock at the same time. He didn't know whether Gabe would live. He'd been shot six times. One policeman had been shot.

Neighbors were being interviewed by the police. TV cameras and police cars with flashing lights crowded the street. The cul de sac had been roped off with yellow tape. Still more cops seemed to be arriving by the minute, more reporters and more flashing lights.

"Where do you think Gabe may have taken the cocaine last night?" the detective asked Edgar again.

"I don't know," Edgar said. "I don't even know where he lives right now. Gabe was my friend. I was here to visit a friend. That's all. Then you and the posse showed up."

"O.K. I'm sure we'll get that from one of the others." The young detective clicked his pen, folded up his pad, and shoved it into his coat pocket. "Wait right here, and I'll have Detective Dennis talk to you."

Once the detective left Edgar alone, Captain Aguilar motioned him over to sit at the small kitchen table. He was drinking a cup of coffee. There was still a tinfoil plate of carne asada waiting for the captain, but he hadn't touched it. He wasn't hungry.

"You hungry? Do you want some coffee?" the captain asked.

"No thanks."

"I remember you used to come by when you were a kid," the captain said. "We haven't seen you in a while. What are you doing with yourself now?"

"I paint. I work at a gallery downtown. I'm a painter."

The captain nodded. He wouldn't have taken Edgar for an artist.

"Have you been hanging out with Gabe since he got out?"

"Before tonight, no." Edgar shrugged. "Tavo ran into me the other day and told me to come by the house, your house, for a welcome-home party."

Captain Aguilar studied Edgar. He remembered the long-haired chunky boy who used to come by on his bicycle and ask if his sons could come out to play. They'd gone all the way through high school together. And they'd gotten into trouble together. But the captain hadn't seen Edgar in years. He didn't know what had happened to Edgar's family. He didn't know why Edgar was there.

"Edgar, did Gabe ever say anything about me?"

"What do you mean?"

"Did he ever say whether he liked me or not?"

"Liked you?"

The captain nodded.

"No. Not that I can remember."

Gabe had never really said much about his father. Edgar knew they had struggled as a family when Gabe went to jail. He didn't know who to blame that on. Gabe's dad was known to be strict. Everyone had been afraid of him growing up. He was a migra agent. But it was a job. Edgar could understand why many Mexican Americans in the area went into the Border Patrol. Especially if they could speak Spanish. They knew the area well. It was close to home. It gave them social status when they had none. It was a physical job, invested with authority. The pay was pretty good, with a chance for advancement, as Edgar was taught to say by his high school counselor. Even though most Mexicans in the area ridiculed the Border Patrol, Edgar remembered a few of his most criminally minded friends from high school talking about going into the police, customs, the Border Patrol, or the FBI. There seemed to be enough jobs for everyone in law enforcement. Even Lalo had always said he wanted to join the FBI. But not Gabe.

Edgar looked up and thought the captain looked defeated. Like a soldier who had lost the war. Edgar supposed they were both prisoners of war. They wouldn't be allowed to leave the house until Detective Dennis released them. It must have been frustrating for the captain to be a prisoner in his own home.

Gabe's mother had locked herself in her room and wouldn't let the detectives in to search for evidence of cocaine. There had been a lot of shouting back and forth through the door. Then Detective Dennis intervened and bought her some time.

It looked like the whole scene had quickly become a narcotics investigation. That would be the easiest way to justify the shooting. Which made Edgar feel responsible. He had convinced Miranda to go to Detective Dennis and tell everything, including the deal last night with Gabe. But he wasn't going to admit to anything yet.

"I'm sorry I can't tell you anything else, Captain."

"I understand," the captain grimaced. "Me and that boy...we just never clicked. He resented me, I think, because I was always working. He felt abandoned. I know he did. I don't blame him. But I didn't know how to—"

The captain gripped his coffee mug tighter.

"—how to understand it. I was never violent with them. Sure I disciplined my boys, but I never beat them."

Captain Aguilar knew no other way he could have handled the situation. He'd gone by the book. Maybe that was the problem. The book—whatever book it was—didn't mention how you should feel. You weren't supposed to feel for your job. You were supposed to work. You were supposed to defend the law. Even if it meant arresting your own son.

Detective Dennis came over to the table and poked his finger into the tinfoil plate. "You get enough of this?" he asked Edgar.

Edgar didn't respond.

The detective told Edgar to wait outside in front of the garage. Someone from the police department would be with him.

Edgar got up from the table and turned to Captain Aguilar, putting out his hand.

"I'm sorry about Gabe. I hope he'll be O.K. I'm not sure what else I can do to help. Say hello to Lalo for me."

"Thanks, Edgar." The captain shook Edgar's hand. "Take care of yourself."

Edgar let go of Captain Aguilar's hand and left the house.

"What's going on with Edgar?" Detective Dennis asked the captain. "You know him?"

"He used to hang around with Gabe and Lalo when they were younger," the captain said. "You say he had something to do with this Miranda?"

"Well, as far as I know, that's her boyfriend," Detective Dennis said. "Or one of them."

"There seems to be a lot of interest in the drugs my son was supposed to have bought off this woman named Miranda Cascabel," Captain Aguilar said. "Is she related to the DOA Cascabel?"

"Yes, she is. They're cousins. And partners."

"But I thought you guys were here looking for guns."

"The judge issued a search warrant for firearms and narcotics," Detective Dennis said matter of factly. "Based on the information we got from the boys you brought in last night."

"So now you all are tearing up my house and terrorizing my family looking for something you're not even sure is here? Can you explain that to me, please, Detective?"

"I can't tell you that, Jorge."

"What about this Miranda? Do you have her in custody?"

The detective stepped back. He adjusted his tie and leaned over to speak closer to Captain Aguilar.

"We're in contact with her," he said confidentially. "She may also have sold some coke to your son last night. Close to a kilo she apparently stole from some very dangerous people. If this is true, this case could get much bigger than the whole fiasco that just went down."

"This isn't making any sense," Captain Aguilar said. "You're saying Gabe is a dealer now? Why didn't you tell me this before?"

"Procedure."

"If there's a lawsuit to be filed, I'll have my attorney—"

"Look, Jorge, I know you're under a lot of stress, but don't forget Gabe shot one of my men." The detective had not wanted to get angry. He cleared his throat and tried to remain on task. "I'm not sure what's all gonna come out of it, but until we get your wife out of the bedroom, we aren't going anywhere. She may be written up for tampering if she doesn't come out in the next five minutes. You've got to get her out of there."

Captain Aguilar was going to say something in response, but decided it was no use. The detective had his own job to do, as well as his own motivations that the captain didn't feel like debating. He got up to walk over to the hallway.

"Let me see if I can get you and your wife a hotel for the night on the department, Captain."

"Don't do us any favors, Detective."

"I think that would be best. I'll have one of the squad cars take you to the new TraveLodge down the street. Sound all right?"

The captain walked away without answering. He didn't care which hotel they took him to, he just wanted to sleep. Maybe when he woke up the whole nightmare would end.

He stood before the door of his room and knocked softly.

"Gina? It's Jorge. Let me in, honey. I need to talk to you."

There was no answer. The captain knocked again.

"Gina? Open the door, honey. I need to come in. It's just me. No one else."

Still no answer. The captain knocked louder.

"Gina, we need to talk about what we're going to do. We have to get out of here. Open the door."

The captain pounded on the door.

"Goddamnit, Gina, open the door right now!"

"IT'S OPEN!"

The captain stepped back. He hadn't even thought to check. He turned the knob and walked in. His wife was lying on the bed in the dark. He could see her shape in the center of the bed. She was not covered by the blankets. He wanted to touch her, but thought twice. Instead, he sat down next to her.

"We have to leave, Gina," the captain said, patting her shoulder. "We have to let the police do their job. They're gonna get us a hotel. We can stay there until they finish."

She turned away from him.

"You go."

"C'mon, Gina. Don't be like that."

"You go, Jorge. I don't want to. I don't have the strength."

"It's not that hard. I'll pack for you."

She didn't respond.

"Baby, what do you want me to do?"

"Just leave me alone. If you're going to leave, do it. But they're not touching anything in my room."

"We should cooperate."

"What if I don't? Are you gonna arrest me, Jorge? Are you going to arrest your wife, too?"

She sat up. They faced each other in the dark. Captain Aguilar was afraid to yell. He didn't know if he could control his anger once he let it out.

"Please, Gina—"

"NO! I'm not leaving. I'm not cooperating. I'm not letting you off that easy."

"You think this was easy? You think I wanted it like this? He's my son, too."

"Why did you have to bring the police? Why couldn't you let the family handle this?"

"You act like I killed him."

"You just might have done that."

"The hell I did! You saw me, Gina. I tried to get him to surrender. I tried to keep him from overreacting. But he—"

"You brought the police here, and you put him in danger. And what for? That's what I don't understand. Why? Why would you betray your own son?"

The captain was silent. He didn't know how to answer. He had stuck to what he knew. He wanted to follow the guidelines. He had a role to fill. The law was above them all.

"We'll wait to see what the doctors say."

"You may have killed your son, and you're going to have to live with that, Jorge. So maybe you should leave."

"Gina—"

"Go on."

The captain got up from the bed and went to his closet. He switched on the light inside and looked for his duffel bag. He found it behind a few boxes of shoes. Inside the bag was his extra gun. He took the bag to his dresser and filled it with a change of clothes.

"Please come with me."

"I'm going to stay with my sister. But I'm not leaving until you're gone. So go."

She was doing this, he felt, to spite him. Well, he deserved it. He wondered if he would be reevaluated after something like this. People who were reevaluated at his age and seniority were offered early retirement.

Detective Dennis was waiting for him in the kitchen.

"She's going to let you guys do your work in a minute," the captain said. "Soon as I'm gone."

"Thanks, Captain. I've already arranged a room for you at the TraveLodge."

"Thanks. I'm on my way."

Detective Dennis stood with his hands on his hips.

"FYI, Captain. Ballistics just phoned. Alfredo didn't kill Cascabel."

That was good news to the captain, even if he had been proven wrong.

"But don't worry, Captain. He'll still be dead when you wake up tomorrow. Now get some sleep."

I'M NOT SURE IF I DID THE RIGHT THING. I THINK maybe you were also trying to cover your ass by making me put mine on the line. I never would have gone to the police if you hadn't convinced me. If you hadn't persuaded me. Whatever. It's done now.

I saw on TV that Gabe died. I'm sorry. I know he was your old friend. I wonder if you are in trouble? I hope you are O.K. I guess I'll just keep going until something happens. Until I find something. Or until it finds me. You know, like the way you paint. You have an idea, and then you just do it and see where it takes you. You said something like that once. You said to trust your instincts, or something. I don't know.

I have to go. I don't know why I can't hang up. I keep thinking that there is something I haven't told you. Something I need to tell you. But when I try to think about it, my mind goes blank.

I'm not good at explaining. Something about explanations are fake, I think. It takes too much thinking, too much remembering. Maybe it's a waste of time. Because you only hear what you want to hear. ¿Verdád?

I just thought how strange it is that you got to hear my whole life story yesterday with Detective Dennis, but I don't know who your first girlfriend was. I never met your mother. Your father. Or your sister. I'm glad you told me the story about them, though. I mean, I know you, even though now all I can remember is your studio and your smell. That's all that I can remember. Everything else is just a blur.

Oh, fuck it.

Goodbye, Edgar. Don't look for me. I don't want you to find me. Because it won't be the same, even if you found me. I'm starting over. And I don't want to think about you. It would be too complicated. I don't want to hurt you, but I've got to take care of myself and Alejandra now.

I know you understand.

Edgar could hear cars passing before she hung up. There was no clock on his answering machine, so he had no idea when she'd called. He was actually surprised she'd left a message. It wasn't like Miranda to be so considerate, nor so reflective.

He envied Miranda's toughness. Perhaps it was good to have a bad memory. You couldn't suffer regret that way.

Now there was only silence in his studio, the messy bed where he and Miranda had branded and cut themselves after they'd made love, the half-smoked bag of pot, and the coke-speckled porcelain plate. The unfinished mural to his sister.

Miranda hadn't met his mother or his family. That was the way he'd wanted it. There would be nothing to forget that way. Nothing but him for her to remember.

He had been lucky she hadn't testified. He had been lucky she'd left him out of her story. Even if Detective Dennis didn't believe her.

Edgar guessed Tavo was in Mexico by now. He'd return. No matter how far south he went, he would resurface. Because hot air rose, and Tavo had always been a high flyer. But Gabe was gone, and Edgar was lucky. Just lucky enough to be bitter.

I don't want you to find me.

Even though he was angry and overwhelmed, Edgar thought he would see Miranda again. There seemed to be this bitter force pushing their lives together and then breaking them apart as if to molest them. Perhaps some day a dark energy would draw Miranda back to Tijuana, back to the border. Back home. Until then she would haunt his sleep. Their relationship had been two-faced and criminal. Like the bars she had carved on his leg. Just like the border. Tough and afraid at the same time.

It was a cliché, he supposed, to have been abandoned, yet to remain unable to erase her taste, smell, and touch from your memory.

Edgar cleared a space on the bench that held his painting supplies and sat down. He stared at the portrait of his sister and thought of Captain Aguilar asking him what Gabe had thought of him. An explanation was needed, but Edgar decided to paint instead. He didn't waste time trying to think of someone to blame. Blame was just another explanation. It was better to paint than explain. Besides, he would have plenty of explaining to do when the detectives came. □